Can Openers

Mal Jones

First published 2014
By Rowanvale Books Ltd
2nd Floor
220 High Street
Swansea
SA1 1NW
www.rowanvalebooks.com

A CIP catalogue record for this book is available from the
British Library.
ISBN: 978-1-909902-81-7

I would like to thank my friends and work colleagues for giving me the confidence to finish the book.

Particular thanks to my family: Kate, for her useful tips and support, and Babs, who has spent hours listening about my ideas and reading my manuscripts, offering me encouragement and support throughout.

Prologue

Two teenagers sit on their bikes, their voices getting louder – they're arguing. One of them throws his bike in anger against a metal gate and it crashes with a loud bang.

Down an alley a piercing, frightening scream echoes in the night air, a deadly silence, an eerie chill descends. Both youngsters stop and look at each other.

Out of the alley, a shadow is running and disappears in the mist. The teenagers instinctively walk slowly down the dark, damp, dirty gulley. As they get towards the end of the alley, they see a figure lying on the ground.

One of the teenagers treads in something that clings to his trainer. He lifts his foot up and touches something sticky – blood. He is nauseous and vomits. The other teen sees a body with a knife pushed into the stomach. A circular red patch has formed on the clothes and blood is around the wound and on the concrete ground.

'Oh God.'

Chapter 1

The automatic doors slid open silently. As Iris walked down the noiseless corridor, she could hear the tip-tap of her heels echoing down the hall. The brightly painted walls and colourful pictures of sunsets and beaches did nothing to lift the sense of gloom and despondency she always felt pervaded the place.

As she walked, Iris tried to calculate how many times she had visited here, coming every day since her mother, Lilian, had been admitted in 2019, just over three years ago. She gave up when she thought of her visit the day before. She felt a deep sense of loss; it wasn't the loss of something that had passed but a loss that hadn't yet been realised. Iris challenged herself to rationalise her thoughts. She forced herself to remember that death had always been a shock; but she knew that what hurt her the most, what gave the Centre such a deep air of gloom, was how death manifested itself here. The option of death and the subsequent agreeing to the lethal injection brought immediate grief to those left behind.

Iris stopped three quarters of the way down the corridor. As she turned to open the pine wood door to her right, she gathered herself and forced a smile. Inside, she found Lilian in the chair next to the bed. The room was small but bright. The window was uncovered, letting in sunlight and displaying a perfect view of the car park. Iris glanced at the family pictures on the top of the chest of drawers and sniffed at the cloying, heavy scent of lavender spray in the air. It occurred to her that the lavender in the room never quite masked the faint, sweet smell of urine coming from the hall outside.

Iris put her bag down on the end of the bed and shrugged off her coat. She smiled and bent down to eye level with her mother.

'Mum, why do you want to take the injection?' Iris asked.

Lilian had completed a Hope in Golden Age Assessment at sixty-eight years old. This was when she had been still fit and healthy and living in her own home. A year later she had suffered a mini stroke and, although she made a good physical recovery, her memory had never quite been the same. Iris was worried; she couldn't understand why her mother agreed to have the injection.

'It's Sarah, you know, the nice lady, she's the manager here,' Lilian said. 'She's a trained counsellor you know? She's a very clever lady. She's my End Your Life with Dignity counsellor. I think she said that I've been assessed. She told me my memory loss and health will get worse. She was ever so kind about it. I don't want to be burden to you, love. I think it's for the best. They've tested my capacity, they were good. They said it would be my decision, so I think it's for the best.'

Iris felt tears welling up in her eyes. She didn't want to get upset in front of her mum. Iris coughed away the choked feeling in the back of her throat and quickly changed the subject. After they had chatted, Iris rose to leave. She put her coat on and reached for her bag at the end of the bed.

As she bent over to kiss her mum on the cheek, Iris quietly said, 'I know it's your choice, but let's talk about it more when I come next time.' Iris opened the door into the bright, bleak corridor and left.

Iris worked in a different care home and had researched the Old Age for Dependency department, so she understood the procedures. She knew that everyone sixty-eight years of age needing a state pension, or any state support, had to complete a Hope in Golden Age Assessment. Studies in Scotland and England commissioned by the State Dependency Department led to a further huge scientific study on age, disability, and life span. The study concluded that old age was too costly a burden for the State and mortality management needed to be more efficient.

Iris was annoyed that the company that was awarded the contract for the Hope in Golden Age Assessment was Bihem IT, the largest IT company in Europe and, infuriatingly, Dibble Care had a twenty percent stake. Iris felt sorry for her mother who was given a computer when she was sixty-eight and required to answer hundreds of questions. If her mum did not use the computer or failed to answer any of the questions, she would be deemed ineligible for her pension. She also had to have a medical and was seen by a dependency doctor. The medical predicted her future health and noted that at seventy two years of age she will not be able to walk upstairs and will have a stroke and at seventy six lose her memory. Iris considered how onerous it must be for so many elderly people to have to be subjected to the process. Her mother did not understand one of the questions so had to ring a call centre. The advisor would only refer to her by case number, never by their name. It irked Iris that the process was so impersonal. Iris also found out that centre workers had to reach daily, weekly, and monthly targets or suffer punitive action by the Department. Iris wondered how on earth the call centre workers could possibly use the Objective Fair Analysis system under such conditions.

The final part of the Hope in Golden Age assessment was to log and store Lilian's future physical and mental health on the Department database. Lilian would then receive tokens and a personal budget intended to last to the end of her life. Iris tried not to dwell too much on how precise and coldly clinical the whole process was.

The stroke had come completely without warning. It shocked Iris to see her mum struck down the way she had been, still, so Iris thought, relatively young. In the course of recovering from the stroke and needing extra care and treatment, all of her mother's allocated personal healthcare budget had been spent. Despite Iris's efforts to appeal to them, the Dependency Unit took the view, and stated it quite clearly, that it had been Iris's mother's own fault that she had a stroke, as the original assessment outcome noted it should not have occurred until she was at least seventy-two. Iris remembered how stunned she was when the call centre advisor told her that her mother had "obviously made bad lifestyle choices in her younger age". The call centre had no compassion at all, telling Iris "the only person to blame is herself," and asking, "did she eat a lot of fatty food or drink too much or not look after herself since the assessment last year?"

Iris knew that her mum really had no option. With no more personal budget left, Lilian would have no choice but to submit to a Residential Home Positive Choice assessment and go on to a number 3 route. Lilian, at the same time, was also informed of the Ending Your Life with Dignity option available only to those over sixty-nine years old.

As a result, Iris became even more obsessed in researching the system for her mother. Every evening after work and increasingly into the weekends she studied and read everything she could about the process. Iris had started to suspect that companies were making a lot of money from the Ending Your Life with Dignity scheme. Lilian moved into the residential home soon after the assessment had been carried out. This meant that Lilian was officially classified as a "burden on the State", that this was her own fault and therefore all her assets were to be frozen. In the event that Lilian died, the State would get all of Lilian's savings and anything she owned that would be passed on to Dibble care. Dibble had lobbied the government about this in the past and had argued that as the State, and Dibble in particular, were taking on the responsibility of looking after people, then Dibble needed the funding to provide that service.

This knowledge nagged at Iris all the next day. When she finished work Iris went back to the care home to her mother. This time Iris sat on the edge of the side of the bed so she was slightly above her mum's eye level. Iris took her mum's hands in hers and rubbed her wrist gently with her thumb.

'Mum, will you come and live with my family and me? We have a room. You'll have privacy.'

Her mother's head drooped. 'I do not want to be a burden on you, love,' Lilian said quietly and sadly.

Iris put Lilian's hands onto her lap. 'But Mum, why would you be a burden? You've almost fully recovered from your stroke.'

'Sarah said I have to think about the future. She told me that by the time I'm seventy-six I am going to be very ill, she said I'd lose my memory.' Lilian paused. 'I don't want to be like that.' A tear slowly rolled down Lilian's downy cheek.

'How does anyone know that?' Iris asked.

'Because it is in my Hope In Golden Age Assessment,' Lilian said, brushing the teardrop away.

Iris could feel herself getting annoyed and knew it wasn't fair to her mum. It was the care home and harsh assessment process that Iris was angry with; she didn't want Lilian thinking that Iris was angry with her. They chatted some more before

Iris left. Iris stood up and once again leaned over to kiss Lilian on the cheek. She gently rubbed off the slight lipstick stain she left behind. 'It's okay Mum, don't worry. I'll see you soon.'

As she waited for the automatic doors to slide open to let her out of the home, a short dark woman wearing the care home uniform brushed against her, in a rush to start work. When Iris reached her car and she felt in her pocket for her car keys, her fingers touched a scrap of paper. Iris realised it must have been slipped in to her pocket by the woman who rushed past her in the doorway. On the paper was a hand written note asking to meet Iris away from the care home. There was a phone number and a hastily scrawled name on the bottom of the note.

The next day, as soon as she was able, Iris phoned the number on the note and arranged to meet the note giver in a quiet back street café called Alan's. Iris recognised the woman from the care home straight away. She introduced herself as Vicki. Other than Vicki, Iris, and the man behind the counter busily cleaning the coffee station, the café was empty. Vicki and Iris sat at the corner table furthest away from the counter. Iris had to lean forward to hear what Vicki had to say.

'The number 3 option is a con. The Dignity of Life counsellors and the manager are given incentives to push for the positive choice injection. We, as care staff, try to stop the residents from going for the option, but if we're found out we get disciplined and sacked. We can also get taken to court and could be imprisoned. Dibble Care will say we're going against the Dignity of Life policy, stopping the residents from having a choice, abusing the residents,' Vicki whispered.

Iris listened in stunned silence. She wasn't entirely surprised by what she was hearing but she had never realised how the staff were manipulated and bullied.

'When residents choose the number 3 option, Dibble pockets thousands of pounds. The State pays Dibble in ten-year block contracts per person. So, say your mother came in the home at sixty-nine and then opted for the injection at seventy-two, Dibble would pocket another seven years of funding, plus the money from anything of value and savings your mother may have.'

Iris shook her head, incredulously. She knew it made sense; she read that, ten years ago, the average age in a Dibble home was eighty-six, now it was seventy-five. It didn't take a genius to work out that Dibble was making money by bringing the age down of residents and putting a positive spin on it by saying it was costing less.

Iris decided there and then to go to the home that afternoon and take her mother out, whatever cost her financially or health-wise.

Vicki made Iris promise not to tell anyone about their discussion. Iris reassured Vicki and thanked her.

As soon as she left the café, Iris went straight to the care home and again sat with her mother. This time Iris was determined.

'Mum,' said Iris, 'I need you to please come and stay with me. Come on, let's go now.'

Lilian looked up sadly at Iris. 'Look, love, I do not want to be a burden and I can't go anyway.'

Iris stood over her mum. 'Why not?'

'I have already signed for the injection,' Lilian said.

'Well, tear it up and come with me,' Iris replied, anxiously.

Lilian looked down at her lap. 'I can't, she said I wasn't allowed to do that.'

Iris turned on her heel went to find the care home manager. Iris quickly found Sarah in her office and told her that her mother wished to withdraw from the number three option and that she would be taking her mum home. The manager continued tap-tapping away at the keyboard on her desk and didn't look up as she told Iris that her mother could not withdraw from the option. She only stopped typing long enough to face Iris and explain that once the decision was made and the resident was assessed as having full mental capacity, it's placed on record with the Hope call centre and there is no going back. She coldly and calmly told Iris that the program could not be changed under any circumstances. Iris went home and decided to phone the call centre the following morning.

Iris got up early the next day. She dressed quickly without washing and rushed to the phone. After a few rings the call was answered. The call centre worker told Iris that once a number 3 was put in place, there was no going back. That it was a positive choice and if they stopped a number 3 due to family pressure or other reasons then the personalised choice will be taken away from the individual. The call centre worker then asked Iris if she was aware that the injection was to be administered that day. Immediately Iris became distraught, choking and crying. The call centre worker was sympathetic and advised Iris that she could make a complaint as the home should have given her 24 hours' notice before the injection was administered. She asked if Iris wanted a complaints form. Iris slammed the phone down.

As Iris raced to the home, her only thought was to stop what was about to happen. She jumped out of her car and, as she ran to the front door to the home, she passed a Chaplin as he was leaving the building. Iris looked across to another door marked "fire exit"; the door was open and an ambulance was parked just outside it. Iris could see a blanket stretched over a body on a gurney, just as it was placed in an ambulance. Iris knew she was too late. They were taking her mother's body to the morgue. The manager saw Iris and came up to her.

Sarah took Iris's hand. 'At least you know she suffered no pain.' She led Iris to her office. Iris stumbled over her words as she told Sarah through tears that she wanted to complain. Sarah looked sympathetically at Iris and told her that the information the call centre had given was incorrect.

'The law is there to give older people rights over their own lives, so they can make as independent a choice as possible. I know this is difficult for you,' said Sarah, 'but things have not gone completely to plan. The call centre should take seven days to authorise the injection and then there is a Form 3 for Old Age to be processed, this has to be added to the Life Plan. If a family member makes contact then this has to go on the computer program. It may hold the injection up for about two weeks. The difficulty is that some residents make the decision but then have to wait, they get scared and are worried about the final solution, waiting for the final day to happen. They panic, you see, and try to withdraw their consent.' Sarah paused and handed Iris a tissue to wipe her tears. 'This cannot be withdrawn, because now their fear of death and their emotional state would overturn the rational decision they made about the biggest choice of their life. Having the injection earlier was better for her mental health and more humane.'

Iris said nothing. She realised that death had become so matter-of-fact to these people, so routine, that at the same time as she was talking to Iris, she was also dealing with a matter of a stolen purse and talking to the office clerk about the residents' lunch. Iris realised that what had happened to her mum was, to the care home, just another management decision. Iris felt physically sick. She noticed a large sign on the office wall headed "Dibble's Mission Statement" in large red letters.

HOPE, HAPPINESS, FULFILMENT, AND CHOICE – THE DIBBLE WAY.

Chapter 2

It was a hot day in May. In the garden, the purple and red flowers and the apple blossoms looked glorious, and signs of new life pushed their way through the soil. Spring had finally arrived. The light, happy voices of children echoed through the still air, followed by the deeper, richer sound of a man's laughter, children and their father playing together.

Most of the neighbours, who watched the father and children play, would see a family full of happiness and joy. It was a pleasure to live next to such a respectable and stable family so well suited to the area.

However, appearances were not all they seemed. Like looming storm clouds on an otherwise clear spring day, dark shadows lurked behind the family's closed doors. The difference between appearances and reality would ultimately seal their fate.

Frederick, a family man of sorts, was in the back garden cutting the grass and playing with his children. Zeta, his six-year-old daughter, came up from behind and squirted him with water; they chased each other while he jokingly shouted that he was going to hang her from the nearest tree. She ran around the garden laughing as her father pretended he couldn't catch her. Zara, his eight-year-old daughter, shouted something out of the bedroom window but no one heard her, so she gave up and went back to the computer.

The next-door neighbour put his head over the garden fence and called hello to Frederick; the neighbour commented on a conversation they had previously.

'When I worked for the department, there was still some hope we could help people.'

'Well things have moved on over the last ten years,' Frederick replied. He then went into the house, irritated by his neighbour who stared at him moralistically. Eventually, Frederick calmed down and realised that it did not matter what his neighbour said. The seventy-year-old man had retired in 2012; being out of work for over a decade invalidated the old man's opinion.

Frederick lived in an area made up of identical three bedroom detached houses, all of the owners trying to create their own identity in their own mortgaged space. The street only came to life on weekends and in summer evenings; the rest of the time it was like a ghost town, the residents were in their own individualised space with no sense of community. An area built for the disengaged middle class. They worked longer and harder for less to keep their status and identity. A neo-liberal age at one time provided the material wealth but, for many, those aspirations were gained on credit. After a decade of economic stagnation, during which time endless amounts of credit had turned in to onerous debt, life had become a treadmill of work with Sunday the only day of rest.

Frederick loved his children. When he was with them, it was the only time he ever showed any care or compassion. He was never very happy and he felt like he deserved a better life. He was resentful of most people and bitter about those who he would describe as scroungers or work-shy. He wanted to be someone others would look up to, to be seen as a trendy executive type. Although he was over six foot, he had never learned to carry himself well and looked gangly and clumsy as a result. His suit never quite fit him properly; he looked seedy, as though he had slept in it all night. Though he cut a rather pathetic figure, in his own mind, Frederick was a legend; at work he liked to flirt with his younger co-workers. Behind his back, however, many described him as creepy, some even called him a 'perv'.

Lidia, Frederick's wife, worked at the local shop on Sundays. He wanted his wife to stay at home, but to have enough income to afford a luxury, all-inclusive holiday every year, and enough to have the latest décor for the house to keep up with the neighbours, they needed the extra cash. He resented the people he knew who seemed to manage without having to work as hard as his family did.

10

Can Openers

Lidia greeted Frederick with a kiss on the cheek. Despite the illusion of a happy family, there were difficulties between Lidia and Frederick. Since the birth of their last child, their sex life had virtually disappeared. Lidia had never felt fulfilled with regards to the physical aspect of their relationship. She got bored with Frederick's fumbling in the bedroom and she kept a vibrator in one of her bottom drawers. The difficulty for Lidia was that she had married Frederick after he accidentally got her pregnant. She hoped that she would grow to love him, but her heart had always been with someone else.

Lidia would often try to be the model wife that Frederick wanted, and in many respects she was. At dinner parties she would dress up and many people found her very attractive; she was slim with long, dark brown hair and a gentle face. Lidia was a good hostess, a listener who wanted to be liked. She never wanted to get in arguments, chose instead to agree with a view rather than say what she thought. Some discovered, while in conversation with her, that her responses were limited to one-word exchanges and were eventually compelled to seek out someone more interesting. She was a good mother who looked after her children. For the most part, she managed to hide her irritability and ongoing irritation with Frederick, though was sick to death of the cheap, sweet-smelling aftershave he slapped on. Lidia considered there were probably many other people in worse situations, so she lived her life from day to day. Unfortunately, the façade could not always be kept up and at times she ended up depressed and angry. Lidia recently started to change, however; she now questioned and argued.

After this particularly trying day, Lidia was feeling combative. When he came in from the garden with the children, she pestered Frederick about the promotion he kept promising he would be getting soon. She was angry; he kept saying he was going to be promoted but it never happened. This was developing into a typical Sunday evening argument. He had insisted that he be the only breadwinner to her doting wife, went as far as forcing her to quit teaching. She resented him for it.

Eventually the argument died down, the children went to bed, and Frederick and Lidia, as usual, sat on the settee watching TV, a large space between them.

Samuel Booth, the Minister for Dependency and head of Frederick's department, was the focus of a news report. Booth was saying that the Dependency Unit had saved money from the public purse; the savings were so large that there was going to be an increase in the number of Dependency Programmers. Booth went on to talk about how the privatisation of the Opportunity Planners had been successful. Lidia remarked that it didn't seem right that the Opportunity Planners were now working for Dibble, the largest multinational supermarket. Frederick snapped at her, annoyed both because she was talking while he was trying to concentrate and because he didn't think she understood the issues involved. He ranted about how she wouldn't believe that people were trying to rip off the system and getting something for nothing. He explained how hard they worked, whereas other families were just taking and taking from the State. She nodded but didn't agree with the argument.

'Don't you think it's wrong that people with no money or with limited resources have to shop at Dibble?' she asked.

Infuriated, Frederick shouted, 'Look, I'm trying to watch TV. Anyway if they're increasing posts in the Dependency Unit it could mean a promotion for me.'

They both sat silently on the settee.

Lidia hated Sunday nights; a sense of despair always came over her. Frederick never listened and treated her with contempt. She felt as though her opinions were of no value and that she was treated no better at home than at the shop, like a pretty trinket, just another commodity. At times she became so desperate and frustrated that her thoughts grew very dark. Tonight those feelings, for some reason, came to the forefront of her mind.

'It's time for bed,' Frederick said. He was treating her like a child, which she hated. He always insisted that they go to bed together and, when they were in bed, they could not get farther away from each other; they slept on opposite edges of the mattress, each in his or her own world.

Frederick was usually very tense and restless in his sleep on Sunday night. He shouted as though he were very angry. What worried Lidia was when he got out of bed in the morning he paced and shouted, as though he were preparing for battle. The truth was that Frederick was going to battle. He had a sense of satisfaction that when he went to work he was on the front line, saving thousands of pounds from those scroungers and fakers. She found this odd, and it was difficult to sleep next to him on these nights.

As she lay in bed, she grew more and more frustrated. She could not sleep. She was upset with her situation and her thoughts grew darker than the cloudy night sky. At 4 AM, Lidia got up, tense and full of hatred towards her husband. She wanted to be finished with Frederick.

Lidia went downstairs to the kitchen, in the dark. She put the kitchen light on, opened the drawer where the cutlery was kept, and found the sharpest knife in the house. The whole time she thought about everything Frederick had done to her over the years, things that only she knew about. She grabbed the knife and pulled it out of the drawer.

Chapter 3

Jane lived with her son and daughter, Daz and Jackie. Jackie was seven-years-old and her son was nine. Jane's partner of ten years had died sixteen months prior, after developing a brain tumour. They had always struggled with their finances but had somehow managed. Jane had a part-time job working in a canning factory when she could get work and Phil, her deceased husband, had been an electrician. Jane saw the best in people; she would often be seen as a mediator and would consider other viewpoints. She would talk calmly and would hardly ever swear. Jane became a dependency figure, the pressure from which caused her to lose sleep during the week leading up to her dependency review.

Although she spent three days a week at the canning factory, this in no way was sufficient to keep the household going, particularly when her housing relief had been stopped.

Dibble Housing Association raised the rent and Jane needed extra support. She needed to pass her dependency review.

Late afternoon on a spring day, Jane was in the front room of her three-bedroom terraced house with her two friends, discussing the next day's meeting and how to pass the dependency interview. Jane needed the small amount of cash the State would give her in order to supplement her income, otherwise she and her children would go hungry.

Gina, Jane's friend, knew all about the dependency system. She had come originally to the UK fleeing oppression from a West African country. She was tall and although she recently had put on some weight, she still looked athletic. She had a slight scar on her cheek that, unless someone looked closely, would not be noticed. She liked to chat. If one person had been treated as a lowlife by the dependency system, it had been Gina. If it hadn't been for Jane, Gina would probably not have survived. Her story was one of horror but also one of survival. Gina explained to Jane how the dependency system worked.

'The Opportunity Programmers will come out with the laptops and when they question you, they put your answers on the computer system which goes to the system mainframe at the local office. Their leader, or manager, back at the office just works by numbers, you know,' Gina said. 'Each question has a number allocated to it. The whole system is based on getting over fifty percent, which is the manager's main target, you know. Zero percent is total dependency and 100% is total self-reliance. The nearer the 100% mark, the better their targets. It can mean substantial bonuses for those higher up in the Dependency Department.

'Fifty percent is important because anyone who gets an outcome over this percentage will not be able to get any cash or income. Sometimes people at this point will get food vouchers to spend at Dibble, and others get told what to eat and have no choice as to what to buy. People then get shifted on to the Obesity Helpers Scheme.'

She carried on and explained that, when there are very serious issues, children and adults can be moved from their homes. 'When children are removed from their parents all the support income the parents received will be taken off them or, if they are working, they will have to pay a substantial amount of their income to the children's new parents. The families where the children stay are called the Florence Families; they are trained in moral education opportunity. These families do not cost the State very much money; usually the Catholic Church and other charities pays a top-up to them if they are struggling, but the main income comes from the families who have had their children taken off them.'

Gina went on to explain, 'When the most serious outcome happens, when children are removed, a large number three comes up on the large screen in the Dependency Managers' office and starts flashing, you know. This ironically gives a macho credibility to the Development Programmers since they get credit for this. Tomorrow, you'll see the workers, they manage, called Opportunity Planners, who have been privatised and now work for Dibble.'

Jane was dumbfounded; it all seemed very complicated.

'Don't worry about it; we can get you through it. We can get you under the 50% again. At least there is one good thing about it, at least the sexual favours have stopped,' Gina said.

Jane, bemused and flabbergasted, looked at Gina. 'What sexual favours? What are you talking about?'

'I don't know if you've heard,' said Gina, 'last year there were a few Opportunity Planners who claimed sexual favours for putting the right answers in the computer, but there was scandal. Do you remember last year when an injunction and censor was put on in a court case regarding an Opportunity Planner?'

Jane remembered and nodded. Iris, who was also listening silently, nodded as well. Iris was opinionated and would be stigmatised by the others at times for dressing and acting like an old hippy. This was unfair; though she was passionate about her beliefs, she was well read and could be articulate and down-to-earth.

'Well the case involved a person on Block Seventy-Two, just two blocks from here, and I know this because the person happens to be a cousin of mine, you know.'

Jane was becoming very interested at this point.

'This family had been on the forty-nine percent mark for over two years. The Opportunity Planner had fixed the answers to the questions asked so as to keep the family under fifty percent, so they could keep their benefits. Unfortunately, now there is less flexibility because the outcome of the court case was that the Opportunity Planners work on a new computer program so they cannot easily manipulate the system,' Gina explained.

Knowing that Gina always liked a good story, Jane was eager for her to get to the point.

'What happened was that my cousin provided sexual favours to the Opportunity Planner to keep her below the forty-nine percent, you know. She was so desperate, poor and vulnerable that she could not afford to go over the fifty percent mark.'

Gina said the favours started with a massage and then the Planner wanted more and started to insist on a blowjob. Gina continued, 'But one day, as she got his big fat penis in her mouth, she bit it so hard part of it came off right in her mouth.'

Can Openers

Jane was startled.

'My cousin couldn't believe what she had done. It was a moment of madness. She spat it out, went to the fridge and got out some ice cubes to put around it. In the meantime there was blood everywhere. She called an ambulance and the Planner was taken to A&E. The ambulance driver then took the bitten off bit of penis wrapped in ice cubes and a towel to the hospital. The Dependency Department had a problem.'

As Gina was talking, Iris, who had been sitting silently and listening, said, 'It's ideological you know.'

'Everything is ideological to you, Iris. How can having someone's dick chopped off be ideological?' Jane asked.

'Get it right, it was actually bitten off not chopped off, Jane.' Gina said, 'The Dependency Department has a moral code regarding who deserves what. Remember, it started around the turn of the century when politicians made statements regarding people who smoke not getting as good health treatment as others. And how asylum seekers should get less money than anyone else and how if you get old and had not saved any money and were in poverty then it was your own fault.'

Gina tried to prove her point, 'Like how euthanasia is now legal, and people have a positive choice of when to die. The choice is that they can have a legal injection that puts them to sleep, forever.

Iris always got frustrated with Jane around this point. 'I'll come back to that point, particularly as the State on the face of it have now come under budget and are saving the most money from dependency in old age. There was an article on the government website last week explaining the savings.'

'What's the moral question?' Jane asked.

'Well, for the dependency culture to exist there has to be an acceptance of at least some of the ideas by those people on the receiving end of the Unit. The best way to gain acceptance is to make all those people around either more or less deserving than you, making those who are in Gina's situation at the bottom of the heap. This creates divisions where the poorest in society look at each other and fight for the meagre resources available, often feeling they deserve it more over other groups.' Iris was so desperate to get her arguments across, her voice rose. She wanted to help Jane but also needed her support in a campaign against the dependency unit, which could be risky. The more Iris could show how bad the system was treating people, the more she thought it would persuade Jane to get involved.

She carried on speaking with perspiration appearing on her brow. 'Those people who are planning and arranging the system encourage this division, it makes it easier to argue that the divisions are natural and they are using evidence based science to prove the theories that they want to be seen as objective. Those in power put themselves on a moral high ground blaming the poor for their own position in life. There is only so much money to go round and there are the deserving and undeserving poor. This all goes out of the window when the decision as to who deserves what resources relies on a blowjob.'

Gina and Jane shook their heads.

'Imagine,' said Iris, 'people would start asking questions, including those who never speak out and are slightly sceptical of the system. It could lead to distrust, they'll feel like they have been lied to. This could cause a protest against the dependency system itself. Ironically, a blowjob could be a catalyst. Do you remember how the 2011 revolutions in Tunisia started by a stall holder burning his stall and setting fire to himself? Why can't a revolution start in 2022 with a blow job that went wrong?'

Jane looked at Gina and asked, 'What happened to your cousin?'

Gina said, 'She got a six-month suspended sentence as long as she kept quiet and told no press or officials. She also got a one-year support automatically from the Dependency Unit.'

'And what happened to the Opportunity Planner?' asked Jane.

'Well he got a good pension, signed a clause not to repeat what had happened,' Iris said, laughing, 'And he will never make such a prick of himself again!'

The three of them discussed the interview assessment that was to take place tomorrow.

Jane said that if she talked about the grief and loss she felt from her partner passing away and explain to the opportunity planner the trauma she went through afterwards, that could only help the percentage going towards the zero percent mark. Gina was very worried that Jane was being naïve.

'That will make not the slightest difference. There is no justice, it will go against you; it could even work the opposite way and push you over the fifty percent,' Gina said.

Jane could not understand this. Gina was getting frustrated.

'Look how you helped me. You knew how wrong the identity laws were, the laws on welfare are exactly the same,' Gina said in exasperation. She couldn't understand why Jane could not see the hypocrisy and contradictions of the system.

When it came to others, Jane was very supportive and sympathetic. But when it came to herself, it seemed as though she thought the system could not treat her as anything but fair and the Opportunity Planners would see her as a deserving poor in the end. Jane still thought the system was democratic with an elected government capable of justice.

Gina said to Jane, 'Look at what happened to me. Do you remember that local youths were being whipped up by the Defend the 33 Gang?' Gina described how some youths came across and pulled Gina's headscarf off, spat and punched her, and threw dog faeces at her. Jane and her friends were absolutely disgusted. Gina went on, 'Do you remember when we discussed how some politicians, and the press since the turn of the century, talked about there being a view that the white working class was under threat and the press emphasised the threat of immigration on jobs and whipped up the War on Terror? If you listened to all these politicians, the white working class had racist views that had to be acknowledged. All of these ideas went into the Identity Act. This affected the outcome of what happened to me.'

Jane and Iris recalled that when Gina was attacked the local press had gone into frenzy. The headlines had been "African woman encourages violence", "White youths attack alien to defend their own culture." The journalists had gone on to slate Gina for daring to look different, for encouraging race war. Others, at the time, said she purposely did not fit into society, and how the poor white youths had been forced to violence, how the people should be proud of these youths. Such headlines had been in the papers for over a week. Gina had gone to court, was then charged with encouraging an affray, and the white youths were given victim support. However, Jane saw how wrong this was.

'You managed to get the workers in the local canning factory together, some of them who were parents of some of the youths,' Gina reminded Jane. 'Ironically, some of the youngsters felt there was something wrong. They became suspicious when the press and magistrates were all supporting them, particularly when both usually attacked them. They hated the sentencing that magistrates would give them, particularly the new laws that allowed doctors to give them injections if they were seen as unruly or organising themselves outside of school. The magistrates ordered them to be tagged and forced curfews on them yet, at the same time, press encouraged them.'

Iris and Jane knew Gina was right. They remembered how the youngsters had started to question the person from the 33 Gang who had encouraged them to attack Gina. This person had agreed with the police strategy of tagging youths. The young people had become fed up with the leaders of the 33 Gang talking about the need to respect authority when no one respected the youth. Jane organised a public meeting where members of the 33 Gang had turned up. Jonno, one of the leaders of the gang spoke, 'The only victim here is Gina.'

Gina, remembering out loud, said, 'When I went to Court, the whole community turned out and the gang members who attacked me were there picketing the court, supporting me. The magistrates, lawyers, and police could not understand it. Even the press was confused.'

Iris said, 'That is because they had been taken in by their own ideology.'

Gina responded, 'Here we go again, talking about ideology.' They all laughed.

Jane commented that it made a mockery of the identity legislation and had caused such a rumpus that there were now anti-identity campaigns cropping up all over the place.

Gina knew that Jane was an inspiration and she was trying to convince Jane that it was the same State that provided the Dependency Unit. Gina was certain of the need to organise and fight the dependency laws as they had started to fight the identity laws.

Gina now tried to persuade Jane that her sense of justice was misplaced; hoping that by reminding Jane of Gina's plight it would cause Jane to question her attitude towards tomorrow's meeting.

Jane understood precisely what Gina was saying about the identity laws but how could anyone not be sympathetic to someone who died of cancer?

'When they ask you about the reason you need relief, what you say is that your partner dying of cancer has made you a stronger person, making you less of a burden on the State as you now work for three days and you do not want the support. That will take you nearer the zero percent,' Gina said.

But what Jane wanted to say was that the stress and grief and having to work three days a week had pushed the family so much to the edge that she could not be there for her son and daughter when they needed her most.

'Balancing all these things shows why I need support off the State for a while,' Jane said.

Gina knew this wouldn't work. The Opportunity Planners would interpret Jane talking about stress as a sign that she was trying it on, manipulating the system to get something for nothing. It was only the people who declined the support who were accepted by the computer program as needing the most support. Jane may become a dependency statistic, but at least she would get some money to keep her going for a while.

Gina again tried to explain to Jane how the system is designed for people to get absolutely nothing. Iris then went on to discuss how all the newspapers, TV, and Internet sites were arguing that dependency in old age was gone forever; no longer, they said, was there an issue about paying for the older generation. Iris thought if she could show how bad the state even treated older people, it might convince Jane how bad the system was overall and make her realise there would be no justice.

'That's because they are killing them all off,' Gina responded.

Jane argued that voluntary euthanasia, for those over seventy years old, gave older people a choice in their own lives. If one was suffering from a severe illness, why not be put to sleep by the Human Choice injection?

'You know that I work as a care assistant in a Dibble Home,' Iris said to Jane. 'Let's look at what happens when you retire at 68 years of age. My mother, for instance, got leaflets through the door, all entitled 'Choice in the Golden Age.' As you know, she had arthritis and had started with the early signs of dementia.'

'What I don't understand is why your mother decided to take Option Three?' Jane asked.

Jane and Gina listened in stunned silence. After telling her story about the last four years of her mother's life, she ended by quoting the Dibble mission statement. *Hope, Happiness, Fulfillment, and Choice – the Dibble Way.*

Iris then looked at Jane. 'Are you still convinced there's any fairness at all when it comes to dependency welfare?'

'I have to be honest,' said Jane. 'I think I may have been taken in by all the press coverage saying that there's no longer a financial crises in elder care and there is now more choice.'

'Look Jane,' said Iris, 'the State saves the money in looking after people in the community and by having block contracts with Dibble. And Dibble makes millions of pounds through underpaying staff, poor terms and conditions and, like with my mother, saving seven years' worth of money by having Option Three.'

'Jane, it's getting late,' Gina interrupted. 'We need to go through the meeting that you're having tomorrow. The first question they're going to ask you is if you are creating dependency. You have to prove to them that you're not. Their pseudo-science believes that by the state offering benefits and support it creates more poverty, creating an underclass of feckless individuals with no morals. Poverty and inequality is the individual's fault, the individual is psychologically prone to accepting support. By being naturally greedy and selfish, the poor will take anything they can. So, Jane, you have to show them that you may need support at the moment, but that you'll never want it again; show them that your tragic loss and grief might be affecting you, but that it will not be creating dependency.'

Jane nodded trying to take it all in.

'In the 1940s, the Welfare State was created to supposedly support people from the cradle to the grave,' Gina said. 'This changed in early 2020 when the Government said it would only support those who have not created or caused their own dependence or health needs. The State can't support those who should have the knowledge to make the right choices in life. People have no excuse, as they can access the Internet and the Government Information Service gives all the information people need to make the right lifestyle decisions.'

Jackie and Daz came in with a bag of chips and went straight upstairs.

Iris watched them, sighed and turned to Jane. 'Whatever you do tomorrow,' she said, 'do not let that happen with your children. You will fail the Obesity Option. They will not give you cash; they'll give you tokens which you'll have to take to a Dibble supermarket. You'll be made to go and see the Dibble advisers who will tell you what to eat. They will make you have a health check on your kids and if their fat versus body mass is wrong, they will fine you.'

'Also be careful about your house,' Gina said. 'If your house is dirty, they will argue that you are purposely becoming dependent. But if your house is too tidy they will argue that you have too much time on your hands. What you have to try and meet is the mean tidiness rating, the nearer to the mean then the better.'

Jane, Gina, and Iris discussed late into the evening. Jane was pleased with the support, if not slightly overwhelmed.

Chapter 4

The knife lay on the floor, surrounded and dotted with specks of blood. Lidia stared at the knife trying to regain some composure. She felt guilty and helpless and regretted what she had done, but when she cut there was a sense of relief, as if all the pressure evaporated out of her body and up into the heavens. But now there was regret.

'Why did I do that? I'll never cut again,' she whispered. She looked at her leg and thigh where she had cut herself. The wound was deep; she needed something to stop the blood. She reached for a tea towel and some tissues, now desperate for the blood to stop. She didn't want anyone to see this, especially her children or her husband, who would wake up in about two hours. She spent these two hours trying to staunch the flow of blood, cleaning up the floor and knife of blood. She wrapped a long, loose dressing gown around her body.

Lidia felt so very stupid. Her leg was in an awful mess. Lidia took such pride in her appearance and now questioned what she had done. Lidia could never understand that contradiction of wanting to look good but then making her body so ugly. Lidia thought there was something wrong with her.

The door opened. Zara stood there and started to cry.

'I heard a bang, and it scared me,' she said

Lidia kneeled down to Zara's height and gave her daughter a hug. Her eyes filled, expelling a lone tear. She turned awkwardly, checking to see if her daughter could see through her gown. Zara could not understand why her mother kept lifting her head, repeating "I love you darling", and constantly asking "Are you sure you were not watching

Can Openers

Mummy?", confusing her daughter. Mother's human emotions contrasted to the neat and tidy clinical kitchen, everything in its place, work surfaces glistening in the light, and the little round table with kitchen chairs around it in precise symmetry. Lidia was warmed and comforted by the unconditional love Zara gave her, however felt regretful, guilty, and paranoid that anyone might find out what she had done, feeling the loneliest she had ever been.

Lidia had started preparing the breakfast for the children and Frederick when he appeared. She worked quietly, feeling like a ghost in the room, looking and watching but unseen. He was doing his usual Monday morning stare, concentrating on what was to come. He seemed hyped up, as if he was coming out on the pitch at an FA Cup Final. Lidia had joked about it once, 'Anyone would think you were the captain of an FA cup team instead of being the manager in a poxy Dependency office.' She hadn't joked about it since.

Luckily, this morning Frederick didn't notice Lidia. He had his coffee and cereal, gave his two children the ritual kiss, and left the house.

Their house was at the far end of a close, away from the main thoroughfare. As he walked down the road, Frederick's thoughts started to make him angry. For him, going to work was like going to war. He would never openly describe it this way, but it wasn't just a job, it was a crusade. Frederick walked out of the estate, turned right on to the High Street, and headed towards the train station at the far end. The area around the station had the scars of dereliction. The station itself was modern, but outside on the street there were people lining doorways, some with outstretched hands begging for change. Frederick would never give. He believed to do so would just be encouraging them.

'Thank God' he thought, 'that common sense has prevailed from the old days when there was sympathy for these people.' Frederick recalled how a few years ago, even some managers in his position at the Dependency Unit felt the druggies and the alcoholics should be helped, as though their problem was some kind of medical issue. At least now, he thought, there was no such view. These people chose to live that kind of lifestyle and the State could no longer afford to support those lifestyle choices.

Frederick boarded the train with an increasing sense of bitterness; no one had sympathy for people like him, upright and honest citizens. He was burdened with a 150-year mortgage, but at least his children and grandchildren may benefit. Unfortunately, the sacrifices made by him would also have to be borne by his children, while those good for nothing layabouts expected something for nothing, just sitting outside the station sponging on society. He was handed a leaflet, which he unconsciously in to a bin. He banged the metal bin with his fist as he passed.

Frederick arrived at the office at 8.30 AM, fifteen minutes early, as always. He entered the building, passed the main security, and walked upstairs. Lifts were for the lazy.

When he got to his floor, he punched the code into the door entry system and walked along the corridor to his office at the far end. He passed a large, open plan office where there was a huge bank of TV screens fixed on the wall; they were watched in shifts, around the clock, by officers employed by Camera Eye's Children's Safety Unit. Families put into the "Problem Family" category had cameras installed in their homes that relayed pictures to the bank of TV screens. Microphones were also installed, allowing staff to remotely intervene in any situations.

Camera Eye specialised in the surveillance of the underclass, Category A. Frederick was always polite, saying good morning as he went past. He was relieved he didn't have any responsibility for Camera Eye; he routinely overheard staff members moaning about how many screens they were expected to keep watch on at once.

Just before he entered his office, Frederick passed Marcus, who was also in early. Frederick sat in his office looking out at the open plan floor through the internal window. Frederick glanced at Marcus, a man who had been a thorn in Frederick's side for over a year. That day, Frederick intended to bring Marcus to his office for an interview about his attitude and insubordination.

Marcus was in his 20s and lived, until relatively recently, with his white mother and black father. He was raised in a political household; many times, when he was a child, he had been dragged to various marches. Over time he had developed an allegiance to, and maintained contact with, the Identity Campaign. He had also, at times, dared to question the policies of the Department. This was very difficult to do as everyone who works for the Dependency Unit was told that the mission statement and values of the Department have been scientifically proven by evidence-based practice. It had been made clear to Marcus that if he criticised the Department then he was criticising the customers, and the customer was always right. The Department claimed they always consulted their customers who supported the welfare reforms.

For Marcus, little of what the Department told him made any sense. He had worked for the Dignity in Old Age Section since leaving school, and had already been disciplined on two previous occasions for telling carers they should go to the press about issues they had about Dibble Homes.

At the appointed time, Marcus went to Frederick's office. Frederick stopped him at the door.

'Give us another hour before you come in, the Head of Human Resources is on his way and we both want to interview you regarding an incident. This is a contact number for support if you want it and here is the number for the union,' he said. He abruptly handed Marcus a piece of paper with two numbers on it and shut the door.

Before the interview with Marcus, Frederick went through the figures for his team. He was anxious as the figures were close to 48%, and he realised if two or three cases came in with the correct percentages it would push the overall figure over the 50%, which could mean a promotion and £5,000 bonus for him. The percentages meant that 50% of people that his unit dealt with would be categorised as nearer the total self-reliant category than the 0% - dependency figure, and they would not receive any money from the State. They would be still on the books for monitoring purposes until reaching the 100%, but the public saved thousands because no cash payments were given over the 50% and nearer the 100% self-reliance goal. Just thinking about it gave him a thrill. He thought Lidia would be very impressed.

Frederick was proud and started to daydream about how important he was to society. He managed the unit that stopped people from committing fraud against the system; he was catching those malingerers and con-artists who were taking public funds.

Although Frederick harassed and bullied staff, he never thought of himself as a bully. He considered himself to be firm but fair, and though his staff may not always like the decisions he made on behalf of the State, he had their respect. They understood he was a corporate man, they knew he had to make hard choices. What he didn't know was that one of his many nicknames amongst the staff was 'the smiling assassin.' The majority of the workers considered him to be an out-and-out bastard, they felt that anyone he spoke to was part of a game, like a cat plays with a mouse; he had no warmth or feeling towards any staff.

Just before the Human Resources manager arrived, a Senior Opportunity Planner knocked on Frederick's door.

'Can I have a quick word with you, Sir?' he asked. Frederick waved him in.

'You're not going to believe this, Sir,' the Opportunity Planner said. 'Two number threes have just come in, one in the Old Age Section and the other in the Families Section. I need you to sign the papers, Sir.'

Usually Frederick would have a quick check of the cases but this Opportunities Planner was experienced, so Frederick simply signed the papers, inwardly bursting with excitement. Once the proceedings in both cases had finished, which could take anywhere from a week to six months, this would go on to his statistics and could even mean a place on the Board. Frederick could not believe his luck. On the very day the Head of Human Resources was coming to see him, he would be able to tell him he had received two number threes. He knew this information would go straight back to the Chief Executive.

Frederick panicked briefly, thinking that he maybe should read the files after all. Before he could make an actual decision, he noticed the Head of Human Resources walking along corridor. He put his worries to the back of his mind and started to enjoy the impending excitement of telling the Head of HR about the threes.

Frederick usually went for the easiest option, some would say the laziest.

As he waited for the interview, Marcus's hands started to shake. He could lose his job, which was concerning because he supported his four-year-old son who lived with his ex-partner. Although he got on with his ex, he didn't know how he would survive if he did lose his job and how this would affect his son.

Frederick, on the other hand, was on top of the world, confident. He started to focus on Marcus. Frederick liked to show his authority, however, he was in such a good mood he may show benevolence. All the staff would see him as fair, particularly as they would be expecting Marcus to be sacked. Marcus was well liked by other staff members; he provided some hope to his demoralised colleagues.

'Good morning, I'm Frederick,' he said to the Head of HR when the other man entered his office.

The other man briskly introduced himself. 'You can take the lead on this. I'll just take notes.'

Frederick smiled. He could now show off; he really enjoyed these meetings. He made sure he stayed calm and cool. He would be the consummate professional manager, would not show any expression that was not planned for the occasion.

When Marcus came nervously in to the office with his representative, Frederick introduced the Head of HR who was sitting quietly with him behind the desk, then started with small talk. He asked him if his daughter was well. Marcus corrected him and said he had a son of four years of age. Frederick carried on as if he had not made a mistake and asked Marcus how his son was. Marcus replied by saying that he was fine.

Frederick continued to engage Marcus in conversation, asking him how he was after his relationship ended, sympathising with him on how difficult it must be to manage, particularly with the finances, while having a son to support and living with his parents.

Marcus was worried. He knew that when Frederick was being friendly it usually meant that something bad was going to happen; Frederick hadn't got the nickname "smiling assassin" without good reason.

'Marcus, what I'm about to say is nothing personal,' Frederick said. Marcus nodded. 'How are you getting on working in the Old Age Dependency Unit?'

Marcus hesitated. 'Well, I'm settled and I know a lot of people.'

'Good,' said Frederick, whilst HR and the rep stayed silent. Frederick got a picture of a woman out of his drawer. 'I just want to ask a couple of questions. Do you know this woman?'

'No,' Marcus said.

Frederick looked directly at Marcus. 'We have it on tape that you have said to carers of families on several occasions that they should make complaints. Also, a manager of a Dibble home is concerned that you have upset a daughter of a resident and that you are saying to people they should have twenty-four hours notice before the positive choice injection. The difficulty that you faced was that although the fact is that twenty-four hours notice is required, the decision had already been made; there was no need to agitate the family further. This misdemeanour, however, is relatively small.'

Marcus tried to hide his shaking hands in his lap. He struggled to remain calm. 'I didn't realise that I shouldn't tell people about the notice period.'

'Although the complaints procedure is there, it is not the thing to tell those who go for the positive choice injection, you have to respect peoples' dignity,' Frederick said, patronisingly.

Marcus started to feel quite angry but never showed it, as he knew that if there was ever a minor complaint about a member of staff on a lower grade the Department investigated it like a murder investigation.

'This woman,' Frederick pointed at the picture, 'is part of an activist's network. The Department knows that she has met families of our customers in a cafe on Spring Rowe. Alan's Café, do you know it?' Frederick had a cold smile on his face.

Marcus didn't know what to say.

'This is just a chat; I just want to remind you that if anyone deceives or lies whilst working for this Department it would be very difficult.' Frederick paused hoping it would unnerve the young man in front of him. 'We could give your name over to the Child Dependency Unit today if we found you guilty. We could show that your untrustworthiness could affect your parenting skills. You are, however, very lucky, and we have instead decided to move you, as long as you agree to quit the silly games, Marcus. You may go.'

Marcus and his rep stood up. The rep nearly fell over him in a rush to leave the room. Marcus returned to his desk. Although relieved that he hadn't been sacked after all, he nevertheless felt demoralised.

Can Openers

The Human Resources manager clicked his pen and snapped his notebook shut, placing both on the desk in front of him. He was impressed with how Frederick handled both his staff and his stats. The latter was nearly reaching 50%, and there were number threes coming in at a steady rate.

'I want to offer you the opportunity to meet the consultants on the project planning board,' the HR manager said. 'Are you interested?'

'Yes, of course,' Frederick said. This was a potential move upwards; the board consisted of those who had the power to make strategic decisions, the insurance health companies and representatives of Dibble Health care. He dreamed of mixing with the movers and shakers. Life was starting to look very rosy for Frederick.

Chapter 5

There was a loud knock, more like a bang, on the door. The children were at school so Jane was on her own and she was nervous; this could be the meeting she had been dreading. She, however, was not prepared. As soon as Jane started to open the door it was pushed open, knocking her over. She was shoved to the floor and a police officer held her face down, squashing her to the floorboards. The police handcuffed her. She could see them going in to other rooms of the house.

Jane was initially shocked and terrified but finally gathered enough composure to ask, 'What are you doing? I have done nothing wrong, what's going on?'

The officer holding her down picked her up and a different one screamed at her, 'You're nothing but dirty low life.' Another poked her in the side. She realised this frightening episode was being videoed. Jane went silent.

The officer eventually loosened his grip on Jane. She got up, disoriented, and almost fell into an armchair.

'This video is being used as a risk assessment,' an officer said. The image was being relayed to a van outside on the street. Inside the van sat two Opportunity Planners who worked for Camera Eye. The Opportunity Planners would carefully analyse the facial expressions, body movements, and any aggressive behaviour that Jane may have shown and input the details into the main computer. They would then receive an analysis with three outcomes, 1 - Proceed with caution, 2 – Proceed, or 3 – Do not proceed. Jane received the number 2. The police had now been mainly privatised, so could afford to take no risks.

Can Openers

Jane was particularly annoyed when she read the logo on the back of one of the police officers vests; "Here to Protect and Serve the Dibble Way."

The police took the cuffs off Jane. They had searched every room in the house. Jane felt violated by this total invasion of her personal space, all she could think was them looking through her knickers drawer.

One of the female police officers decided to speak to Jane like she was a human and may have taken some pity on Jane. She explained that a total risk assessment had to be completed because the police had filmed Jane the year prior while she was protesting against the identity laws. It was on the record that she might have a predetermined disposition to aggression if challenged by authority. All her protesting had involved was sitting in the road for five minutes. As Jane sat in the chair wondering if this was a nightmare, two people came through the door and introduced themselves as Opportunity Planners.

'Hello,' said one, 'I'm Joyce Sokvitch. Sorry about the risk assessment, but its Department rules on Health and Safety grounds.'

'Are the children at school?' The male Opportunity Planner, who did not introduce himself, asked.

'Yes. They should be home at one,' Jane said. 'The email I received said they should be seen at a specific time.'

'I'm glad to hear the children are at school,' Joyce said. Jane nearly responded sarcastically but remembered the conversation with her friends. She remembered that the Opportunity Planners always assumed the worst and most negative about those who needed support or, as the Department saw it, those who were dependent.

'How are the children doing in school?' Joyce asked.

'They both struggled when their father had died and had to catch up with course work,' Jane said. She panicked slightly thinking this might be viewed as a sign of dependency and had to think quickly of a way to recover. 'But they have learnt so much in other ways.' Jane was relieved to see the male Opportunity Planner nod at this. Jane remembered what she had been told the previous night; the assessment began as soon as she started to speak.

'We'll be asking questions based on evidence-based practice and the answers will be fed back to the main computer program. An analysis of the data would then take place and an outcome would be produced in the form of a score. This would then go to the dependency manager who would have the final say,' the male Opportunity Planner said.

'The Department,' he told Jane, 'will be able to work out why you make certain decisions. Remember, we are here to help you to help yourself, to help you develop your life plan.'

All Jane could think to say was, 'Thank you.'

'Let's begin,' Joyce said. 'Are you happy or sad when you go to work?'

Jane said, 'I work three days a week. At times I'm happy and at other times sad.' She then knew that she should have given one answer and they must have noted her uncertainty. Jane was drenched in nervous sweat, something she'd never experienced before. Jane knew that if she answered "happy" they might say she was lying, but if she said "sad" they could put her down as work shy.

Although answers to certain questions were more important than others, there was also a separate box for the Opportunity Planner to write about Jane's reaction. Joyce, who had been doing the job for several years, took the lead and noted how Jane hesitated, thinking maybe she was hiding something suspicious. Joyce did not know if this made Jane any more or less dependent because the comments went back to the main computer and were looked at objectively. Joyce had mandatory training in cognitive objective analysis; she was required to be value-free, recording only what she observed.

When Joyce explained this to Jane, she was annoyed.

'No one can be value-free,' Jane said.

'The assessment is fair, honest, and scientific. The Opportunity Planners guarantee an objective value-free assessment.' Joyce said this in a monotone; she had said it hundreds of times before. Joyce then handed Jane a small card with the corporate mission statement that ended: "All customers to be treated the same."

Jane suppressed a laugh with the thought, 'so all customers get treated like shit.' Jane also wondered how everyone could be treated the same when people were different.

Joyce entered a note on her laptop: "Anti–authoritarian".

Can Openers

'If you won the lottery, would you want to carry on working?' Joyce asked. Jane thought the question was odd and hesitated. Again, there was a small box for Joyce to put comments about the reaction.

'Can you work fulltime and, if not, why not?' Joyce asked.

'There's no fulltime work at present,' Jane said.

Joyce said that Jane received a caution for sitting in the road and protesting. She said this might go against Jane, it showed how Jane was not helping herself, which could be seen as a blemish on her character. However Joyce only marked Jane as "low" on this.

Joyce explained how each person's history is put on to the system and that people would be getting specific questions linked to their personal circumstances. Jane's questions were centred on her political activity and involvement in campaigns. This could be difficult, with regards to her job and her children's moral education.

'I am duty bound to tell you that your children need to know right from wrong,' Joyce said. 'The right way to protest is not standing in the street with others. So the next question is how would you teach your children to manage conflict?'

Luckily Jane had planned for this question, 'In the future, I'll go on to the CIVIC website and explain to them how, if they are not happy about something, they could write to our local MP. If the MP does not answer their query, they could write a letter to our local paper's website, who would publish it.' Joyce seemed pleased that Jane knew right from wrong and, in the future, would teach her children moral values.

Joyce reiterated that to protest the way Jane took away freedoms and affected the local businesses that create the nation's wealth.

Joyce had to put a mark in either the box that asked. "Does this individual have the potential for being disruptive?" or the box that asked "is person easily influenced by others?"

However, Jane was shrewd, just before Joyce went to press the button she said, 'I used to believe that being involved with others and organising would get somewhere, but now, since reading the CIVIC guidance, I understand the structures to go through.' Joyce seemed impressed by this remark and other answers. Unfortunately for Jane, there were endless questions about how to protest. She received a positive tick to most of her answers; Jane had been coached admirably.

Joyce then moved on to discuss safeguarding the children and started with health. She asked Jane to take her to the kitchen. Joyce then looked in the cupboards. There were noodles, beans, a variety of tinned food, some fresh vegetables, spices. Joyce always hated the task of looking at what people ate because she had to put all the brands of the food into the computer. This would then go through to the main Hope Centre. Unfortunately, the system had recently been changed and that was causing delays and confusion. If the outcome was blue then Jane would have to go on to the Obesity Plan and get referred to the Dibble obesity support worker who would help with planning.

For her part, Jane was worried. Gina told her to have all Dibble products in the house and she had not the time to remove the variety of brands stacked on her shelves. Gina said that this was not a scientific test - it was all about getting people to buy Dibble products.

Joyce had to do everything methodologically and by the book. Built into her new lap watch was a recording system that recorded everything that was said. If Joyce went against corporate policy or deviated from the script at all, she would be disciplined. This day was especially agitating because she had the trainee with her who could not check or keep an eye on things for her as a more experienced colleague would.

Joyce had not even finished recording the food items when Jackie and Daz came home from school ten minutes later than scheduled. Jane panicked. Joyce also panicked; she hadn't noticed and so hadn't quizzed Jane for 10 minutes about their lateness. Joyce cursed under her breath; if she had been with her usual partner he would have reminded her of the time and that she ought to start questioning the mother. Joyce could not care about the questioning; her concern was if it had been noted on the computer watch. When she got back to the office, the dependency programmer would ask her why she did not start to question at the children's scheduled arrival time. She could be reprimanded on her report. They would use the course on Positive Psychology she had completed to point out that she did not put into practice the investigating child psychological techniques or the theory of the relationship between lateness, anti-authoritarianism, and the mother's lack of control of her children. These theories may have brought up further information regarding child neglect. Jane should have been put under some sort of trauma for the ten minutes and her reaction should have been studied, yielding statistics to determine whether Jane was at high risk of neglecting. The problem was that the person most stressed was Joyce, with the constant thought that she may be in trouble back at the office. Joyce had a plan, though. It was possible she could pretend the children had arrived from school on time, and therefore would have no need to provide an analysis. Could she trust the person she was with? He may be a corporate spy; he may be checking on Joyce, the company sometimes put plants with staff to make sure they held the company line.

What was she to do? Unless she came up with something, her failure would be picked up on by her boss and used against her.

She needed to refocus quickly. She decided to speak to the children.

'Hello, Daz. And you must be Jackie,' she said. 'I'm Joyce, and this is my colleague, Marcus.

'How do you know our names? What are you doing?' Daz asked. 'We are here to make sure you are safe and being looked after properly,' Marcus said. 'We also need to speak to you both alone.'

The children looked at them dumbfounded.

The procedure which followed usually only ever took place if there was a suspicion that any significant harm was happening to the child. However, times had changed. Over the last few years, anyone working for child welfare was also legally obliged to assume that parents were abusers unless they could prove otherwise. Departmental policy was to monitor the abuse. This assumption had been proven by various studies, the main one carried out by the Dibble research department at the main Dibble sponsored university over the course of four years. Trained psychological processors, who were essentially Opportunity Planners with a special qualification, saw parents classified as abusers.

The study's conclusions showed how the dependency class had a predisposition to violence and abuse. The report was critical of the liberal values of previous generations; government ministers had praised it for making welfare services come back to the values of common sense and decency. Joyce was sceptical about the study, but needed a job so she played her cards close to the chest. She was privileged to have a job. She would not be able to get another with unemployment at a constant high. Not everyone was a scrounger and she could easily, and through no fault of her own, end up a dependency figure herself. This thought sometimes made it hard for her to sleep at night. She was a single parent and could never hurt her child, whom she loved more than anything. However, the evidence-based studies showed that if she lost her job then she could become an abuser just because she was poor, which was distressing.

Joyce hated asking children questions, particularly when they were on their own.

"Are you scared of your mother?" Joyce always found this very difficult to ask. The advice from the Department was for the Opportunity Planner not to get to know the children, but move through the questions quickly to catch them off guard.

'Sometimes,' Daz said. What he meant was that when he was naughty he may get told off and was worried he may get in trouble; the child had not intended to mean that he was scared of his mum. However, this was not noted as the Opportunity Planners training instructed that she input the first answer given. There were numbers Joyce had to press which corresponded to answers: sexual abuse was 5; "scared" was 4, no issues was 0. There was no room for what the child meant by the answer, the question was fixed.

The next question was asked to all seven-year-olds in the country under the remit of the department. It was designed to judge how far the child had developed.

'Which is the heaviest, a kilo of stones or a kilo of feathers?' Joyce asked. Confused, Jackie did not reply, so Joyce asked if Jackie understood the question. Jackie was nervous and thought she had no choice but to answer A or B. She knew they were the same but decided to pick one answer even though she knew it was wrong.

'A kilo of stones,' Jackie said.

Joyce thanked her for the answer but would not tell her whether she was right or wrong. The policy was not to give the child the answer. Jackie was even more confused.

Joyce then asked the children question after question. "How do you get on with your sister/brother?", "Do you have a father who comes round?", "Who do you share a bedroom with?", "Do you eat sweets?", and "What do you eat?"

The questions went on and on and every answer was entered in to the computer.

Children always got restless and often saw no point to the questioning; they therefore didn't often take it seriously. Unfortunately, the dependency managers took it very seriously.

Several hours had gone by and Jane was starting to feel emotionally drained. As she began to mentally switch off, Joyce asked Jane the question she had been dreading, the question which brought back the extreme grief she suffered on losing her husband. The wrenching of the stomach, the searing ache in her heart, the numbness, a sense of detachment from the world, it all came back. Jane did not know whether it was Joyce or Marcus who asked the question but it came as though someone was blasting a loud hailer at her.

'How have you managed since your husband died of cancer?' It was not just the words but how it was asked, no emotion, just a cold consideration of the facts.

The Opportunity Planners had been told that if the questions become value laden and if they showed any sense of emotional attachment to the subjects then they could be disciplined. When Jane heard the term "of cancer" her legs weakened, her hands sweat, and she felt numb. She felt like giving in, but somehow she gained strength and responded as coolly as she could manage. 'It has made me a better person,' she said.

Marcus thanked Jane and Joyce entered her response on the computer.

The remaining 15 minutes of the interview Jane thought were the most bizarre. She was told that the family had to be videoed for a quarter of an hour, that they wanted to film her getting her children ready to go back to school, even though they would only be going back for the short amount of time which was left of the school day. They needed, they explained, a snapshot of family life to study. They even asked her to prepare her children a snack so the interaction of family life can be monitored and analysed.

When she finished recording the video, Joyce announced that the meeting was finished.

'What happens next?' Jane asked.

'If the evidence-based science score was below fifty percent, you will be classed as a dependency figure and the funding will be worked out on the basis of the score, but you would be entitled to state aid,' Joyce said. 'However, no one wants to be labelled as a dependency figure.'

'The dependency Unit wants for you to achieve above the 50% mark. This will mean you moving on to the self-reliance category. Self-reliance is not a burden on the state and shows that you are willing to help yourself and your children.' Joyce did not like having to say that but, as the watchtop was still on and recording her every move, she had to explain it all, and in corporate speak.

Jane thought that the Opportunity planners were being very patronising; they had no idea or understanding of how anyone could end up in her position.

Marcus kept quiet, thinking that working in the Old Age Dependency Unit had been bad, but this seemed even worse. He was getting angry but he managed to keep it hidden. Frederick would be watching and waiting for him to make a mistake, keeping an eye on every move he made.

Joyce explained to Jane the second scale the department used. This scale was scored from one and three. Joyce explained to Jane that she had always been at category number one, but if she went on to a two then it would mean that her case would be transferred to the Intervention Team, who would place cameras in every room and watch her family day and night. If she went to number three, it could mean that her children were taken away and placed with Florence families. Jane would be assessed and would be tested to ensure she had enough for her basic needs, then the remainder of any income she had would be given to the Florence family as an allowance whilst they looked after her children.

Joyce told Jane she could go from a 1 to a 3 if the outcome of the interview objectively assessed for the family to end up that way.

'How likely is it that I could end up a three?' Jane asked, physically and psychologically wrecked.

'I cannot say,' said Joyce. 'The interview is now concluded.' She closed down her watch computer. Joyce knew she should not have closed or logged off the computer until she left the address.

Joyce stood up to leave. She shook Jane's hand and placed a small piece of paper in her palm that Marcus did not notice.

Joyce and Marcus left the house and proceeded down the path. They let themselves out of the gate on to the street. Marcus was annoyed with himself. They should not be treating people the way they had treated that family. He hardly spoke to Joyce in the car before the interview. He had been told to be with Joyce that day. He had noticed her on previous occasions and was strangely attracted to her. He noticed her smile when they first met; it lit her whole face and made him shiver with lust. She was of Eastern European decent. She was a single parent, he did not know very much more about her. He was nervous around her. Marcus, however, was perturbed by the interview. It was morally wrong and too hard. Jane had been treated badly. Yet he was conflicted, 20 years of evidence-based research could not be totally wrong.

The computer said that Joyce and Marcus had to take a 45 minutes break. Marcus asked Joyce about going to a local café, Joyce agreed. There was something about Joyce that seemed warm and sympathetic. He wanted to tell her his thoughts about the interview, but he did not know if he could trust her; one word to Frederick and he would lose his job. Not only that, Marcus knew he would end up on the other side, being assessed by Camera Eye.

Chapter 6

Marcus sat with Joyce, a mug of tea in hand. No one else was in the café; the table where they sat was at the opposite end of the counter.

'How long have you been doing this job?' Marcus asked.

She replied, 'Too long.'

Marcus did not really care how long she had been doing the job for, what he really wanted to know was what she thought about the interview process.

'How do you feel the interview went?' He asked, apprehensively.

'OK,' she said.

A couple came into the café. One of them came over to Marcus, greeted him and said how it was good to see him. Marcus said hello in response and then quickly explained that he couldn't chat as he was on his break from work.

'Understand, man,' said the stranger, who ambled off to be with his partner. The couple went to the other side of the café. Joyce wondered if the couple were gay. This thought was interesting to Joyce, there were very few places straight and gay people mixed and yet one half of this couple had spoken to Marcus with warmth. Before this point, Joyce had felt that Marcus could be a company spy there to monitor her performance and give feedback to the Quality Assurance Department, but now she wasn't so sure.

Joyce had been out to see Jane on previous occasions and was under pressure from Frederick to get her over the 50% barrier. Frederick was obsessed with Jane's case as it was one of the statistics that was stopping his promotion. The day before, Frederick had spoken to Joyce and told her in that relaxed but threatening way he used, that he was expecting good results from the case today. He told her that if she came back with the same stats, he would be forced to give her a performance review. Frederick had then seen her again and, with a raised voice, told her off like she was a naughty schoolchild. He told her how unprofessional her attitude towards Jane had become and how her petty emotions were hindering the way she approached the case.

It was true: Joyce had a soft spot for Jane and hated Frederick. He did not know the names of the people they dealt with, they were just numbers to him. Jane was put in to the category of the 48 and 49 percenters. Frederick did not want to understand Jane as a human being; all he wanted was a shift to over fifty percent. Joyce knew if Jane didn't receive any income from the state, she would not be able to survive and may have to move, possibly even lose her children or end up homeless. Joyce knew the wage Jane received, as a canner, was not enough for her survival.

Whenever Frederick spoke to Joyce she wanted to argue back and stand up to him. She hated herself for not doing so, but she realised she had no power on her own. If she did stand up to him, Frederick would bully her even more. Joyce did, however, have a trump card. She was an IT expert. Even with the new computer program, Joyce could manipulate the system and only someone who was brilliant at IT would be able to work out how and what she had done. For now, Joyce thought she had done enough to keep Jane under the 50%. Joyce hated the fact that Jane probably saw her as a hard person, just a number cruncher. Joyce had wanted to tell Jane that it was not her pushing the policy, a policy that Joyce was fundamentally against.

Joyce found herself starting to warm towards Marcus, there was something she found endearing about him. She now started to let her guard down with him; if he was a spy he was doing a very good job.

She decided to start a conversation. 'How come you worked with me today?'

Marcus was shocked. All he had got from Joyce since the interview were monosyllabic answers. He hesitated and wondered whether to tell her the truth.

'Well, it wasn't my choice,' he said.

'I see. Thanks very much,' said Joyce who couldn't help breaking into a smile. They both chuckled. Joyce wanted Marcus to see the other side to her character and not the dismissive, cold, emotionless person she had been portraying. She liked him and thought that maybe he liked her. She did not want Marcus thinking that she was a hard bastard. So she opened up.

'Mr Smyth is putting a lot of pressure on me regarding the case we just dealt with,' she told Marcus. 'He told me yesterday that I am unprofessional and too emotional; he feels Jane stays under the 50% because of the way I input her answers into the computer.'

The reason I was moved was because I was deemed to be too emotional,' Marcus said. 'This is my last chance.'

Their 45-minute break was nearly up.

'What are you doing tonight?' Joyce asked. She felt pleased that she got the confidence to do it.

'I'm going somewhere you may enjoy. Would you like to come? Text me,' he said.

Joyce had to sign back on to the computer, and then they headed back to the office wondering what they were going to face when they got there. As they entered the office door Adrian, another Opportunity Planner, met them.

'Mr Smyth wants to see Joyce,' he said.

Joyce walked to Frederick's office. He called her in when she knocked. Straight away he asked how her family was. Joyce had only seen Frederick yesterday yet here he was acting as if they had not met for months. She always found his manner inappropriate and he made her skin crawl. Before she had a chance to respond to his question about her family, Frederick said he was concerned about her inputting skills. He then explained that the Department had signed a contract with a new IT firm called Cruise, who still employed some of the department's existing programmers.

Joyce had a vague recollection that this was the firm who had been involved in the upgrade of the new computer program.

'I've asked them to monitor the inputs on case A1021a.'

Joyce knew that he was talking about Jane's case and, to make matters worse, Frederick was trying to suggest that the monitoring was something that Joyce may find helpful. Frederick only spoke in numbers.

'You will be pleased to know we may be able to solve the problem of why A1021a avoids the 50% mark.'

Frederick told Joyce that it was nearly home time, but he was concerned about case A1021a. If they could get the case over fifty percent, it would send the average figure for the department over fifty percent. If that happened, they would get the Supporting Investment in Choice award, and would gain an excellent rating. 'You do understand,' he asked in a patronising voice, 'if we get the top mark, it will help our customers? They will be getting an excellent service; that is statistically proven.'

He then spoke softly in a menacing manner; Frederick loved the mind games he played with staff. He knew in his heart that they would eventually thank him for the wisdom and experience he had given them. 'I do not understand why you dislike your job,' he said. 'You should feel privileged to work in a department with so many awards for excellence. I really think that it would be helpful for you, Joyce, to have an appraisal tomorrow. This will be for you and the department.'

Joyce was too stunned to respond.

'I will be inviting the IT experts from Cruise to the meeting, as well as Human Resources, which is now called Human Care, by the way. They're now a private specialist firm. They advised me to call it a disciplinary interview.' Frederick paused, whether or not it was for effect Joyce couldn't tell. 'Anyway, I will stop at this point as you will be late getting home. We do care about our employees' work–life balance.'

Joyce stood to leave but Frederick stopped her.

'Oh, by the way, before you go, how did you find it working with Marcus? I'm concerned he may have been a bad influence on you. I think the mistakes were due to him spoiling your concentration. Don't worry; if it is shown that Marcus influenced you, we will guarantee you stay in your post, we require your skills, but you may have to go on an Attitude Awareness course. You'll be OK. Goodnight.'

As Joyce left the office with a growing sense of anger towards her boss; she had never felt such an intense hatred toward another individual before.

Frederick was pleased with himself. Life was looking more positive to him, and the Higher Board had recognised his skills. Frederick thought about how, if he could prove fraudulent practice, this would show the Board how he dealt with quality control and they the Board would, Frederick was sure, be suitably impressed.

He was looking forward to telling his wife but just as he was about to leave there was a knock on his door. Frederick would leave late from the office at least twice a week but leaving late today was an exception.

Joseph opened the door and entered Frederick's office. They were the last ones left in the department. Joseph was only in his early twenties, a slim, fresh faced, good-looking young man. He had just been promoted to supervisor in the Old Age section. Frederick waved Joseph over from the door and, even though it was not the usual day, Frederick was getting excited, took off his tie and jacket and draped them over the back of his chair, which he then moved back·from his desk as Joseph moved towards him. Frederick sat and waited.

Chapter 7

The café they had been in earlier turned into a bar at night. As soon as he left work Marcus had texted Joyce, 'Would you still like to meet?' Joyce had texted back and said to meet at the café later that evening.

The café was a place where people met as an alternative to the mainstream meeting places. It had become difficult to find anywhere to go that had an identity, these types of venues had gradually disappeared. Two companies own most of the bars and they chose the music that was played, the décor, and the theme.

Dirk, who owned the café, had difficulty keeping it open as the large leisure companies had tried to either buy him out or shut him down. Dirk always argued the point, as he was tonight with a small group of customers, that when pubs were closed down seven years ago due to the depression, it had also stopped people coming together, which was another way of alienating people. The café was Dirk's way of opposing this but it was a struggle. Public houses were where groups met, organised protests, co-ops, etc. This was nothing more than state control over their activities outside of work, and their social lives.

Joyce arrived at the café early and was listening to a self-assured Dirk's forceful comments from behind the counter. Joyce even plucked up the courage to ask him a question. 'If the authorities and the companies wanted to keep this place closed, why have you not been closed down?'

Dirk smiled. 'People come here from call centres. Many of them talk about how they're bullied and how their self-worth is eaten away at work. Some people will always challenge the system however controlled it is. When people get angry,' he said, 'it is better the steam is let out slowly or else there could be a large explosion. Look at Dibble's Canning Factory and the difficulties management have controlling their staff.'

'How does this relate to the café?' Joyce asked.

'The authorities know that meetings take place here. They let it happen as it is a safety valve. They know where people meet, but they also know who and where any opposition will be.'

Joyce nodded, she saw the point he was making, nonetheless, and perhaps despite herself, she could not help feeling suspicious about him. She wondered if Dirk knew someone who worked for the State or if he was working on behalf of the authorities. Joyce was distracted by Marcus' arrival. He was on time to the second.

'Do you want a drink?' He asked Joyce.

'White wine, please,' she said. When he'd gathered the drinks, they went over to the table where they sat earlier in the day. There were now four couples at the counter.

Marcus told Joyce how pleased and excited he was about meeting her. Joyce asked if he came here a lot. 'I do,' said Marcus. 'Funnily enough, this café is featured in one of the accusations Smyth put against me. He asked if I was meeting a woman here who is acting subversive against the department.'

Joyce said, 'If you wore odd socks you'd be accused of being subversive.' They both laughed.

They chatted some more and, as they relaxed in each other's company, Joyce asked Marcus if he was up to going somewhere very different. He agreed.

They left the café with Joyce taking the lead. They cut across a park and went down some side streets, part way down a darkened street, and came to a door at the side of an old building. Joyce pressed the bell.

'What is your password,' asked a voice through the intercom.

'Billie Holiday,' Joyce said. Both she and Marcus watched as the door opened.

There was short hallway and then steps that led down to a basement where they came to another door. A man sat at a small table with an open tin box. After Joyce and Marcus paid a fee, the man kicked the door with his foot.

Can Openers

They walked into a comfortable lounge where people were chilling out on comfortable chairs and sofas. A sweet smell hung in the air.

'Come with me,' said Joyce as she pulled Marcus through another door and into a large room with various seats lined up in semicircular rows. A young man was on the stage at one end of the room, reciting poetry. Joyce told Marcus that the man on the stage had written the poems himself and anyone could get up on the stage and entertain however they liked.

Marcus asked why there was a need for all the secrecy. 'We don't live under a dictatorship, unless it's work.'

Joyce explained that the club was run as a co-operative but had to change venues. The venue used to be in the main street where all the chain bars were. What was so good about that location was that it was very popular with all ages. The club encouraged local people to put on gigs and it was free. However, at the same time it attracted youngsters who used to fight.

Joyce said, 'we also noticed that the fights seemed to be organised and there were certain 33 Gang members there. Fights were always breaking out. A new venue came up so the committee voted to move. Sadly, we found out afterwards that the 33 Gang was paid by the two large bar companies to go and disrupt the club.'

'No way,' said Marcus.

'Oh, it gets worse. The police were always there very quickly and kept closing the club down. The local press accused the club of being a den of iniquity. We also obtained evidence that local councillors were getting cash payments from the bar companies. As if all that wasn't bad enough, the local police chief, who just retired, is now paid as a consultant for security by one of the companies. And in its place is a theme bar owned by one of the two companies.'

Marcus said, 'I suppose they control us when we are in work and outside of work.'

'They try,' said Joyce, 'but it's not easy for them, otherwise why keep trying to bully us? The evidence-based science may be one part of our life but we have our own subjective reality. When we see some of the narrowest minded, least creative and reactionary individuals getting both supervisory and managerial posts, people know there is something wrong, but what do you do about it?'

'I never thought about it like that,' said Marcus.

'It's getting worse. They have a supervisor who talks like a robot about how the team needs to meet the production figures. He meets the staff one-to-one every day and is always picking on any minor point, turning it into a massive issue.'

'I know who you mean.' Marcus laughed.

'He wants to know what the staff are saying. Did you know that he's said if anyone moans more than twice a day they'll be charged for bringing down company morale? The supervisor is called Joseph. Early twenties and no one knows how he got the post. He's got no experience and, even by our company standards, it's odd.'

Marcus told Joyce that Joseph fitted exactly the type of person the company wanted, a 'do not think, just do' type.'And the other thing Joseph brought in was a badge system. Blue badges and small bonuses were given to workers who were team leaders. Green badges were given to the most productive workers and red ones given to all the rest. This created an atmosphere of distrust. But most of the workers just saw it as a job and stayed with the red badges. We at least knew who not to trust, the ones with the green badges.'

Marcus thought that what Joyce had to say was illuminating but he really wanted to know how she had fared with Frederick today. Joyce told Marcus that it upset her even thinking about it. She explained how he had her tracked down by the new IT Company.

Marcus's jaw dropped. 'Oh no.'

'The other problem,' said Joyce, 'is that he has brought you in to the equation.' Joyce then told Marcus how impressed she was with him as he must have really upset Frederick. Joyce explained how Frederick had said that if she blamed Marcus for their poor result then she would be OK. 'I've got an interview with Human Resources and Frederick tomorrow and they're going to accuse me of fiddling the A1021a case. They're going to say it's my fault that the department will not get their excellent rating and Frederick said it will have a detrimental effect on our customers.'

Marcus thought this was complete nonsense. 'We have to do something about Frederick,' he said.

Can Openers

'We can't do anything on our own about Frederick. The State Company has just offered him promotion to the private board, and he fits everything they want.'

'But he is a bullying bastard.'

'So?' replied Joyce. 'Look, the whole system is made up of bullying bastards. That's what capitalism wants. Those at the top of society have gained massively over the last forty years at the expense of everyone else, and that's why the rest of us have to be controlled so they can better exploit us to get their wealth.'

Marcus could understand what Joyce was saying but still wondered if they could get Frederick in some way. He told Joyce that individuals do make a difference. As he was talking, a band came on.

Joyce grabbed Marcus by the arm. 'Come on,' she said, 'let's dance.'

They danced for a while, watching the others dance around them, eventually dancing so close to each other that their bodies couldn't help touching. They gazed at each other, completely focused on each other as the music beat on.

They danced for a long time. They agreed, when they sat down, that the music took them away from their immediate problems. Secretly, they thought that sexual attraction also helped, but neither of them was quite prepared to admit it to each other yet.

Joyce asked Marcus whether the mass-produced music would have the same effect. 'Does the music the big bar companies produce make us passive or was it just about enjoyment? And then, is there such thing as good or bad music?'

'I suppose it depends on what affects you emotionally,' Marcus said. 'Music can remind you of time and place and be very personal. My grandmother loved Frank Sinatra and so do I, even after so many years.'

Joyce said she liked music that challenges and was progressive. Even revolutionary music could give people confidence. 'It is something we need now,' she said, 'like Beethoven and, my favourite, Billie Holiday.'

As they spoke they were getting more confident and relaxed with each other, sitting closer together, touching slightly and looking into each other's eyes. They were becoming closer physically, emotionally and intellectually.

However, they sensed a cloud on the horizon. Could the bond go any further? Were they too stressed? Joyce had her interview the next day and they both knew she would be asked to save herself at the expense of Marcus.

Marcus fetched them both some more drinks. As he sat down and handed Joyce her drink, she began to talk about oppressed people and how oppression could help formulate ideas resulting in real progressive art and culture. She talked about how the anger and frustration with the status quo could produce the best art. 'Look at Picasso,' she said.

Marcus believed that art can be a thing of beauty in its own right, and that a person didn't even have to like an artist for the work to be stimulating.

'I love the music of Wagner and he was not at times the most caring of men,' said Marcus. Joyce agreed.

Joyce told Marcus how one of her work mates had said, 'We need Norman Wisdom.' Joyce had laughed at this but her colleague was serious and had explained that working for the Dependency Unit was like working for a totalitarian state. Her colleague had said that Albania in the latter half of the 20th century was like the department. Norman Wisdom had been a hero in Albania; he had been a clown, but he had laughed at authority. Norman Wisdom had touched some hearts in Albania, and her colleague had said that they needed to do the same. Their department was a joke, albeit a sick one.

Marcus laughed at this recollection of Joyce's. He joked, 'We should start showing Norman Wisdom films in our lunch hour.'

They were now sitting very close. Emboldened by the alcohol, Joyce ran her hand along Marcus leg and touched his hair. Marcus felt like a teenager again. He hadn't had physical contact with another person since splitting up with his son's mother. Marcus stopped thinking about the rest of the world. He leaned forward and his lips touched Joyce's. They kissed and caressed each other. They both felt the warmth of an emotional and physical bond, in some respects neither of them had felt this way before.

Joyce told Marcus that her flat was empty that night because her child was at her friend's. 'Would you come back?' she asked tentatively.

Without hesitation, Marcus said, 'Great.' They both laughed. They finished their drinks and left the club.

Can Openers

On the way back to Joyce's flat, they could not keep their hands off each other. When Joyce opened the door to her flat, they embraced and kissed again. She led Marcus to the bedroom.

Their emotional attachment pushed them towards each other. They undressed in the dark but within close touching distance of each other. They both stood naked in front of each other, slowly touching and exploring each other's bodies. They kissed again and fell on to the bed laughing. The warmth of their bodies against each other felt luxurious. It was a sexual pleasure and freedom they had never felt before with another person. They forgot the world around them. They didn't speak, there were no words that could be said, and the only sounds were the gentle noises of their lovemaking. The immediate moment was sensational and exciting, they both reached orgasm at the same time. They didn't speak; they kissed again and fell asleep in each other's arms.

Joyce woke early, warm and comfortable. As she was preparing to get up, she panicked. In just a few hours, she would be in a meeting that could decide her whole life and may mean the loss of her job. She was numb and frightened of what Frederick could do to her. She knew he wanted her to blame Marcus and that doing so would save her job. The consequences of what she did would also have an effect on her daughter. Her daughter had to come first. Joyce felt awful.

Marcus woke up and put his arms round her. 'Don't do that' she said.

'What's wrong?' he asked.

Joyce said that she was worried about the meeting that day and was worried about the consequences. 'The only way I am going to save myself is for me to blame you.'

Marcus felt unnerved but tried to put a brave face on. 'If you do blame me, I won't hold it against you. I'll understand. it's this rotten system that's at fault.'

'Maybe Cruise IT is not up to the job. However corrupt the system is, there has to be at least some pretence of evidence,' Joyce said. She explained to Marcus how she had falsified entries in the computer system in support of case A1021a.

'Jane needs the money,' said Joyce. 'I have to be honest when I first met you I thought you may be a company plant. I'm now assuming you're not. If you are, you are good.'

Marcus didn't reply.

Joyce also explained that she was upset that Jane probably thought she was a bastard. 'I come across to her as a cold fish and she must believe I support the company line.'

As the morning went on, Joyce was becoming increasingly nervous, so much so, she could not eat breakfast. However, she was forming a plan.

Joyce had regained some her confidence last night; she had started to feel attractive and worthwhile again. She knew she had to think more positively and to think about her particular strengths at work. The IT expert would have to be good to be able to spot how she had manipulated the computer system. They would need to have a total approach. If they concentrated solely on IT, she just might have a chance. But she kept swinging from optimism to pessimism and back again. Her hands were sweating and she looked guiltily at Marcus.

She knew deep down that her hope was false and that she was going to get caught. Would Marcus forgive her if she sacrificed him to save herself? What would she do?

Chapter 8

Iris called round to Jane's house the day after the horror of the dependency review. Iris had waited until she knew Jane's children had gone to school and went straight round to the house. Iris was in the unfortunate situation of being involved with the Dependency Unit both as a result of her mother's death but also on her own account, so she understood what Jane had gone through.

Iris was in a happy relationship with her girlfriend, Jo. She used to be married and had spent a number of years protecting her daughter, who was now an adult, from seeing the worst of the domestic violence she suffered. Iris was pleased that she had now gained some stability in her life; she knew that she still lacked some confidence due to the abuse she had suffered at the hands of her husband.

She was forty-eight years old but looked younger. She was petite and always looked immaculate. Iris looked up to Jane as she provided Iris with inspiration. She was impressed with the work and effort Jane put into the identity campaigns and how she developed and created the Can Openers.

When Iris was involved with the Dependency Unit, the policy had been that domestic violence had a serious effect on the children and, at times, the family would be issued a number 3 and the children would be removed. The State disapproved if you had no income and could not afford to pay the Florence families because the expense would have to be met from State budgets. At the same time, budgets were limited and the unit did not want to fund the children being taken away. At times there was a conflict between the Department's values and the financial reality. If a child were removed, both parents would have to pay, particularly if they were under a Financial Order. Years ago these had been called Care Orders. So if a family's income was very low, they would have a visit from the Income Financial Adviser. However, IFA was employed by HARP, a large insurance company.

The financial adviser would assess the parents' income and assets such as TV and furniture and they would then be compelled to sell what they could. It was in HARP's interest to leave the parents with as little as they could. The company got a percentage of what income they could raise to give to the Florence families. It didn't matter whether you were the abuser or the abused, the state treated you the same. According to the policy, the woman was to blame just as equally as the man, especially if the woman often stayed with her abuser.

Iris's husband had been a foreman on a building site. Iris worked in a care home. Initially the relationship was very loving, but the toll of their respective jobs and the almost constant financial struggles put their relationship under an intolerable strain. Iris did her best to cope but her husband started lashing out. In time, the occasional slap from her husband changed to serious abuse. Iris still had nightmares from the memories.

As his control over her grew, Iris's husband would play psychological games. His favourite form of abuse centred on food. Iris used to describe her husband as traditional, but what she really meant was that he was a chauvinist pig. In practice this meant that he wanted Iris to have his food on the table when he came home from work, but he never came home without stopping off at the bar first. So when he arrived home, he was always at some level of intoxication. He would demand the food be on the table, if it was not there he would immediately walk over to her and put his large hands on her neck and squeeze, at the same time shouting in the face, 'So you think it is funny to let me starve?'

On other occasions he pulled her knickers down and said to her, 'You're only good for one thing, take this you whore.' This was not a regular occurrence, but he did rape her on several occasions.

Iris left him once and went to stay with a friend. He found out where she was and cried on the phone saying over and over that he was sorry and he should never have taken his frustration out on her. He called time and time again and contacted her by text and e-mail. Iris said her confidence was shattered, that she wanted to believe things would be better. Unfortunately, that had been her big mistake, not just because of the relationship and going back to him for more abuse, but also because the Dependency Unit would no longer support her in finding a safe house. The Unit told her that once she had left him it was her only chance.

Studies had been carried out several years prior, showing that most women go back to the abuser because they have lost control over their lives. Such women also needed financial support and help to get re-established. The studies also showed that a common feature for all abused women was that all their confidence disappeared. Iris's friend, Jo, had told her about the studies and that the Dependency Unit had their own evidence-based practice. The theoretical evidence-based studies were run by the Royal College of Dependency and had been funded by Dibble and HARP.

The Dependency Unit told Iris when she went back to her husband that she had made the choice to be abused. They took the view that she had put herself and her child at risk and they would offer no support to her because of this. The family was now to be classed as a problem family. The Dependency Unit would only give women in this situation one chance and, because she went back home, the Unit said that she was encouraging her husband's behaviour.

When the Dependency Unit assessed Iris, she had been hoping that Camera Eye would get involved but, as her situation did not fit their criteria, they refused. They tended to only get involved with families who had too good a lifestyle but were claiming off the Dependency Unit and therefore could be fraudulent. Camera Eye was not used for domestic incidents.

Iris told her friends that when she had gone back to her husband, he became even more sadistic. He would come home from work and when she put the dinner in front of him, he would say, 'Let me taste this.' He would eat a forkful of food and say, 'Not very good, this.' He would go silent and wait, the tension would become unbearable and then he would explode. He would get up, scream in her face and punch her several times. He would shout, 'How you dare serve me this shit, I am a respected person.' Her ex was respected mainly by some young people who were in the 33

Gang until the gang had collapsed after Gina's court case; this was when Iris had her first contact with Gina.

Iris had been forced to go with her husband to the court. He was a National Socialist and had wanted Gina to be prosecuted. Iris, however, had spoken to Gina and they developed a friendship of which her husband was not aware. It was via this friendship that Iris came to truly know Jane.

Iris's husband would play evil, twisted games. It was not knowing what was to come, whether she would get hit or raped, which terrorised Iris the most; she could not predict what would happen and when.

Over time, Iris made friends with Gina and Jo and went to socialist and campaign meetings, giving her confidence. All of this was very difficult for Iris to explain to her husband. There was no way she could tell him the truth about her friendships and activities, so she used her mother as an excuse. Iris's mother would help by telling her son-in-law how unwell she was and how much she needed support from Iris, and there was more than a grain of truth in this.

Iris still sometimes got a beating for going to see her mother but, for some reason, never stopped going. She believed his satisfaction was giving her a beating when she got back.

Meeting her new friends gave her the confidence to fight back. She made her husband's dinners so hot it would burn the inside of his mouth, but at least she got a beating for a reason. Iris knew that if she went to the police they would refer the case to the Dependency Unit and, as both parents were earning, HARP would carry out an assessment which would result in an outcome of number three and her child would be taken. So instead Iris devised a plan with her friend Jo.

Jo worked as a staff nurse, and then in the lab at the local hospital, but before this she had worked in the care home. Jo was an expert in chemical development in new drugs. It was Jo who gave Iris a drug mixture to put in her husband's food. The drug would become addictive but would also calm him down to the extent whereby, if used enough, it would knock him out. It would also have side effects of itching and blotches on the skin and make him impotent, a wonder drug. The drug would become so addictive he would not be able to come off it unless he took an antidote. Otherwise, ultimately, he would suffer extreme convulsions and possible death.

Jane's husband had also helped by installing hidden cameras in Iris's house. It was all part of the plan.

The time had come for Iris to confront her husband. He had unknowingly been taking the drugs in his food for a while. He had become totally dependent without realising. He started to feel very old; he had no energy and experienced severe pains in his chest.

Now was the time for Iris to challenge him. At teatime she put a special chemical cocktail in his food. Afterwards all he could manage was to sit in his usual armchair. The medication she had used left him with the capacity to understand what was going on while he was effectively paralysed.

Iris switched the TV channel without his permission; he got angry but had no energy and couldn't move. She showed a recording of him raping her. He just stared at the TV screen. Iris told her husband that she wanted him to leave the house; otherwise the video recording would be copied and sent to his workmates, all his friends and even to his boss.

'Fuck off,' he managed to say to Iris. 'If you show anyone that video it'll be you who'll be humiliated, you stupid bitch, not me.'

'Oh, I don't think so,' said Iris. 'In case you didn't notice, my face has been pixelated so all people will see is a brutal man forcing himself on a woman who is saying no. You will be the one who is humiliated.'

At this, he knew Iris had him over a barrel.

'By the way,' said Iris. 'If you want to feel better, it would be in your interests to move out.'

'What the hell you talking about, bitch?' he said with the nastiness only he could manage.

Iris replied, 'You know that you can't move, you're becoming weaker, you're having terrible nightmares when you sleep. It's all due to a chemical I've been putting in your food.'

'I'll kill you,' he said, but he felt so unwell he would do anything to feel better. He was caught in a Catch-22 situation, although he wanted to have a go he could not physically do it.

'By the way,' she said, 'if you start eating other food and not take your medication you will end up with septic shock and die. The chemical is in your system and the only way for you to improve is if you take the antidote for four weeks. So if you think you can just stop taking the drugs I've been giving you, think again, it'll probably kill you.' Iris paused, savouring this rare opportunity to have control. 'However, if you move out I will send you daily tablets containing the antidote.'

Her husband's only response was to gurgle out, 'Get lost.'

Iris left him to sleep in his armchair that night.

The next morning, when the worst of the immediate effects had worn off, he tried to carry on with his daily routine but he quickly collapsed; he struggled to move and could not even get to work. Within hours he got the shakes and started hallucinating; within a day he started to experience a terrible, unbelievable itching and hot sweats, he saw terrible flashing lights that he thought was a sign of his impending death. He could not get out of bed; his legs were immobile. Iris was frightened that if he did not give in he would die.

However, within 24 hours, he was crying, real tears streaming down his face.

'Do you want me to move out?' he asked,

'Yes,' she said.

'OK,' was the only response he could manage.

Iris had beaten him. She tried to make him comfortable and then explained to him what would happen next. She told him she would give him the antidote for two days and he would at least then be able to walk.

'But,' she said, 'I want you out of the house by the end of the week. If you hurt me or our child in the meantime, I will stop putting the antidote in your food and you will end up back in the same state.' She paused to give what she was saying time to get through to him. 'You'll need the antidote for several weeks. When you leave I'll bring the antidote to you on a daily basis and remember I still have the video. Do you understand?'

Her husband nodded, at this point would have agreed to anything. Iris also made him agree to sign a contract agreeing to a separation, that both of them were willing parties to the end to the marriage; he was also forced to agree to never come back to the house again. As his strength slowly returned, her husband took the pen and signed on the dotted line.

Even though he had signed the contract, and despite everything that had happened to her, Iris felt guilty about what she had done. When he moved out she took the antidote round every day and watched him improve. Iris was still very cautious; she posted the medication through the door. She also had the locks on the front and back doors changed.

After a few weeks, he did not need the antidote anymore and Iris stopped taking it to him. However, now that he was well again, his threats to Iris started. Iris realised that drugging him might have got him out of the house, but he did not seem at all concerned about the video.

Eventually he told Iris that he was moving back in and told her she needed to get his dinner on the table; he gave her a time and date when he was coming back.

Iris was on tenterhooks all that day. When the appointed time arrived, her husband knocked on the door. Iris went to the door and opened it. Her husband pushed his way in. 'Where's my dinner?' he demanded as he went into the living room where 14 women met him.

Jo said to him, 'This is just the start. We've seen the video and it will be circulated round the whole area.'

One of the women, a martial arts black belt, went up to him. 'Come on, big boy, want to try and fuck do ya?' she said with a snarl. She then slapped him in the face.

Iris's husband put his hand up to his cheek, which stung from the sharp slap. He hesitated briefly before turning around and running out of the front door. Iris had had no contact with him since.

Because of her experience, Iris had a lot of sympathy for Jane and was worried that Jane was going to have her income taken off her.

Iris asked Jane if the Opportunity Planners had asked about or mentioned the Can Openers. Jane replied that they had never mentioned it at all.

'They didn't mention about your pay rise?' asked Iris. 'I know it's not enough for you to live on as you only work part-time but I would have thought it would go against you.'

Jane shook her head and shrugged.

'So what happened yesterday Jane?' asked Iris.

'Well, the police floored me as part of a risk assessment because I'd been involved in a protest.' Jane shook her head at the memory. 'They asked me questions like "how happy are you from one to ten?" and, after talking to you and Gina, I made sure I scored below five.' Jane and Iris both smiled at this. 'However,' continued Jane 'I think they're going to take my support away. I'll be desperate for a full-time job else I do not know how I will survive.'

Iris tried to tell Jane not to worry and asked how the rest of the interview went.

'The female Opportunity Planner was very hard, a real job's worth,' said Jane. 'And the male looked disinterested and didn't want to speak to me at all. At the end, she put a note in my hand but my palm was so sweaty it just smudged the writing so I couldn't read it.'

'I'm not sure I should tell you this,' said Iris, 'but I and Gina had a little bet. I said they wouldn't ask you about the Can Openers, but Gina said they would.' Iris wanted to ask Jane a question; she also wanted to know more about the Can Openers. 'I want to ask you a favour, some of us who work at the care home, are fed up the way we and the residents are being treated. We want you to come and meet us and tell us how you organised everything in the canning factory and created the Can Openers.'

Jane was surprised but wouldn't mind talking about what had happened with the Can Openers as she knew it would help take her mind off the outcome of the dependency interview.

Jane began. 'The whole area,' she said, 'knew that the Dibble canning factory was like a totalitarian state. Anyone who spoke out would either be disciplined or sacked.'

'So how did you go from a culture of oppression to getting a pay rise and a better shift pattern in one afternoon?' asked Iris.

Jane laughed. 'We stopped and shut down a shift, but it took longer than an afternoon. Do you want to hear the whole story? It may take me a long time to explain.'

Iris told Jane that she was really keen to hear the story. 'You keep promising to tell me, and I promise I will not interrupt.'

Chapter 9

'The plan was to stop work for one afternoon; the stoppage lasted one and half hours and the company accepted our terms. What we did was to refuse to put the cans on the line so production would be held up. The difficulty for Dibble was that each part of their production process was so well timed that if there were a blockage in the system in any of their plants in the world, it could create chaos. Also the company is so vast, they're worried about competition. As soon as there is a gap in the market, another company will jump in and get an advantage,' Jane said.

'So how did you get everyone to agree to take action?' Iris asked.

'Well,' said Jane, 'the first thing a couple of us did was look at the obstacles, and one of them was that the company pays for thirty union negotiators fulltime. They pay them above their working wages. They were on the same grading as middle managers. Over the years, even though most of the workforce was in a union, they became very cynical. Conditions were negotiated and productivity deals were completed. The union officials used to go the workforce with managers after negotiating conditions at the factory committee meeting. This committee was made up of the paid union officials and senior managers. The union leaders then speak to the workforce saying how they've won good conditions and I am sure they believed they had. But our conditions were actually getting worse.'

Jane paused and fetched drinks for her and Iris. When she returned, Jane continued. 'In our small section of forty workers, all of us were on different grades, which was done deliberately to divide us up. Things started to change when management told us they were not going to supply toilet rolls and soap in the toilets unless we paid for them. The union officials said they originally opposed it, but got an agreement that at least the workers are still allowed to go to the toilet. Everyone in the section got very angry. So I went around and we organised a meeting after work. The workers were angry about management and everyone agreed to do something.'

'Go on,' said Iris.

'The following day we all walked off shift at one-thirty,' Jane continued. 'We all decided to go to the loo together and then went to the manager's office where he had put the toilet rolls. Management went ballistic and got the head of the union to come down to negotiate.'

She took a sip of her drink. 'The union head came and spoke to us and we all went out on to the shop floor to hear what he had to say. He agreed with our view and said if we go back to work they will try and get the situation reversed. One of the members shouted out "We're not moving until we get the rolls and the soap back." Someone else shouted, "Let the Battle of Bog Side commence!" The union rep left, to speak to the management, we assumed. Ten minutes later, the union official came back. He told us that management felt there had been some misunderstanding, a communication problem. They had no intention of making us pay or taking the toilet rolls or soap. You should have seen us. Everyone knew we gained a victory and it was the first time the canners had stuck up for themselves. When we went back on the line one of my friends said that we'd now opened a can of worms, a good description. After that I became their unofficial spokesperson.'

'That's amazing, but really funny,' said Iris.

'Yes,' said Jane, 'it had it certainly had moments of comedy. Anyway, a short time afterwards, they moved me to another section. I made sure the section I left had stewards and was organised. Two people came forward. One of the union activists, the one who mentioned the can of worms, said we should organise amongst ourselves across the whole factory. She suggested we call ourselves the Can Openers and the name stuck.'

'Go on,' said Iris.

'Well, as soon as I moved, we had union meetings in the new section and elected people to represent us. The main union official also recognised me as a shop steward. He asked if I would be interested in going for a post with the union, as one of the fulltime officials would be retiring. I made no comment. We were having meetings outside work and called them Can Openers meetings. Anyone could come, we wanted Can Openers acting as stewards all over the factory, and ideally we wanted all workers to be Can Openers. If we could achieve this, then it would be us who decided our destiny. We didn't want any one saying they were going to do it for us and telling us to be reasonable or taking away our hope.' Jane paused briefly. 'Word got round, even though we were being watched closely by management and the union leadership. Ironically, after the Battle of Bog Side, management was less bullying and more reasonable with us than in any other area in the factory.'

'So was that it?' asked Iris.

'Not at all,' said Jane. 'Time went on, but we decided to speak to at least one or two workers from every section. We were Section C and there were over two thousand workers as a whole in the entire factory. We argued that the only way to achieve anything was to do it ourselves. Initially not much changed, in fact things got slightly worse. If the management found out that workers had been to our meetings they would be victimised.'

'What did you do about it?' asked Iris. 'Because I know we'd have that problem with our management.'

'Well,' said Jane, 'we had to make our meetings more general so we talked about other disputes, the nature of society, how society changes, and other topics to keep members interested. The problem was that this lasted about ten months, management kept bullying, and we weren't sure of how confident our Can Openers were. Some sections didn't even know what was happening. But we kept meeting and more and more workers, even if just on paper, joined the Can Openers.'

Jane paused again. 'After about ten months, the issue we discussed previously came up on the agenda. Although we didn't know what went on in negotiations, we had recruited some more shop stewards who were on union committees. We knew something big was on the table when all thirty paid union officers called a meeting with the general factory shop stewards committee. The general works secretary, Dodge Dearly, spoke.'

'What kind of a name is that?' exclaimed Iris.

'Oh, believe me,' said Jane, 'That name suited him. Dodge told us they'd had a long and protracted negotiation with management. He told us that they'd discussed an issue and it needed to be taken back to members. He actually boasted to us, *boasted*, that they'd achieved a situation where there would be no job cuts, but there would have to be pay cuts and shift changes.'

'What did you do?' asked Iris.

'We all said, "Tell management no." The officials said they couldn't do that but would send a ballot out to people's home addresses. We then decided to test our network. We produced newsletters and got word round that we were going to have meetings after work and, where possible, at lunchtime. All the workers were angry, I could feel the tension, and even management recognised it. In the end Dodge decided to call a mass meeting.'

'I cannot believe it how well organised you are,' Iris said. 'We want to have a campaign but I am not certain we could do it in Dibble Care homes. I wish we could have a go against the Dependency Unit.'

There had never been such a meeting in the history of Dibble Multinational; they knew that for too long they had taken their workforce for granted,' Jane said.

Jane clearly recalled what had happened. How Dodge started to speak, 'Comrades, brothers and sisters, he had said, none of us are happy with management but we all need to work together and have some common sense. New products are being developed and the tin cans could soon be outdated.' Jane remembered how he had had to stop there as the heckling was so loud.

'No way,' said Iris.

'At this point,' said Jane, 'the shouting stopped so we could hear a worker who I recognised had become a Can Opener the week before. She said, 'Let's not put the cans on the belts tomorrow afternoon.' Well, the meeting went in to uproar and everyone cheered. One of Dodge's fulltime officials said, 'I agree with the sentiment but we need to go through procedures'.

Can Openers

'Well,' said Jane, 'he also got booed and heckled. Again the meeting let a young female union member speak.'

'What did she say?' asked Iris.

'Get this,' said Jane, 'she said, "I want to put a motion. We stop production tomorrow afternoon and any negotiation with management is done by people voted on at this meeting." The meeting went wild; I and two other Can Openers were voted to go to any discussions with management. After a long debate it was agreed that three union officials would also go to discuss anything with management. The main vote then took place and it was unanimously passed that no cans were going on the line the next afternoon.'

'Wow,' said Iris, 'it sounds really exciting.'

'Oh, it was,' said Jane, 'but it was scary too. Dodge was fuming, but afterwards we got word around by all means possible to our members. Dodge was angry because they had a whole process of consultation that we ignored. They had even signed a voluntary agreement that if any section took industrial action they would ballot their members, and the ballot would not be valid if there was a return of less than fifty percent.'

'That's a stitch up,' said Iris.

'I know,' said Jane, 'everyone in the factory was involved from the loaders to the admin. Ironically, we had had a number of low paid women admin staff recently join the Can Openers. Because of the high level of technology involved in timing the products as they go out to the stores and customers, every second in the production cycle counts. If there was any hold up at the stores, a rival firm would get to know about it and push the product up in their stores. Remember, this is Dibble's largest canning and food plant in Europe. Well, the rest is history. We stopped work at one-thirty. Dibble agreed to all our demands and agreed we could have a mass meeting in two weeks.'

'So that was that?' asked Iris.

'Not quite,' replied Jane. 'The members wanted us all to stay out and demand a three percent pay rise. The meeting was split and we agreed to go back to work as long a discussion took place with management over the pay rise. We were back at work by three with no shift change, no job loss, and no cut in wages. The following Monday, management offered us three percent pay rise to be reviewed in six months. We were jubilant and so was the workforce. Everyone wanted to join the Can Openers.'

'That's amazing,' said Iris, 'and at least your position is secure, they would not dare touch you after all that. Besides, you're a hero to the Can Openers.'

Jane said, 'I may be but I still don't think they'll give me the five days a week I want. They still have their ways and means to get revenge and I'm still reliant on the bloody State to make ends meet. I was the only part-time worker involved in the discussions and, in some ways, the most vulnerable.'

Iris asked, 'Can't you get the Can Openers to support you going on five days a week?'

Jane replied, 'I couldn't ask them to do it just for me but we could look at arguing to make temporary workers permanent.'

Iris said, 'If the Opportunity Planners had a go at you too much, they must not realise what support you have.'

'Things have settled down,' said Jane. 'The union members' confidence has gone up and the middle managers are laughed at and ridiculed. The disciplinarians have stopped; they're worried the Can Openers will disrupt production. I've never known a time when it is such a pleasure to go to work.'

'Jane, can I speak to you about my situation and ask for help?' asked Iris.

'Of course you can,' Jane said.

'Look, it's like this,' said Iris, 'the care home I work for has now been taken over a hundred percent by Dibble Care and a number of us who work there are very concerned about how the residents and we get dismissed or disciplined. They say we're going against all the scientific research. I've been discussing with others that the science they use and the evidence-based research is ideological. It just fits the needs of big business and the state that supports the one percent at the top of society who have gained billions of pounds at our expense.'

'Good argument,' said Jane.

'Even though not all the staff agrees with me on every point, they do feel that there is something very wrong and certainly concedes to most of the points I make. Something else I wanted to discuss with you, just between you and me, but I feel people who come in to the care system at seventy years old and have the injection are getting murdered.'

'That's a very dramatic thing to say,' said Jane, although she certainly had more sympathy than she had previously and agreed with Iris on most of what she said. Jane also saw how Dibble, when they could get away with it, treated workers so badly that it could make them both physically and mentally ill.

'I know it sounds emotive, but I'm concerned,' said Iris. 'But listen, I've got a number of colleagues who want to organise a meeting with you and other Can Openers; remember these care homes are like factories, they're big and employ a lot of people. I think I can get a number of staff to join the Can Openers.'

Jane's mobile rang. As she screened the number, she knew it was the call she had been dreading; it was the Opportunity Planner with the outcome of yesterday's interview. Jane shivered, how was she to survive if she was to be classed as self-reliant? She took the call.

Chapter 10

Frederick waved goodbye to his children before he left for work. That day was going to be important for him and his family. He was pumped up. He was going to interview Joyce. The A1021a case had been an irritation to him for a long time. He knew there was something wrong with it, but couldn't see what.

Frederick had planned to meet the IT experts that morning. He decided to get in 20 minutes early to study the case. If he could prove that Joyce was affecting the outcome he would make her suffer and, at the same time, would be able to punish Marcus. He would make an example of her. Frederick decided he needed to show his authority; he would sack her on the spot. If all went to plan, Joyce might even implicate Marcus. That would send out a clear message to the rest of the staff; they wouldn't dare question anything again, his control would be complete. Frederick felt he was justified in his actions; it did not matter to him about Joyce being a single parent, she was an adult who knew right from wrong; she needed to be responsible for her own actions.

Frederick was excited. On the way to work, he practiced his facial expressions. He would lead Joyce into a false sense of security, play with her like a cat played with a mouse. She deserved everything she got. Frederick took what Joyce had done personally.

He believed in the values of the Dependency Unit. He believed it was his moral duty to stop the abusers of the system. Frederick genuinely believed that the customers of the Dependency Unit chose their fate.

A couple of years ago, around the area of the station where he caught the metro to work, there had been riots. The rioters needed a moral focus and, with the church in disarray, the Dependency Unit could provide that focus. People in Frederick's position would impress upon the underclass the need to have boundaries; he acted as the moral policeman of the poor.

Frederick knew that all the scientific evidence backed him up. He was a very proud man. How could anyone question him? In his office, the computer systems could now predict customers' behaviour; those who questioned were very stupid individuals.

He then considered his own family, how his children were in the scouts, how they saluted the flag and how his family respected him because of his discipline and values.

Frederick made sure his children supported the genuine poor, the genuinely deserving. He made them do charity work. They collected money for the local hospice. Ironically, it was the same hospice where A1021a's husband had died, not that Frederick was aware of this. He had sympathy for cancer sufferers, but not for those who were diagnosed with depression – they should just cheer up and get on with it. He liked that he had such strong moral values; it put a spring in his step as he walked from the station to his office.

Frederick arrived early, waiting for IT. But at the scheduled meeting time, it was not IT that arrived but Herbert, his boss. Herbert was in his late 50s and a pragmatist. He had always supported Frederick.

Herbert sat on the Management Board along with some very powerful figures. There were two Sirs on the Board, and the Head of the Dependency Unit for the region. Because it was a partnership grouping, the Head of Dibble Care also sat on the Board, as did Maggie Brown, OBE. Lord Dibble even made appearances from time to time.

However, despite the number of people who sat on the Board, in reality only a few people controlled the Board, the Head of the State Development Unit, the Head of Dibble Care, Sir Harpa, and Lord Dibble, who was a Director of Dibble UK.

Not all of the Board supported Frederick. The Head of Dibble Care believed Frederick to be, what he called, a loose cannon. Herbert, however, felt Frederick really believed in what he was doing and that was why he got the best figures. Although some members of the Board were concerned about what they saw as Frederick's evangelical crusade, they also knew he came up with results. The system was set up and he always came up on top. The Board members knew they would have no choice but to sooner or later to bring Frederick on as a member. People could be seconded on to the Board but they had no voting rights. This was the appointment that Frederick hoped for. He also knew if he got the position it would come with a substantial bonus paid by Dibble Care.

'Hello Herbert,' said Frederick. He was always nervous around his superior. Because Frederick really wanted to please and impress Herbert, he would sometimes bumble his words and almost become inarticulate. Herbert always turned up unannounced.

'How are you getting on, Frederick?' asked Herbert.

'I'm fine,' he replied. Frederick was not happy to see Herbert. He wanted to sort out the situation with Joyce and had been looking forward to stamping his authority; he had it all planned out in his head. He could not understand why Herbert was there, at that time. If he had sorted Joyce and the case out then he would have expected Herbert, but not before the meeting had even started.

'Would you like a coffee, Herbert?' asked Frederick.

'No,' Herbert replied. 'Anyway, I want to tell you why I am here.'

Frederick tried to remain calm but he inwardly thought he could feel his stomach liquefying. He felt like a naughty schoolboy. He was, in fact, an intense coward. Perhaps, thought Frederick, he wants to know why the one case has been on less than fifty percent for over a year; maybe he doesn't know that the case is being sorted today.

Frederick became so nervous he felt his pants get wet from perspiration. He had to go to the loo, he was sweating, and he started to shake. Frederick managed to excuse himself and he rushed to the toilets. As he sat on the toilet, Frederick slowly composed himself; he knew the only way he could get through the meeting with Herbert was to calm down. Frederick washed his face and went back to his office to face Herbert.

'Are you ok now?' Herbert asked.

Frederick responded saying that he didn't feel very well and he may have food poisoning.

Can Openers

Frederick,' said Herbert. 'I believe you are meeting one of your Opportunity Planners today.'

'I am,' said Frederick, 'and I think things are going to go well.'

'Well, I am going to give you some good news. We want you to come on to the Board.'

Frederick was stunned into silence; this was the very thing he had planned for, dreamt of. However, he was puzzled. He hadn't yet reached his target, perhaps they knew the case he was dealing with would be a foregone conclusion, they must have the information from IT. Frederick knew that now he was really going to sort Joyce out. It was his moral duty to do so; in fact it had now become as important to sort Joyce out as is his promotion was to him.

Herbert explained, 'Dibble are going to be offering you a £7,000 a year bonus.'

This was more than any person had been offered in his position. Frederick could hardly believe it, after all these years he was now finally being recognised, he was so proud.

'There's one small thing we want you to do.'

'What's that?' asked Frederick, thinking they probably wanted him to sack the deadwood Opportunity Planner.

'We understand you're seeing that Opportunity Planner this morning. What's her name, Joyce, I think; well, when Joyce gets here, and I know IT is coming—I've told them to come later so we could talk first—we want you to find her innocent and no case to answer.'

Frederick laughed, thinking Herbert was joking. 'Look,' he said, 'I'm going to sack her and make the A1021a case go over fifty percent. I want to come on to the Board as the most successful dependency programmer and manager.'

Herbert, however, was not joking and he found it disconcerting that Frederick would act in this way. He shouldn't have to explain the bigger picture to someone of Frederick's calibre, it irritated him to have to do so, but he knew he had to make Frederick understand the situation they were all in.

Herbert said that he understood that he believed in the science behind the practice and in the Dependency Unit, and so did Herbert, but it was important to understand that sometimes the goal posts had to be moved for the benefit of society. The problem for the Board, Herbert explained, was that because they did not have room to be flexible, they could only make slight adjustments. The system had become very rigid and too scientific. Most of the time this suited Dibble, but when there was a crisis the lack of flexibility made it almost impossible to make responsive adjustments to the system.

There had recently been a crash on the stock market; it had been stable over the last few years, primarily thanks to the welfare bubble. With the welfare state being broken up ten years prior, the private insurance/venture companies and risk assessors had made millions.

Dibble made more profits than most firms and were seen to be the organization to invest in. Although Dibble had big rivals, it was the main player. Their shares had just crashed for the first time in ten years. Dibble needed to sort out the crisis.

Herbert became firm; he said that Frederick had to find Joyce innocent. Frederick was perplexed and frustrated; he could not understand why Herbert talked about the economic crisis or where Joyce came into it.

He decided to disagree with Herbert, the first time he had ever challenged authority, but he was confident they could not turn him down. Before Frederick had a chance to say anything, Herbert told him to leave his office for ten minutes. Frederick went outside and hovered by the door. Most of the staff didn't notice Frederick outside the office except Joseph who watched from the other side the room.

Inside the office, Herbert phoned Phil from IT, who was on his way to meet Frederick. Herbert asked Phil what the IT evidence was against Joyce.

'She is one hundred percent guilty and we have the evidence. Frederick should be dismissing Joyce on the spot,' said Phil.

Herbert knew this posed a problem for him. The IT Department was run by Cruise, another large company. Herbert knew it would be in Phil's interest to pass his knowledge on to his superiors, but Phil was also in a position to make a recommendation about how serious the offence was and if Joyce should be dismissed. Herbert was also aware that Phil was the only person who liked Frederick; they had the same values, although Phil was not so radical in his views.

Can Openers

Herbert told Phil he had taken orders from Head Office that Joyce should not be dismissed.

'Get stuffed,' Phil said, 'I don't work for your organisation and, as far as I am concerned, she should be sacked.'

Without a further word, Herbert put the phone down on Phil and angrily dialled another number. After a short delay, Herbert spoke to Phil's boss. Five minutes later, Phil sent a text to Herbert informing him that the Head of their organisation in the UK had personally phoned him and told him he had to take orders from Herbert.

Phil had never before met or spoken to the Head of his organisation but it was more than his job was worth not obey to his instructions. Phil thought the situation was completely bizarre.

Whilst Frederick stood outside of his office, he noticed Joyce at the far end of the open plan room. He also saw Marcus. Frederick grinned.

Now, he thought, is the chance to get rid of two for the price of one. He really wanted to fire Joyce; he took it personally that she had been manipulating the system. This not only had an impact on the Department, but it had kept Frederick's figures low for such a long time. He wanted revenge.

Herbert asked Frederick to come back into the office. 'Sorry about that, Frederick, I just needed to speak to my boss.'

A knock on the door interrupted Herbert, Frederick opened the door and Phil walked in.

Whilst all of this was going on, Joyce watched from the other side of the office and saw the different people going in and out; she was worried that all the to-ing and fro-ing had to do with her. She feared the worst.

As soon as Phil entered the room, he was asked by Herbert what evidence was there regarding Joyce.

Phil said, 'Joyce has been able to use a slightly different coding system, allowing case A1210a to always come under the fifty percent. I've got all the data; we can prove it, categorically.'

'Thanks, Phil. Would you mind if I have a word with Frederick alone.' It was a statement, not a request.

As soon as Phil was out of the door, Frederick said, 'Before you say anything, this woman is as guilty as sin and I am going to dismiss her. No one can say that I am wrong.'

Herbert wasn't used to being spoken to in this way. He got angry, his face became redder and Frederick could see a vein twitching in his neck. Frederick had never seen Herbert in this mood before and wondered if he had overstepped the mark.

Herbert said angrily, almost aggressively, 'You will not get your promotion, and you will be stopped from coming onto the board if you dismiss Joyce. I want you to accept the evidence, but give Joyce the opportunity of getting it right next time. Anyone can make a mistake. You will say to Joyce that she got too emotionally close to A1201a and you will make Joyce go out and see her again to reassess without IT monitoring.'

Frederick did not understand, was suspicious. He had never thought of questioning the integrity of the Department before. They were protecting Joyce but could not understand why.

Frederick tried a different tack with Herbert. 'If you let Joyce off the hook it means the A1210a case will not move to over fifty percent and the Department will be paying money out for a scrounger.'

'We are aware of that,' said Herbert. 'However, you need to go in and interview Joyce with Phil and you will insist on seeing all the evidence. But if you choose to dismiss Joyce, you will not get promotion to the Board or get your bonus. We also have information that you were going to use the case to possibly dismiss another Opportunity Planner, some young man called Marcus. You therefore would be using one person to get someone else; that could be seen as discriminatory and could lead to you being investigated.'

Frederick could not believe what he was hearing. Despite being wary of Herbert, he had always been supportive and encouraging with regards to the actions he took against staff, including recently Marcus, and indeed Herbert had actively encouraged it.

Herbert said, 'Enough is enough. You need to see Phil and then see Joyce. It is your choice.'

'What choice do I really have?" thought Frederick. The motto of the Dependency Unit was to offer choice to customers. "Where's my choice?" he wondered. Frederick felt very strongly about what happened. Joyce needed to learn the consequences of her actions. This was the first time Frederick had felt confused and unsure about the situation he found himself in. How could they go against the value-free science? How could they allow him on the Board without getting the A1201a case over the fifty percent? It was so confusing.

When Herbert left the room, Phil entered again. Frederick composed himself, determined to focus on the task at hand. He wanted to see all the evidence. Phil then spent thirty minutes using technological language that Frederick did not understand to describe how the system had been manipulated.

Phil told Frederick that he didn't know why Joyce manipulated the system but, he said, 'That is why the system needs people like you who are professional.'

Frederick nodded in agreement.

'You keep your distance seeing cases in numbers, making you completely objective,' Phil said. Frederick was under pressure; he always believed that staff saw him as firm but fair. To be fair for everyone, the only principled position would be to sack Joyce.

Joyce had now been waiting for two hours to be seen. Frederick pressed the button on the intercom on his desk and asked another staff member to fetch Joyce. As so much time had now elapsed, other staff in the office had noticed something was wrong, they could feel the tension in the air.

As Joyce walked through the long open plan office to get to Frederick's office, there was a deadly silence and everyone stared at her. Joyce entered the room. Already there were Frederick and Phil, Herbert had left, and Human Resources hadn't arrived. Frederick explained to Joyce that any actions or decisions would be taken by him and the IT expert Phil and they would let human resources know the outcome. Unfortunately, but unbeknown to Joyce, this was not completely true; Human Resources had contacted him Frederick to say they would not be attending the meeting.

As soon as Joyce sat down, Phil began. He loved showing how clever he was and how exceptionally knowledgeable he was about IT. He talked Frederick and Joyce through the system and how it proved that Joyce had been manipulating the system.

Frederick knew by the rules of the system that Joyce should be sacked. Was Herbert testing him? He then wondered if it was a test to see how loyal he was. Frederick decided that he had always been principled and needed to remain so, so he would do what was right.

Joyce just stared at Phil; she knew she had been caught. It also saddened her that Jane was going to lose out. Joyce kept quiet, hoping they wouldn't catch her out on everything. She decided to stay quiet until spoken to.

Frederick looked at the IT expert and said he could not understand too much of the argument, he looked subdued. Frederick asked Joyce whether she understood what was being said to her.

Joyce understood it very well but answered, 'No.'

'I will now play the video of the interview.' When looking at the video Phil asked why they could not see A1201a.

'We only need to see Joyce because when I make a decision I do not want any kind of sympathy regarding the case – it has to be value-free. If, for instance, he saw a person crying it may affect his emotional decision making,' Frederick said.

Joyce came across as very corporate in the video, which Frederick said needed to be taken into account in mitigating circumstances. He was, however, intrigued to see what A1201a looked like and thought he might ask the video team to unblock her face; he would need to think of a reason why. He didn't realise yet, but Frederick was starting to become obsessed with the case, something he had tried to avoid his entire working career.

Frederick snapped back into focus, he told Joyce that the video and the IT evidence were contradictory and that he would need to discuss with Phil where they went from here. Frederick had thought of a principled get out-of-jail resolution, but he hated Joyce and had really wanted to sack her. However, Frederick did have his usual chance to intimidate the interviewee and put fear into the Opportunity Planner.

Phil and Frederick were left alone. When they spoke it was like they used a different language. Frederick started by saying how important it was to have as many people as self-reliant as possible, that the State could not provide handouts as it would mean others will have less choice. According to Phil, case A1201a has reached 55% which meant her State benefits had to be stopped. According to inputs Joyce had made, the case was at 48%, thus meaning that 7% had been stolen from the Department for over a year.

Frederick said he thought Joyce may be on the make and queried whether they should investigate every case she had been involved with. Phil kept silent, which unnerved Frederick as Phil was usually keen to agree with him on most things. The only people Frederick had anything in common with were Phil, and Joseph, in more ways than one.

Frederick also knew the Department relied on competition between staff to help keep everyone in line and it actively encouraged complaints to help ensure everyone behaved impeccably. There was also distrust amongst your closest friends.

Frederick told Phil he thought they should discipline Joyce and, as the case was so serious, give her notice of dismissal. Frederick thought if Phil was on side then he would take the risk that Herbert was testing his loyalty. By sacking Joyce it would show what a brilliant employee he was. If he was wrong, it would be difficult for Herbert to go against the statistics and against Phil's evidence. Frederick strongly believed that Herbert was testing his loyalty and, if he did not dismiss Joyce, he would lose Herbert's trust.

Phil still hadn't responded.

'So Phil, shall we dismiss?' asked Frederick.

'Sorry, Frederick, I don't agree.'

Frederick could not believe his ears. 'We always agree, Phil,' he said.

Phil then explained how he had been getting pressure from his Department and that they had ordered him not to recommend any dismissal of Joyce. 'Do you think,' asked Phil, 'that she's a plant put there by the department? Who is she spying on? I am suspecting, but we have to let her off the hook.'

Frederick struggled; he had a clash in his head. Should he dismiss Joyce and take the consequences on the grounds that the ethics of the department was at stake? Or should he go along with authority of Herbert's instruction? Frederick felt that both choices were outside his control. He had somehow lost his sense of humanity, unsure whether he was being controlled by a system or by those in authority but the effect was just the same.

Phil broke the silence, 'I will respect any decision you make.'

This only served to put extra pressure on Frederick as Phil had now effectively distanced himself from the decision-making. Frederick was also well aware that having respect for a decision was not the same as agreement with the decision.

The situation was left to Frederick. He asked for Joyce to come back in to the office. Frederick led the interview. 'Well, Joyce we have decided that there is evidence against you,' he began. He hesitated, having considered the issues, and felt he had to make the right decision. However, he was still not certain of what that was. He looked at Phil directly in his eyes; he could see the tension in Phil's face waiting for the decision to be made. He turned looked at Joyce and then he panicked and suddenly blurted out, 'there are difficulties and we will be taking no action.'

He paused and gripped his fists in anger with himself for a moment as he felt weak out of control. Still unsure of his decision, he knew at least that this was the most secure move he could have made, considering his own position. He then looked at Phil, forcing as much self-composure as he could manage so that Phil did not think he was a coward. Frederick thought that the calmer he acts the better, but knew he'd made a panicked and rushed decision. Though he tried to convince himself otherwise, in the end he'd cowed down to what Herbert had asked and tried his best to accept authority, as he always has done, hoping his quiet worry that this was all a test was nothing more than paranoia.

Frederick did not even mention Marcus. He went on, 'We want you to contact A1021a and give her the outcome of the decision by phone today, she is only on 49% and so maintains her income. She has still not reached the self-reliant barrier. But, as she is so close, we want you to go back in about four weeks' time and complete another review.' Joyce looked at him dumbfounded. 'You can go now,' he said firmly, almost aggressively. Frederick was drained physically and emotionally, his shirt wet with sweat and his body aching all over.

As she walked back down the open plan office she managed to speak to Marcus, but only fleetingly. 'Nothing happened,' she whispered.

Can Openers

A short while later, Joyce and Marcus managed to arrange to meet up that night. Marcus was pleased and relieved about the outcome, but he wondered why she had been let off and whether it was because she had implicated him.

Joyce contacted Jane later that day. Jane wasn't in work that day and had a friend with her just as the phone rang. Jane was expecting the worst news. She felt it was a travesty that she could not survive on her wage, even though she did only work three days a week

Joyce greeted Jane briefly and then informed her that the outcome of the assessment was that she came under the fifty percent and that the actual result was forty-nine percent. She told Jane she was a dependency figure and went through the corporate speech, this required Joyce to inform Jane that she was taking from the State and becoming a burden.

Chapter 11

Frederick arrived to observe his first Board meeting; the Board was by now aware of the outcome of Frederick's meeting with Joyce.

Frederick had never been to a Board meeting before and he was unsure how they were run. Before the meeting, Frederick was asked to meet the Head of Dibble Care and the Head of the State Company. Frederick always panicked when he had to meet someone important. It was unfortunate that no one had invented a book on etiquette focusing on how to grovel to your superiors. Frederick would have been first in the queue to buy it.

He went to a glass pyramid structure on top of the building where the meeting was to take place. As he came out of the lift, he stepped into a corridor that was decorated entirely different from his floor. The area was plush with modern decoration; the reception was like that of a five star hotel.

The uniformed aide behind the reception desk said with perfect enunciation, 'Both Sir Harpa and the Head of the Dependency Unit need to see you urgently. Please take a seat while I let them know you are here.'

Frederick sat down as requested. His mind was racing, wondering why they wanted to see him. Many in this situation got very paranoid, especially when working for the Dependency Unit. Frederick was no different, and his thoughts turned paranoid. He was convinced that he had been tested and he had failed. He should have dismissed Joyce; he should never have gone against the structures in place. He should have kept to the percentages and figures and not let Herbert put him off. He knew he had failed the test

Can Openers

and, in his view, he deserved to suffer. He had never been so worried about his fate before.

Chapter 12

Joyce kept her post and Jane was still a dependency figure, they both had something to celebrate.

Jane phoned Gina and Iris and said, 'Let's go out.'

Meanwhile Marcus had arranged to meet Joyce in the café. He was already there and, whilst he waited, he contemplated his present circumstances; he felt uneasy.

When Joyce arrived she wanted to talk about what happened earlier that day. She explained how worried she had been and how she waited for hours whilst the IT man and someone more senior than Frederick were in the office.

She told Marcus that the IT man had worked out how she manipulated the system. Marcus asked if she had been given a hard time and if he had been mentioned.

Joyce said, 'That is what I do not understand. I was worried that Frederick was going to sack me and, because of the way he talked when I last saw him, he clearly wanted me to put the blame on you, but this time nothing was said about you.'

Marcus was curious. 'Why do you think he hasn't done anything considering the IT expert knew everything?' Even though Marcus tried to pretend he was all right his tone of voice gave him away.

Joyce was perturbed. 'Don't you believe me?' she asked, sharply.

'I do believe you,' protested Marcus, 'at least, I want to.'

Joyce got angry. 'I don't think you believe me, but it's true. What do you want me to do? Change history? Throw away my job?' Hot tears started down her cheeks. She was hurt.

Marcus felt guilty for doubting Joyce. He briefly wondered again whether she may have been working for Quality

Can Openers

Control, but almost immediately, he felt bad and realised how insecure he was. He knew he shouldn't take this out on someone he was falling in love with. He told her he was sorry.

'Don't worry,' said Joyce as she wiped the tears away. She took a sip of her drink and took Marcus's hand in hers. 'It's the system we are working for. It creates distrust between everyone. I don't blame you. Anyway let's move on to the Co-Op club, they've got poetry on tonight. We can stay there till eleven and you can come back to mine after if you want. I've got wine in the fridge.' Marcus smiled and leaned over to Joyce, they embraced and kissed and then left to go to the club.

Chapter 13

The kids were settled for the night and the babysitter had arrived. For the first time in a long while. Jane relaxed. She arranged for Iris and Gina to meet at her house before going for a night out. They were going to the Harp music bar, a themed bar. Gina had promised to take them somewhere different later on. Iris and Gina arrived at Jane's house together, all three friends agreed to go straight out.

They arrived at the Harp in good spirits and Jane gave them her news about the outcome of the assessment as they enjoyed their drinks and then decided to move on. They messed about walking down the street making Jane tell them over and over again about the Can Openers stopping production for hour and half, thinking it was funny.

Gina took them to the alternative club. They had to go through a door and down some stairs and pay some money to a man at a table before going through another door, through a large room and into another room with a large stage at one end where someone was reciting poetry. Gina told the others that the club was run by the members and not some multinational company. They ordered a round of drinks and laughed at each other's jokes. Jane couldn't remember when she had last enjoyed herself and had such a good time.

'This is our one night out, thought Jane. At least I can now survive and not worry about feeding the kids.

Chapter 14

The boss of Dibble Care, Sir Harpa, and his fellow Board member, Sir George, sat waiting for Frederick to meet them. Sir Harpa was a multi-millionaire. The previous year he had received a two million pound bonus. Sir George also lived very comfortably; he had made half a million pounds in the past year and in some ways was even more powerful than Sir Harpa. He was head of the State Dependency Unit. Although they both supported each other, there were often disagreements between them. One such disagreement was about Frederick. However, one thing they both agreed on was that it was interesting how Frederick had made waves at the top level without Frederick having even realised it. This situation was unusual.

Sir George, Herbert's most senior boss, felt Frederick was an asset to the Department. He was also convinced that Frederick believed in the mission of the Department, that he had an evangelist's zeal for the cause and his moral crusade helped the Unit.

It was Sir Harpa who had been responsible for himself and Sir George getting together and developing their working relationship. In fact, it had been Sir Harpa who invited Sir George to the meeting he intended to have with Frederick.

Sir Harpa was a hard-headed businessman; he had gone to Yale University Business School and, after graduating, had gone straight into managing Dibble Care. Sir Harpa liked to feel he had got to where he was on merit and that his position had nothing to do with the fact that his mother was related to the Dibble dynasty and his father was an eminent and highly respected trust lawyer.

However, Sir Harpa was pushing Sir George about the Department's statistics and Sir George was not a man who liked to be pushed. As he sat down Sir Harpa asked, 'Where are we up to with the plan?'

Sir George replied that there would not be any difficulties.

'I do hope not,' said Sir Harpa, 'as we cannot make any mistakes. We are talking about a serious recession or depression both in Britain and the rest of the world if this plan backfires.'

Sir George nodded in agreement.

'We cannot open the markets up to unnecessary competition, it will cause chaos.'

'I agree,' said Sir George. 'Any blip in the market will set the UK economy over the edge.'

'Can we trust Frederick?' said Sir Harpa. Sir George explained that Herbert was one of their best men and that he had recommended Frederick and had complete faith in him. Sir Harpa told Sir George that he wanted to see Frederick for ten minutes maximum.

Sir Harpa expressed his concern that, based on what had been reported to him, Frederick was a loose cannon. 'Frederick believes all the propaganda we put out but, in the end, this is a business, not a moral crusade.'

Sir George was forthright in his reply, 'That is what Frederick is employed to do and, remember, the Dependency Unit propaganda may be bullshit to you, but it has made the Dibble Corporation healthy profits over the last ten years, so be careful what you wish for. If it wasn't for the cuts and the privatisation of the welfare budget, your company would not being having growth figures year after year.'

Sir George was not going to let Sir Harpa dictate to him and was determined to make his point. He explained how Herbert had given him his view on how to deal with Frederick. 'We need to praise his accomplishments, we then reward them. We will put him on the Board as an adviser with no voting rights. We will also put him in a PR role. His passion for the post will come through in the media, he will not put a foot wrong and, as he believes all the bullshit, he will argue for the Department in the press.'

There was a knock on the door. Herbert arrived and was asked to give his view. 'He's no loose cannon and there is no reason to worry. We will also keep him with twenty percent of the responsibility he has now.'

Sir Harpa rang his secretary and instructed her to send Frederick in. Frederick had been waiting outside, getting increasingly nervous. He sat there wondering and worrying about why the two most powerful men in the Department wanted to see him. Every conceivable possibility went through his mind and he was really upset he had not sacked Joyce; he should have realised it was a test.

The secretary led Frederick into a vast office. There was a large, old-fashioned writing desk at the far end in front of large windows offering a panoramic view of the city. There were sculptures in alcoves in one wall and modern contemporary art on another wall. There was a leather sofa and an easy chair, as well.

Sir George was sitting in the easy chair and Sir Harpa was sprawled out on the sofa.

Sir George spoke first; his voice was deep with an air of confidence and superiority that only comes from with a public school education. 'Please sit down, Frederick,' he said indicating a space at the opposite end of the sofa to Sir Harpa. 'I believe Herbert has given you the conditions attached to your new post?' Without waiting for a reply, Sir George continued. 'The reason you are here is because we wanted to acknowledge that your statistics have been consistent and we feel the rewards need to fit the hard work you have given to the Department over the years. You have created a culture where it is no longer acceptable to see not working as somehow a lifestyle choice. You have encouraged and helped many customers to become self-reliant, something that must make you very proud.' Again he didn't give Frederick a chance to respond, 'You have saved the tax payer and the hard working majority thousands of pounds.'

Frederick felt an almost overwhelming sense of pride at being praised by such great men.

Sir Harpa watched Frederick's reaction very closely and now it was time for him to turn on the charm and draw Frederick in. 'We are being most remiss,' he said to Frederick, 'we haven't yet offered you any basic hospitality. Would you like a coffee?'

'Yes,' Frederick squeaked. Sir Harpa stood up, walked over to the large desk and spoke into the intercom to order the secretary to fetch coffee. He then leaned his back to the desk and nodded to Sir George.

Sir George leaned forward and, in almost a whisper, said, 'I understand Herbert told you not to dismiss one of our Opportunity Planners?'

Frederick's heart raced and his stomach flipped over. This is a trap, he thought.

'The reason for this unusual step was not because he went against the evidence-based science that has taken years to develop. On the contrary,' Sir George purred, 'we can now predict people's future behaviour. As you are aware, one of our great theorists, Franz Ink, proved that poverty was the result of a person's psychological profile and the way individuals see the world. So we are proud of you Frederick, being one of our greatest advocates of the dependency approach.'

Sir Harpa coughed theatrically and held up a hand to Sir George to signal to him to stop as the secretary had arrived carrying a tray loaded with cups and saucers, a coffee pot, sugar bowl, and cream jug. She set the tray down on the expensive mahogany coffee table in front of the sofa, poured coffee into each cup and then left the room.

'This leads us to the Opportunity Planner who was putting the wrong inputs in to the computer. We are aware she should have been dismissed, but we have found out some serious news about this particular Opportunity Planner,' Sir George said.

Sir George paused to take a sip of coffee. Sir Herbert picked up the story. 'We have reliable information that she has been planted in our company by another multinational company; she's an industrial spy. We took the decision not to dismiss her so we are now in a position to use her to feed whatever information to the other company that we want. We believe it is better to know we have a spy in the company and use them for our own purposes. We want to thank you personally.'

Frederick had been holding his breath and suddenly breathed a huge sigh of relief. A great weight had lifted. He was able to speak, although only briefly and said how he fully understood the situation and thanked both Sirs for seeing him.

Frederick had such deference to authority that, as soon as someone as important as Sir Harpa and Sir George spoke to him, Frederick would just accept what he was told. Frederick was relieved, as he had been worried that he may be in trouble; but here he was, speaking to the big boys, and he suddenly felt ten feet tall. Frederick was immensely pleased; he could hardly wait to tell his wife about the promotion. However, there was other business to deal with first.

Sir George asked if Frederick had any questions for them.

Frederick said, 'None, thank you.'

Sir George said, 'You may go now.'

Frederick wasn't used to being spoken to in such an imperious manner; he was so overwhelmed and intimidated he bowed as he left the room.

When he left the room Sir Harpa spoke. 'Do you think that did trick?' he asked.

'The man was very nervous,' Sir George responded. 'I'm sure he'll not say anything, especially after you told him about the secrecy of the action we are taking and how important the project is. He seemed impressed with authority.'

They both laughed at this.

'Did you see his face when we told him that it was only ourselves and those at the very top who knew about this information?' asked Sir George.

Sir Harpa nodded. 'He would probably agree to anything if we asked him.'

'Yes,' said Sir George, 'he has a sense of duty. We had better let Lord Dibble know the outcome.'

The Board meeting had been delayed due to the meeting with Frederick, and started fifteen minutes late. The standard agenda items were discussed, statistics and targets were gone through, PR issues were brought up and the latest research considered.

Frederick had been asked his view on a few occasions; he had never felt so important. When the meeting finished he rushed back to his office and phoned his wife. Frederick told her what had happened and how well he had done. Lidia didn't sound as elated as he thought she would but he didn't think too much of it; instead he suggested she arrange for a babysitter for that night so they could go out for a meal.

While Frederick was speaking on the phone to his wife, Sir Harpa and Sir George went to see Lord Dibble who had an even bigger, more sumptuous and luxurious office than the one Frederick had so recently been in. Lord Dibble listened while Sir Harpa and Sir George explained how the meeting with their man Frederick had gone. When they were done, all three men agreed that the first stage of the plan was in place. Lord Dibble ended the discussion by saying he wanted to meet as soon as possible to formulate the next stage.

Chapter 15

Four weeks had passed; Joyce was on her way to reassess case A1201a, once again accompanied by Marcus. Just as they pulled up outside the house, the emergency alarm that was built into the dashboard of the company car started to bleep. Joyce had only ever heard the alarm go off on three other occasions.

Joyce contacted the controller and was informed that there had been a serious incident and Marcus was required to return to the office. The controller advised Joyce that there was no need to wait for the police to get to the house, as it had only been four weeks since the client had last been seen and therefore the previous risk assessment was still valid and current. The controller instructed Joyce to see A1021a alone, but that she was to leave if any incident occurred.

They both got out of the car. Marcus made his way back to the office. Joyce locked the car and walked down the path to the front door. She rang the bell and Jane answered the door. Jane invited Joyce in and to sit down.

Joyce began by going through the standard introductions and then went through similar questions as before in the same professional manner. This time, though, Joyce knew she would not be able to help Jane.

The interview went without incident and then just as they were reaching the end, something very unusual happened. Joyce was just inputting Jane's response to a question when her computer system crashed. This had never happened to Joyce before. At first Joyce thought she had pressed the wrong key but quickly realised that wasn't the case. She started to panic, hoping she wouldn't get blamed for this.

Can Openers

Whilst Joyce was trying to work out what to do, there was knock on the door.

Jane went to the door. There was a uniformed man with a letter in one hand and a small electronic device in the other, like the old recorded delivery system. Jane had to sign her name on the device and press her fingerprint on to the screen. This must have been the first recorded post she'd had in years.

Jane took the parcel and closed the front door. She looked in to the living room and saw that Joyce was still absorbed in trying to fix her computer. Jane was intrigued to know what was in the letter, so she snipped it open and read it. It was from Dibble Canning, they were offering her a fulltime position five days a week. Jane was so astonished she had to read the letter at least three times before she could believe it. When it finally sunk in, she then thought what a shame it was that she hadn't got the letter sooner, it would have saved her the embarrassment of going through the patronising interview.

Joyce had just partly got the system going again when Jane returned to the room. Jane felt like telling this Opportunity Planner to get lost but she was pragmatic enough to know that she may need the Dependency Department again in the future.

Jane told Joyce her news. 'Don't worry about the interview, I've been made fulltime.'

Joyce congratulated Jane. 'That takes you to ninety percent self-reliant. What I need to do is record it, and then this will take you off the dependency system.' However, every time Joyce tried to enter Jane's changed circumstances, the system crashed again. This was frustrating, as most of the interview had been recorded. Although she could not manipulate the computer system any more, there was no need for her to try as Jane now had a fulltime job. Despite her frustration with the computer, Joyce felt pleased for Jane and not a little proud that she had helped Jane at a time of crisis; she had been able to help Jane feed her children, even though no one knew.

'I will just need to check how I can record that you have now been offered the post,' said Joyce. She phoned the office on her mobile and was put through to Phil.

There's no need to worry,' he said, 'it's recorded. There's been a problem with the computer main frame.'

Joyce ended the call to Phil and turned to Jane. Joyce informed Jane she was no longer a dependency figure. 'Well done.'

Jane was relieved and very pleased. It was an acknowledgement that she could stand on her own two feet even though, deep down, she knew it was meaningless.

Joyce packed her computer away, shook Jane's hand and left. With the interview finished, Jane video-conferenced Gina and Iris with her good news.

When Gina heard the news she was sceptical; she could not understand why Dibble Canning were taking Jane on fulltime now after what she had done in organising the Can Openers. Jane reasoned that maybe they had decided to have more of a human approach, after all, the bullying had lessened and they had given the workforce a pay rise.

Iris's response was short and to the point. 'Bullshit,' she said, bluntly. 'The only reason they're showing a human face is because of the collective action the workforce took. If you stop or let your guard down, they'll go back to acting like a totalitarian state again.'

Jane wasn't convinced. 'There are better ways of managing staff and they've learnt their lesson.'

They ended the call by agreeing to meet up to celebrate Jane's good fortune.

That evening Iris and Gina arrived at Jane's house to congratulate her. They continued their discussion from earlier.

'What you need to realise about managers is that they're only employed to get the most out of you for the best outputs and profits by any means necessary,' Iris said.

Jane shrugged. 'If they're meeting their targets but at the same time treating us with respect then so be it.'

'They can't afford to give you too much respect because you and the rest of the workforce might question why you need them,' retorted Iris. 'Let me tell you, they will have to either make cutbacks or pay less as they're in competition with other employers.'

'Come on,' said Jane, 'what about a fair day's work for a fair day's pay?'

Iris shook her head. 'There's no such thing. You create the wealth and they steal it off you. If you get rid of the

Can Openers

Directors who earn millions of pounds, you still have the machines, you still produce things. You do the work, if they got rid of you what would happen? I'll tell you, the firm would collapse.'

'This is all well and good,' said Gina, 'but I think your news is brilliant Jane. We have to go out and celebrate later, but for now I need to get home.'

Jane thanked her friends for calling to see her and saw them out. She decided to treat herself to a glass of wine and took it in to the front room. She sat and watched a TV panel discussion about the low economic growth since the start of the teenies. There had been more and more very large companies controlling the market and all of them were in very intense competition with each other. Due to increasing technology and more readily available information about the movements of the markets, a slight blip could have a dramatic effect on the economy. A workforce that was flexible helped keep the system stable. The so-called experts droned on. Jane switched channels. She watched the international news. There were new struggles in Egypt and one commentator was remarking that the situation there was similar to that in Russia between 1905 and 1917.

The commentator saw the Egyptian uprising in 2011 as a prelude to the more organised resistance today. She described how the two state solution was causing its own problems in the Middle East. Jane had become much more interested in world affairs and, since being part of action at work, she seemed to feel more of a connection with the outside world. She could not quite grasp the reasons why she felt this growing connection but it was undoubtedly there.

The phone rang, it was Gina. She had contacted Iris and was now calling Jane to see if she wanted to go out with her and Iris later. Jane readily agreed. As she went upstairs to get herself ready, she suddenly realised that she was humming a tune to herself; she couldn't remember the last time she had done that.

Iris, however, was not so happy. She was worried for Jane; she could not understand why Dibble had taken Jane on full-time considering that Jane had been such a thorn in their side, it didn't make any sense to her.

Later that evening, they all met up at Jane's again for the second time that day. The last time they had met in celebration was because Jane had been told she was still a dependency figure, which meant Jane would be able to survive on part time pay with State support. Now they were celebrating a complete reverse of fortune, Jane was to be taken on fulltime at the cannery.

Iris said again that none of the last four weeks made sense to her.

'It's barely made sense to me,' said Jane. 'So much has happened in such a short space of time. But I wanted to ask you something, Iris. When we went out last time, we were at that music bar. As we were arriving, we passed two people who were leaving. It was only afterwards that I realised who they were since it was dark in the club. They were the two Opportunity Planners who came to assess me. The woman came to see me today. When we were in the club I wouldn't have paid them any attention but there was something about what happened that played on my mind. Iris, you spoke to the male. Why did you speak to him? Do you know him?'

Iris said that she did not remember because she had been so drunk. 'I speak to everyone when I'm drunk, you know what I'm like.'

Jane shrugged and said she was also drunk, but she didn't pursue the conversation.

Chapter 16

The day after Jane was given a five-day-a-week contract, Lord Dibble finally met with Sir Harpa and Sir George in his office. It impressed them; they envied it for its size and sumptuousness. As the two Sirs entered, Lord Dibble asked his PA to leave. She raised an eyebrow in surprise; she was usually required to sit in on most meetings taking notes.

Dibble, Harpa, and George were all aware of the sensitive nature of the discussion.

Lord Dibble asked, 'Have the fish taken the bait?'

'The fish have indeed,' Sir George replied.

Sir Harpa said they met the Dependency Program Manager who had done exactly what they had wanted. 'We all have different views about him but he did not go against our man Herbert.'

'Does anyone suspect?' asked Lord Dibble.

Sir George replied, 'We have our information and sources and as far as anyone is concerned, no one suspects.'

'What about our IT expert?' asked Lord Dibble. 'Can we rely on him?'

'He has had a nice cash reward,' said Sir Harpa.

Lord Dibble snorted. 'Offer enough and anyone can be bought. Now the fish have taken the bait we need to follow the process.'

The other two nodded.

'And let us not forget,' said Lord Dibble, 'whatever is said within these four walls stays within these four walls. I've spoken to the Minister for Stability, he is keeping the government in touch.'

Sirs Harpa and George murmured.

'As you are aware, the economy has taken a severe dip into crisis. The spark to this is the instability at Dibble Canning. We have an agreement with trade union leaders on a stability pact, however the problem is that the Can Openers are so well organised they can hold production up for two hours. This has created such a problem that the whole system virtually collapsed.'

Dibble put his hands down on his desk and looked at the two Sirs in turn. 'The cartels have truces with each other, each agreeing to their share of the market. The Ministry for Stability has organised this all. Unfortunately, gentlemen, this fell apart as soon as other firms heard that the Can Openers may go on strike. Rival firms broke the peace and went in like vultures to steal Dibble's share of the market, as any hold up in production would create a gap in the market that could be exploited. Other firms produced extra and, in the process, over produced, which created a mini crisis in trying to fill the gap. The other difficulty is that more firms are finding that what the Can Openers have done is spreading – other workers are now making demands.'

'I understand,' said Sir Harpa.

'It was inevitable,' said Sir George, not to be outdone.

'Let me continue, gentlemen,' said Lord Dibble. 'Due to the market being flooded with commodities, the stock exchange went in to free-fall. Fortunately, gentlemen, we have a plan. The plan is to take out the ringleader of these Can Openers. If we challenge them directly we could have problems, and we do not know how many of them are out there. We could have serious disruptions. So how do we cut off its head? What we need is for the workforce to lose respect for A1201a. If the Can Openers lose trust in her they will lose confidence in themselves. We are looking at various ways we can go about this and get the situation under control. What we cannot do is victimise her.'

'Sounds sensible,' said Sir Harpa.

'Perfect plan, totally realistic,' said Sir George.

'Yes, yes,' said Lord Dibble, mildly irritated at being interrupted. 'Her name is Jane, or A1201a, and that is how we will refer to her from now on. As you are aware, it was imperative that the Opportunity Planner, some personnel called Joyce, was not disciplined, and it seems that this went to plan. I am also pleased that the Dependency Manager has taken the offer of promotion and hopefully he can be relied on. Our plan has already been put in action, and now we can move to Phase B.'

Sir George said that the Opportunity Planner had gone out yesterday.

Sir Harpa said he offered A1201a a five-day-a-week position. 'The letter of confirmation,' he said, 'went out exactly at the time the Opportunity Planner was interviewing her. We also arranged for the computer system to fail at the same time.'

'Excellent,' said Lord Dibble, 'I have a report that the Opportunity Planner contacted the IT department, unfortunately the message was not recorded and our man in that section has conveniently forgotten about any contact made. So A1201a's benefit money is going out in three weeks, as she has not told the department of her change of circumstances.'

'How unfortunate,' said Sir Harpa.

'Most regrettable,' said Sir George.

'Indeed, gentlemen,' said Lord Dibble. 'Then our man, Frederick, who will be keeping twenty percent of his work, will get an anonymous tip off saying A1201a is working five days a week but still getting cash from the department.'

The three honourable gentlemen chuckled.

Lord Dibble continued, 'Frederick is completely unaware of the plan. When he finds out about this benefit cheat, the idea is that he will be angry and all his evangelical instincts will re-emerge; the same person who he saw as keeping his figures down will be revealed as fiddling with the system. It helps that he does not even know who A1021a is. So, technically, he will be acting honourably. The only information he has been given is that his Opportunity Planner is working for another company. Sir George, it is your job to make Frederick feel everything is as normal as possible.'

'Of course, Lord Dibble,' said Sir George.

'So, gentlemen, in a few weeks the press will find out. Imagine the headline: "Leader of the Can Openers and fighter for justice defrauds the state system". No one will believe her anymore, mud always sticks, and people will lose faith in her. We can then tell our moles in the canning plant to highlight the issue and hopefully the Can Openers will fall apart. We will then only offer a pay rise on condition that we deal only with the union officials, and then congratulate the union in a joint statement to say that industrial relations are back to normal.'

'And what about the ring leader?' asked Sir George.

'Well,' said Lord Dibble. 'We suspend her on full pay while we investigate serious allegations of fraud. This should put a stop to any further activity by the Can Openers. We can then get Sir Harpa's people negotiating more productivity deals with the official union leaders.'

'Of course,' said Sir Harpa.

Lord Dibble nodded at him. 'The minister wants this plan to work and is relying on us, gentlemen. However, due to the serious threat to the economy, we have two other plans if this does not work. We will call them Plan B and Plan C.'

'I've always admired your thoroughness,' said Sir Harpa.

'I never doubted it,' said Sir George.

'Yes, of course, gentlemen,' said Lord Dibble, 'Plan B is that the leader of the Can Openers is offered a management position. At the same time, we offer rewards and career development to the canners by creating numerous supervisor roles. This gives the chance to the canners to get promoted and should lead to competition amongst the workforce. As we are promoting their leader, it shows that we are working with the staff and want to offer a socially moral approach. We tell them we want more teamwork and push decision-making down and let the supervisors have the responsibility of reaching the targets. This will create another structural divide among the Can Openers. We also want workers to have an individual plan to help their career. Every supervisor will see workers alone every week so as to individualise the job and encourage him or her to look after themselves if they are to have any chance of promotion. We concentrate on each worker's weaknesses and strengths. Over time, this will undermine their confidence when they try and take collective action. Let's be clear, in this situation we are selling the package to the workforce. We're showing them how serious we are by putting their person in charge. We have to let the workers believe that if she gets the manager's post then she will be on their side and raise their expectations. However, the difficulty we have is that she may not accept the position.'

'Hence Plan C,' said Sir Harpa.

'Always good to have a contingency plan,' said Sir George.

Can Openers

'Which indeed brings us to Plan C,' said Lord Dibble. 'This plan is going to rely on the trade union leaders. They are being pushed by the Can Openers to act. They are mostly men, conservative by nature; we can do business with these people. They enjoy the status of being in boardrooms with us. They even copy my style of dress and wear the same colour suits. I will not comment on the quality of their suits beyond saying they bear no comparison.'

Lord Dibble laughed at his joke, Sir Harpa and Sir George laughed, too.

'We have to accept that they still have to have a relationship with their members,' Lord Dibble said. 'So we end up in endless discussion with them, sometimes they shout and get into arguments, but usually we get what we want and they get some tokenistic changes they can sell to their members. However, since the Can Openers have started, the union leaders have had to make radical speeches against management and this has enabled them to just about hold their positions, although we have lost two of their leaders to the Can Openers. So our third and last resort is for the Can Opener's leader to be offered a fulltime post as chief negotiator for the union and we pay her a good salary. This is a risk, but we have spoken to our research department at Dibble Care. The psychologists and organisational experts argue as soon as these people get these positions their reality changes and it becomes important for them to protect their new position.'

Lord Dibble paused as he flicked his cigar butt into the waste paper basket under his desk. 'Our experts have told us that whatever political or human perspective they come from, as soon as they shift away from the frontline and the shop floor, the union becomes more important than the members, the union becomes everything. Therefore, gentlemen, in this scenario, the Can Openers will become secondary. Demoralisation will set in amongst the Can Openers, and our problem is solved. So our last option is to get the present union leaders to support the leader of the Can Openers in getting a position. If our first position does not work we may need to have a mixture of B and C.'

'Inspired,' said Sir Harpa.

'Genius,' said Sir George.

Lord Dibble held the view that modesty was only for those with something to be modest about, he therefore nodded vigorously in agreement. 'In the meantime, Plan A is now moving forward. When Frederick finds out that A1201a is deceiving and committing fraud, he will be looking at it and, if he thinks we are supporting him, he will be ruthless. What we need is for Frederick to feel secure and important. We will also tell him the department is going to look at every case. Tackling fraud will be our priority over the next few months. A1201a is to go fulltime on Monday, the button gets pressed and it goes to the press in four weeks.'

'We need to make sure Herbert supports Frederick, but we do not tell him anything about the plans,' Lord Dibble said.

'Good, good,' said Sir Harpa.

'Good, good, good,' said Sir George.

Chapter 17

Jane was pleased as she was going to be paid in two weeks. She was also pleased to be able to go fulltime; her three previous requests to do so had been had been rejected. However, it seemed to Jane that management had become less bullying and there seemed to be a fairer way of recruiting. No one she spoke to ever thought Jane, the leader of the Can Openers, would ever be taken on permanently. It was interesting times for the Can Openers. The union was being forced to have regular meetings with the shop stewards and nearly all of them had joined the Can Openers. However, the Can Openers also had separate meetings and spoke via speaker networks. The Can Opener movement was now spreading across the country, from workplace to workplace and from strength to strength.

Jane poured herself a glass of wine and thought about the local issue of the Can Openers. Management had offered a 4% pay rise but the Can Openers wanted the pay rise backdated for the years when they did not get a raise. The official union position was to go for 5%. The union called meeting after meeting, something they had never done before. The Can Openers felt that even if they only got half of what they were asking for, it would still be more than the 5% the union recommended. The union leaders argued that it could mean a long campaign of strike action to get what they were asking for, that they wouldn't get strike pay or state benefits, and would be entirely dependent on whatever solidarity donations they could get.

One member had argued that the bosses had stolen money from the workers.

'We make their products,' he said, 'and, as Karl Marx said, they own our labour.'

Jane had tried to be at every meeting. She felt confident and invigorated by the debate that often went further than a discussion about a pay rise. They often debated what a better future for their children would look like.

Jane would now describe herself as a socialist; she read books ranging from *Das Capital* to *The Ragged Trousered Philanthropists*.

Life had changed for her. She had become the leader of the Can Openers, she was working fulltime, work had become less strict, and she was no longer a dependency figure. She was self-reliant and not a modern version of a Dickens character. When she thought about the Dependency Unit she got angry. Even though the dependency system's objective was to get people back to work, it did the opposite. It undermined peoples' confidence, it left them with a feeling of powerlessness and completely alienated from any sense of human dignity.

Jane spent the first three weeks of being fulltime going to meetings going out with Gina and Iris. She was even thinking of taking her children on holiday for five days, later in the year. Jane, however, was nervous that she was seen as a leader of the Can Openers and at times could not believe what happened. Iris had told her that she had started a rank-and-file movement. At one meeting someone had called her "Larkin". Jane had never wanted to be a leader, it wasn't what she had set out to be; she just felt that things could get better. She had found herself speaking at large meetings and her humility and her passion lifted the crowd.

There were times she wished someone else was the leader, and she really believed the old socialist view that everyone could become leaders. Every individual could make a difference. Jane remembered reading an old post card where everyone had finished work and were walking out of a call centre. The picture seemed to reflect a sense of conformity, there was a conversation between two of the people in the picture and one said to the other: "under socialism we would all be the same". Jane felt that in this unequal society, as a worker she had lost her individuality.

Jane sipped some of her wine and thought about the impact her role as leader had changed her. Now, for the first time in her life, she felt a responsibility not just for herself and her children but also for her workmates. She had discussed this with Iris who had said she also had responsibility for human history.

Chapter 18

From the time of his promotion, Frederick felt a renewed confidence. Lord Dibble and Sir George had spoken to Herbert about improving Frederick's confidence. Herbert in turn had spoken to Frederick about how important he was to the organisation and how proud they were of his achievements. Herbert also took the opportunity to tell Frederick how the Department took fraud very seriously.

Over the following three weeks, Frederick looked at the case notes of all Opportunity Planners trying to find any clues that even hinted at fraud in the system. He felt that if he could catch any of them, he would get the complete support of his seniors and would be seen as one of the best employees.

Frederick's home life had also improved. It looked as though Mrs Smyth would be able to give up working at the shop, or at least cut back on her hours.

Now that he was on the Board, he felt he finally had the status he had always deserved. When anyone spoke to Frederick about it he glowed with pleasure and pride. The situation with Joyce was now behind him. As far his work was concerned, Frederick was on a mission. He believed in getting dependency figures down more than ever before.

The only thing that could complete his happiness was to see Joseph more. Frederick went to Joseph's flat every week where their affair continued. Frederick hated himself and felt that it was wrong to do it but, at the same time, he enjoyed the company and sexual pleasure he gained from his visits to with Joseph.

Frederick, however, recognised and appreciated the increased sense of stability to his life. He thought about going on holiday, going to the Maldives for two weeks with Lidia. They both felt they deserved a rest.

Lidia, one night, even became closer to Frederick emotionally, and they restarted the physical relationship that had been missing for years.

Frederick's life was one of calmness at home and crusader at work. However, there were still issues underlying the relationship between Lidia and him. Lidia felt that Frederick was very harsh about people and felt that people sometimes found themselves in poverty under circumstances that weren't their fault; but he would still maintain that going into poverty was a lifestyle choice and people needed to change.

Three weeks had also passed since the three Directors had had their meeting. At their behest, Herbert had regular meetings with Frederick and it was now time for Frederick to get the tip off about the A1201a case. The tip was that the female claimant was claiming from the State even though she was working fulltime.

Chapter 19

Frederick was feeling both confident and happy, he felt more relaxed than he had in years. After finishing work one evening, he decided to stop on the way home and get some flowers for Lidia. Luckily there was a flower shop open. Frederick got some glorious looking multi-coloured carnations and also bought a very expensive box of chocolates. He then took his usual route home, taking the metro and again getting irritated with the homeless man who played the tin whistle outside the tube station. Frederick thought, as always did, 'one of these days that bloody dog of his will have to be kennelled.'

Frederick walked up the street to his house. The sun was setting and a cool breeze made the evening really pleasant. Frederick arrived at his house went inside and shouted for Lidia, flowers in his hand. As he went into the downstairs lounge, there was Lidia crying and shaking and in despair.

'What's wrong?' Frederick asked.

'I don't know,' she snapped.

'What do mean you don't know?'

'The fucking bastards,' she shouted at him. 'And you work for the same department, you fucking bastard!'

Frederick was stunned by the outburst, 'But I thought things were getting better, why are you being like this?'

'It's the kids, you stupid bastard,' she said.

'Stop calling me that. Who do you think you are?' He turned his back on his wife and walked through the house into the back garden shouting the children's names. Lidia followed him, telling him he had no chance of finding the children.

Lidia tried to calm down. 'There's no life with you without the children.'

'What do you mean? What are you talking about?'

Can Openers

Lidia calmed down enough to talk to him. She told him that two people from his Department had come to the house that day. They had said their children would not be coming home after school and that they had been transferred directly to a Florence family. That, unless there was any significant change, they would be staying with the Florence family. Lidia started crying again.

Frederick couldn't believe what he was hearing; he couldn't quite make sense of it. 'This cannot be true, I run the department.'

'Frederick,' she said through her tears, 'they gave me a letter to say that the decision to move the children went to the highest level. Our children reached a number three risk level.'

Frederick said, 'Calm down, there must have been a mistake, something must have gone wrong. Or perhaps those people are not actually working for the Department. They must be con artists. I know the structure; we have done nothing to even be on a level one. I know that way back in the past there was a mistake on the system and children were removed in error – maybe that happened here. I've got Herbert's number, I think I'll ring him to try and get this sorted.'

Frederick was completely confused about the whole situation. He thought that the new computer system, linked as it was to the evidence-based science, was foolproof. If this was a mistake, and not people pretending to work for the Department, what a coincidence that it had happened to him.

Frederick phoned Herbert, but there was no answer. He left a message on the answer phone. A short time later Frederick tried Herbert's number again; still there was no answer.

Lidia said she would contact Sophie, Herbert's wife. Frederick asked how she knew Herbert's wife. She explained they had been friends ever since she and Frederick had held a dinner party several years ago, and they had kept their friendship to themselves.

Lidia said, 'We didn't want to compromise you and Herbert because he's your boss. We went for girly nights out.'

This wasn't a time for Frederick to either worry or care about whom his wife made friends with. 'Phone her, then,' he demanded.

Lidia reached for her phone, shaking with nerves. She dialled the number and waited anxiously. Sophie answered.

As Lidia spoke, her voice cracked; she apologised straight away for phoning but she needed a favour.

Sophie was much younger than Herbert. She was a gentle, caring person who completely supported her husband. She considered Lidia her best friend and felt a strong sense of loyalty to her. She listened as Lidia said that she was desperate.

'It's the children,' said Lidia. 'They've been taken off us, it's a terrible mistake. Frederick needs to speak to Herbert urgently, he's been trying to call him but there's no answer.'

'That's terrible,' Sophie said. 'But of all nights, of all the bad timing! Herbert's gone away for the weekend. He's staying in the South West of England on a golfing tournament and won't back until Sunday. All Frederick can do is keep ringing him.'

Lidia thanked Sophie and ended the call.

Lidia told Frederick what Sophie had said. Frederick didn't know what else to do. He wondered if it was the Dependency Department or people pretending to be working for the Department. He asked Lidia to get the letter she had been given, Frederick wanted to take a good look at it. If it was not official or was in any way suspicious he would call the police straight away. Lidia handed the letter to Frederick:

Dear Sir or Madam,

This is to confirm that your children have been removed on a Dependency Order.

They will be staying with a Florence family and will have all their moral and physical needs met.

We note that this action is only ever taken and used in the most extreme circumstances; where there is a risk of significant harm physically, emotionally, and/or morally. It is our department's duty to keep children with their families rather than becoming a dependency statistic, as this does not help a child or the family.

The Department will be contacting you in due course to explain further procedures, however it should be noted that, as this is the most serious level, Level 3, your children are at the most risk. We, therefore, will assume that you understand the reason why your children have been taken into a permanent Florence family.

Yours faithfully,

Lord Dibble

Can Openers

It looked official and Frederick knew that Lord Dibble's name was signed off on every letter. He was confused. He had always believed that these letters were fair.

The view of the Department, and indeed of Frederick, was that when a family had their children taken, the families knew deep down why this was the case and understood they had harmed their children in some way. Gone were the days when you had woolly liberal social workers finding excuses in wider society for the situation when the families knew exactly what happened.

Lidia interrupted Frederick's thoughts. 'What are you going to do now? You need to sort this out!' she said. 'You're high up in the Dependency Department, what's going on?'

Frederick explained that because it was the weekend, it made it difficult to get answers from anyone. 'I'll keep trying to get hold of Herbert but I may have to wait until he gets back.'

He tried to speak with contacts he knew at the Department without success; in the end he spoke to the police who confirmed that it was the Department who removed the children and not imposters.

It was the worst day of Lidia's life.

Frederick tried to calm things down. 'As soon as I can, even if it means waiting till Monday, I will get this sorted.'

The flowers and chocolates lay forgotten and unnoticed on the kitchen table.

As the evening progressed, the stress and tension between Frederick and Lidia reached breaking point.

'Have you done something to our children that I don't know about?' Frederick asked.

'Of course not,' Lidia gasped, shocked at the question. 'How could you even think that?'

'The whole basis of the Dependency Department is fact.'

'It's ludicrous. How dare you accuse me!'

They argued into the night, going to bed very late and struggling to sleep. Before getting into bed Lidia swallowed some tablets. She and Frederick lay restlessly, neither of them drifting off to sleep until very early that morning.

They were woken by a loud knock a few hours later. Lidia got up, wrapped her dressing gown around her, and rushed downstairs to answer the door. She opened the door and found a uniformed man holding a letter for her to sign for. The man explained that he needed Frederick to sign for the letter, not her.

Frederick rushed down the stairs to the front door and took the letter. The uniformed man, Frederick knew, was from Dibble Post. The man laughingly asked Frederick if he had won the World Lottery. Frederick didn't appreciate the joke but didn't utter a word. He signed for the letter, which was in the form of a memory stick to insert into his computer. He shut the door on the Dibble Post man. Lidia followed Frederick in to his office and watched as Frederick put the memory stick into his computer.

The computer screen lit up. Frederick found the connection and opened the letter. He had been summoned to the headquarters of the Dependency Unit at 10 am on Monday morning. The instruction was not to go to his usual office but present himself on the fourth floor of the headquarters. There was nothing else in the letter.

Frederick was shocked and wondered why he was being summoned.

'What is all this about? I don't trust you. You get a promotion and now our children are removed; you're a bastard. What have you done? I'm going to sleep in the children's room tonight, keep away from me.'

Frederick didn't know what to say or what to do; none of it made any sense to him. He always believed that in this situation at least one of the parents was guilty. He tried to speak to contacts in the department but no one got back to him. He also considered going down to find Herbert but realised the system had no room for mistakes and Herbert would not be able to help. Herbert would have to record Frederick seeing him and not waiting until Monday would be going against procedures. He knew the system could not be wrong, so his wife must have harmed the children. He also knew that he had to keep cool, as any stress could be interpreted by the system as guilt. He froze and felt momentarily useless and angry; he was like a rabbit caught in the headlights. In many ways, knowing the system made him even more powerless. Trying work with it was an unenviable task.

Throughout Saturday both Lidia and Frederick continued to blame each other, there was no trust between them. Their worlds had narrowed; Lidia shouted and screamed at

Frederick to do something, and he shouted back at her, demanding to know what she'd done. At one stage he nearly broke his hand in frustration, smashing his fist in to a wall. Frederick was lost as to what else to do. Even in his high ranking position, the system was out of his control.

Frederick knew what people would say about him; they would gossip about him being an abuser and that he was the Head of the Dependency Unit. The sad thing for Frederick was that he had told everyone about his promotion and gained respect, he thought, amongst people who had high status in society. Even Lidia had gained a new respect for him, but now everything had fallen apart.

In the afternoon, Frederick noticed some cuts on Lidia's arms. He asked her about them. Lidia had always hidden her self-harming from him but decided now to tell him truth. After all, it didn't matter now that she didn't have her children.

Frederick asked Lidia if she had cut herself before or if this was the first time.

'I've cut myself on several occasions,' said Lidia. 'It makes me feel better. I never get to feel any better about anything when I'm with you.'

Frederick never usually drank in the day but now he left the room, he went into the dining room to the sideboard where they kept their spirits, wine glasses, and tumblers. He took out the whisky bottle and one of the tumblers, sat down and poured a drink. He started to wonder what would happen at Monday's meeting and what they would say to him.

So many thoughts whirled through Frederick's head; he couldn't understand why Lidia was cutting herself. He couldn't understand why the children had been removed and began thinking through the different scenarios of how all this could have happened. He thought of his own experience in dealing with all the other cases in his department and came to the conclusion there could only be two answers to what had happened. If abuse had happened, it was due to his wife having done something serious to his children. He thought to himself that if she had cut herself, did anybody know about it, and what effect it could have on their children?

For the second time in recent months he had started to question the Dependency Department's ideology. He questioned the Department's policy in not giving any information. According to the Department, the risk assessment and the evidence-based science would inform the Department of the facts about the families they were dealing with. As far as the Department was concerned, the perpetrators would have to come to terms with what they had done.

However, when he looked at his own situation, he did not know where and when any investigation had been carried out about his children. For half of the cases in the Department, he knew that evidence came from different sources and that all this went into the computer program. A decision would be made based on what was put into the computer. This practice he now started to question.

What Frederick could not understand was how a decision could be made on a Level 3 case without it being investigated first. They were usually checked and double checked, and it was very rare for a Level 3 to just come out of the blue. What Frederick also couldn't understand how this happened given that he ran the Department and everything came via him.

Lidia was not close to any family. She had a sister who lived abroad and a father who had been in a Dibble Home until he decided to take the End of Life option at only seventy-two years old. She had lost her father too young. His physical health had deteriorated but mentally he was alert. He made the choice to take the injection because the counsellor in the Dibble home explained to him about the poor quality of life he would have in the future. Lidia's only remaining family were her sister and her children; Frederick may as well have been a complete stranger to her.

While Frederick was nursing his whisky and his thoughts, Lidia contacted Sophie again. Sophie suggested Lidia to go round to her house for a couple of hours. Lidia agreed and left. Frederick was now alone with his thoughts.

As he got more intoxicated, he started to feel sorry for himself. He had always supported the Department and Department policy and had felt that, when any employee put the Department in a difficult position, it was only right that the employer dealt with those employees harshly. However, the situation was different. It was his children who had been removed and, although he blamed Lidia, he was still not certain. He desperately needed more information.

Frederick left another message for Herbert.

Can Openers

Lidia knocked on the door and Sophie answered. She looked at Lidia, who looked a complete wreck. As Lidia walked through the door it was clear to Sophie how distraught the woman was.

Lidia blurted out that she could not live without her children. 'The Dependency Department is terrible. I love my children; I've never done anything to hurt them. I've never even smacked them and hardly ever raised my voice to them.'

Sophie hugged her. 'I know how brilliant you are with your children.'

'I can't be with Frederick anymore,' said Lidia. 'He believes in all that rubbish about the Dependency Department. He even talks like a corporate man, he never questions anything.'

Sophie put her hand on Lidia's arm. 'It must be awful for you. At least Herbert questions things. I know he goes along with the ideological concepts of the Department's welfare policy at work, but he sees himself as like a foreman in a car factory. He will accept it at work, but knows a lot of the policy is very contradictory. It makes it easier for us, though in some respects he is probably more dishonest than Frederick. He plays the game so in the end we can all have our holidays, the nice life style, and have enough money to support the children.'

'What do you think happened?' Lidia asked.

'I don't know' said Sophie. 'I'm sure it's just one of those terrible mistakes. It will get sorted and everything will be all right.' Sophie had listened to Lidia's complaints about Frederick for months. However, Sophie conceded that, considering how bitter Frederick was about the world and the way he treated everyone else, he clearly loved his children; with them he seemed to become a different person.

Lidia agreed with Sophie but couldn't take her mind off what she was going through. 'Frederick thinks either there's been a mistake or it's my fault. He said I must have abused the children.'

Lidia told Sophie that Frederick had a meeting the next day. 'Hopefully we will have more information then. Even if we get the children back next week, I decided to leave him.'

'It's about time,' said Sophie. 'But what a shame it's under such tragic circumstances. There's never a good time for a relationship to break down, but it's even sadder under these conditions.'

Sophie and Lidia talked for a couple of hours more. Sophie told Lidia she would help her in every way she could. She even offered Lidia the use of the apartment she owned in Spain for however long she wanted, and told her that she should have not left it so long to leave Frederick.

Lidia said, 'Perhaps you're right, but there is no such thing as should. I make my decisions in the here and now. However bad things are, change is very hard, it brings uncertainty and that is such a great fear.' Lidia explained that fear had stopped her from leaving Frederick years ago. She said how she hoped the next day, when Frederick got to work, she would find out what had happened to her children.

In the meantime, Frederick had consumed two thirds of the bottle of whisky and was flat out on the sofa. When Lidia arrived back home later that evening, she went straight up to the bedroom.

Neither of them spoke that night. They got through the night without each other, Frederick dazed and drunk, Lidia sleepless until late in the night.

They were both awake early the next morning. Frederick was weak and nauseous; his head felt as if a bolt had been passed through it.

The couple distrusted and held contempt for each other but they both realised a truce between them would be the best way forward. Lidia was keen for Frederick to contact her as soon as he found out why a department that prided itself on evidence-based practice could make such an awful mistake.

Frederick, however, knew deep down that the meeting this morning was separate to the children being taken. Despite this, he would do everything he could to find out what had happened. The difficulty was that he had no idea who would be at the meeting. Also, for the first time in his working life, he was totally focused on his children. Everything else, including his moral crusade against those who chose not to work, his zeal to ensure that those who needed it got a push to get motivated, and his determination to champion the ideology of the dependency department, no longer seemed important.

Can Openers

Frederick wasn't going to be early to work this morning. He didn't notice the beggars, the street hawkers, or the man with the tin whistle and the dog. The world had changed around him. He had momentarily lost his anger with everyone else. All he could think of was the meeting and whether Lidia had done something to his children. He feared the worst; he feared the nightmare of not getting his children back. Frederick had never felt so confused and uncertain.

Procedures had changed over the last five years. In the past, if an allegation was made against a staff member, that person would be suspended on full pay and an investigation would take place. This had changed. If the department deemed any allegation as a serious breach, or a gross misconduct, the staff member would be summarily dismissed and would have to lodge an appeal in order to trigger an investigation. The concept of unfair dismissal eroded to the point where it was no longer recognised. What existed now was an assumption of guilt; one had to prove one's innocence.

Frederick had always believed in the disciplinary procedure, it was robust and if anyone disagreed with or questioned it, he would feel that individual was being disloyal to the Department. But now Frederick was very frightened. He wandered up slowly to the office where the meeting was to take place. He went to the secretary's desk to announce himself and she led him to an office. The secretary knocked, she opened the door, and said, 'He's here, sir.' She stood to one side and allowed Frederick to enter.

Frederick perspired and, as he walked into the office, his legs trembled. Behind the desk was Herbert, and next to Herbert were two men who he did not recognise. Herbert introduced the two men, they both worked for the Quality and Performance Department. To Herbert's left was the Department head and to his right was a representative from the Legal Department.

Straight away Frederick blurted out to Herbert that there had been a big mistake. The person to Herbert's left told Frederick to be quiet. 'We will tell you what is happening,' he said. He said that if Frederick spoke again without permission, the meeting would be suspended. Frederick could not believe what was happening.

'We have information that your family has triggered a number 3 risk,' The Legal representative said. 'Your children are therefore are at risk of significant harm. Only you know the true facts and what has put you in this position.'

He looked directly at Frederick as he continued, saying how they were not interested at this moment in time in the issues or the abuse that had occurred. 'You have your confidentiality. What we are interested in how this looks for the department, and we have to consider your responsible position and that you are a beacon for the department.'

Frederick swallowed but said nothing.

'You will understand,' said the Legal representative, 'that we have to uphold the values of the Department. We therefore have to be just and fair. We do not want the Department to be a laughing stock.'

The Head of Dependency said, 'We regret to inform you that from the end of this meeting you are dismissed from the Department.' Frederick's stomach felt like it had dropped. 'You will receive your full pay for one month without bonus. You are not allowed on Dependency Department premises unless invited. If you have contact with anyone whilst they are at work or you come on the premises without permission you will be committing a serious offence and will be prosecuted. All of this will be confirmed to you in writing. Do you understand, Mr Smyth?'

'Yes,' he responded, 'but can I ask—?' However, Frederick was interrupted before he could ask his question by the legal representative who told him to leave, the meeting was now over.

Frederick couldn't believe what was happening. He felt a sudden surge of different emotions, confusion, shock, panic, and anger, all at the same time.

'No!' shouted Frederick as he moved towards the desk. 'I need answers.' As he did this, two uniformed security guards, tall, well built, their biceps bulging through the sleeves of their shirts, entered the room, grabbed Frederick by his arms, and almost marched him outside.

As they took him outside the office the biggest of the security guards said to Frederick, 'Calm down mister, we're only doing a job.'

The other guard said, 'Maybe you could e-mail your issues, just calm down.'

Can Openers

Frederick looked at the security guards who were both twice the size as him.

The bigger of the two guards spoke to Frederick again. 'You need to be searched before you leave the premises and we have to give you this envelope. The information in the envelope tells you where to send your ID badge.'

The guards then escorted Frederick to an office in the basement, it was windowless, the walls were bare and the room was lit with strip lighting. Frederick was searched; he was asked to turn out his pockets, was patted down, and was told to open his briefcase, which one of the guards then went through before handing it back. The two guards then escorted Frederick back to the ground floor and watched as Frederick went out of the door.

Frederick seethed with anger. He had no answers. He thought to himself, there are real scroungers out there claiming benefits, why have I been singled out? Why have I been picked on? Why me? I've done nothing wrong.

His anger went from blaming nameless, invisible people, those who were always scapegoats, to blaming Lidia. He became increasingly angry towards her.

Frederick walked down the street. It had started to drizzle. By now it was lunchtime, but Frederick didn't notice. He remained too stunned and dazed to notice much at all. He walked past someone on the street and hardly noticed as that person put a leaflet in his hand. Frederick carried on walking. As drizzle turned to a steady rain, Frederick decided to enter a small takeaway food shop that had a few tables and chairs. He ordered a coffee and sat down at one of the tables. He looked at the leaflet in his hand. It had a headline written in capital letters:

"WHY SHOULD THE HARDWORKING FOLK SUFFER AT THE HANDS OF LAYABOUTS AND SCROUNGERS? THEY ABUSE OUR KIDS AND EXPECT HANDOUTS. COME TO THE MEETING TO FIND OUT WHAT CAN BE DONE".

The leaflet advertised a meeting taking place that afternoon, organised by the 33 Gang. Frederick liked the back of the leaflet and what it had to say, particularly the bit that said "homes for heroes not for scroungers".

Frederick couldn't face going home just yet to explain to Lidia what happened. He decided to go to the meeting instead. Frederick left his coffee and backtracked along the street. He found the building where it was due to be held, opened the door and went inside. There was a small lobby and then a door that led to a hall.

Outside the door to the hall was a desk with two men standing behind it; they looked like security guards. They asked Frederick to sign in, handing him a pen and pointing to a book on the table. The book already had a list of names all written in different handwriting. Frederick signed the page.

Another male, who Frederick thought was probably in his 60s, showed him into the meeting hall. Frederick walked inside. In front of him, seated on a platform, was a large man who looked like a bouncer; he was wearing a very tight-fitting suit, but anything would look tight-fitting on the man's frame. The man looked pumped up, as though he had been lifting weights for years and popping steroids. His head was disproportionately large with a neck that was width of his shoulders. Frederick realised, once the meeting had started, that the man with no neck was the chair. He was sat next to another male on the platform who had no distinguishing features except that he was of medium height, slim build, in his 50s and looked almost anorexic compared to Mr Big.

Frederick was intimidated as he sat in the hall but he put it down to the fact that he had never been to a meeting like this before. He noticed that, since the meeting was in the middle of the day, there did not seem to be many office or factory workers in attendance. The room had scattering of people, mainly men, who seemed to know each other. Some wore coats that looked like a uniform of some kind.

The no neck man on the stage stood up and called the meeting to order. 'Can you all stand and show respect for the speaker.' Everyone in the room stood up.

As the thin man rose from his chair, the people in the hall sat back down. The thin man folded his hands together and started to speak. Much of what he had to say was very close to Frederick's views and principles.

The speaker knew how to speak to his audience, he gestured with his hands to emphasise a point, and he sometimes spoke quietly to get across the seriousness of another point. Another time, he shouted. 'It is now time that no money is given to those time wasters who don't work. And those perverts who, when they are found out to be child abusers, these sexual thugs, they need to be taken out. Punish them I say, don't give them charity.'

Sitting next to Frederick was a pale-faced man who looked about 30 years old. As the speaker paused in his speech, the pale-faced man leaned over to Frederick and said, 'we've got a list of perverts right and we're going to smash their places up. If you want to help, if you're interested, see me after the meeting.'

Frederick didn't know what to say, fortunately for him the main speaker carried on.

"These vermin should have no rights,' said the speaker. 'These aliens coming in to our country, wrecking our culture. And those people who abuse our kids, those who take their innocence, they are cowards; they should plead guilty and take their punishment like men. Those who are dependency people should not be pandered to.'

Frederick realised he was being stared at. He was uncomfortable and paranoid; he realised that he had lost his kids and it could be him the speaker was talking about. Frederick knew he hadn't done anything wrong, but if these people knew or found out about what had happened to him, feared for the consequences. Frederick was nervous and frightened, for the first time it dawned on him that he was to become a dependency figure. This was the worst day of his life. Frederick left the meeting.

By now the rain had cleared. Frederick started drifted slowly to the Metro station. He wasn't conscious of having got off the train; he had wandered aimlessly and found himself at the gates of the local park. He found a bench and sat down and put his head in his hands. His hands were quickly wet from tears.

Eventually he stopped crying, wiped his eyes with his handkerchief and blew his nose.

He sat there numb and not noticing anything around him at first until a man came and sat on the opposite end of the bench. It was, Frederick realised, the man who played the tin whistle near the metro station. He was holding a short flute and his dog was with him, lying on the ground by the man's feet. The man's hygiene was not the best, he had an odour that could only be described as sour milk mixed with urine.

The man looked at Frederick sympathetically. 'Times are hard.'

To his surprise Frederick found himself replying, 'They are indeed.'

They had a further brief exchange this time about the weather, and then Frederick, not even noticing the smell, started telling this complete stranger his life story to a man who would normally either be invisible to Frederick or a focus of his bitterness about the world.

When Frederick finished pouring his heart out, the man on the bench asked him if he had any enemies. Frederick replied that there were some who did not like his style. The man asked if he thought he had been set up. This had never occurred to Frederick before. He had always had a belief in the system that it was value-free and could not be manipulated. A few weeks ago Frederick had questioned the system for the first time and, while sitting on the bench talking to the man, he began to wonder if he had been set up.

The man said, 'Life goes on. Maybe you need to ask questions. The whole of human history is not predetermined, anything can happen. If you accept your fate and don't believe in yourself, which is what happened with me, you'll end up the same as me, in the gutter.'

Frederick looked at this man. He was unusually articulate. Frederick thanked him and offered him some money. The man shook his head and said that he didn't want any money, but that he wished him well as Frederick stood up to walk away.

Frederick decided to walk home. Sooner or later he would have to face Lidia. He still felt that she must have done something to the children. He still believed in the values of the Department, therefore she must know what happened to the children.

Frederick also thought about the words of wisdom from the man on the bench.

As he arrived home Frederick felt calmer; he told himself that Lidia was not the enemy that he just needed to know what she had done. Lidia was there waiting for him when he walked in. She asked him what had happened. Frederick, hesitantly at first, started to explain.

Lidia, however, became increasingly agitated. 'Why didn't you ask anything about the children?' she asked in bewilderment.

'I tried,' he said, 'but there were two bouncers there, they just dragged me out of the room.'

Lidia put her hands up to her cheeks and shook her head in disbelief. 'This is disgusting,' she said. 'Where's the justice?'

Frederick didn't know what to say to her, he didn't have answers to either of their questions.

Lidia became upset. 'They've stolen our children!'

Lidia then stopped and more calmly asked what the Florence families were like. Frederick told Lidia that every Florence family was different but that they did their duty. Lidia thought about this and nodded.

Neither of them said anything for a while, and then Lidia told Frederick that the video post-delivery had called that day. 'They wouldn't give me the information, the letter needed both our signatures.'

'Shall we go and get the letter together?' asked Frederick. 'The office might still be open.'

Lidia looked away from Frederick. 'I've already signed. you go get it. I'm going to a friend's.'

Frederick left the house and walked the short distance to the Dibble Post Office. It was clear from the activity inside that the office about to close for the day. The woman behind the counter sighed at the inconvenience, but located the electronic signature pad and found Lidia's signature. Frederick signed his name underneath Lidia's, as requested. The woman went through to the back of the office and came back after a few short minutes carrying a padded envelope, which she handed to him.

As soon as he left the Post Office and was back out on the street, Frederick tore open the envelope and read the letter. Two Opportunity Planners from the Children's Section would be visiting his house the next day. Maggie Brown OBE signed the letter.

Frederick knew Maggie; she was in charge of the other district, which meant his case was going to be dealt with by this other area. The letter also gave him a case number he was required to quote when having any contact with the Department. They were now to be known as case number c421.

Lidia went to see Sophie again. They had spoken several times since the children had been removed. Sophie had been a great support for Lidia; she had contacts including an acquaintance looking for someone to help run a bar. Lidia had already spoken to the bar owner who, it turned out, also knew of a flat with cheap rent. Lidia had also made enquiries and had found out she had a chance of being transferred to another shop, which offered extra hours. Lidia's plans were progressing; all she needed was to sort things out with Frederick as soon as possible, and decided to talk to him the next day.

Chapter 20

Tuesday soon came around and, as the couple ate what little breakfast they could manage, Lidia wanted to discuss their future, or lack of one. Somehow she managed to keep herself calm.

Lidia felt their relationship had been strained for a long time; that it only slightly improved over the two weeks before the children were removed. Ironically, it was because of the children that she had stayed with him. For her children to be taken off them felt like a death.

'I'm not a stupid person, Frederick. I've read up about the dependency system. I know that when the system gets to a number 3 there is unlikely to be any turning back.' She paused. Frederick said nothing. 'My life is finished without my children and I know in my heart that I will never be able to see them again.' Lidia took a deep breath to stop herself from crying. 'I don't want to be with you, Frederick, and I can't live a lie. Without the children we're nothing.'

'What about the meeting?' asked Frederick, quietly.

Lidia said that at the meeting she would show unity. The meeting was the most serious meeting of their lives.

'If that's what you want,' was Frederick's only response.

She was worried about Frederick's reaction. She would have preferred not to have said anything to him until after the meeting but the tension had been unbearable and she couldn't take it anymore.

Frederick was surprisingly calm, almost spaced out. He thought about what Lidia had said to him. In some respects they hadn't been honest with each other for years. They would have to tell the department that they were separating, they would find out everything anyway and honestly, he thought, was the best policy. For them, as parents, losing their children was their worst nightmare.

There was a loud bang at the front door like it was going to explode. 'Open the door, we have a warrant. It's the police,' demanded a voice through a loudhailer.

Frederick rushed to the door and opened it. In came a large uniformed officer who immediately started directing other officers. 'You take the upstairs and you the downstairs,' he ordered two officers. 'You two, sit down,' he ordered Lidia and Frederick. A small camera was attached to the officer's lapel. Everything was being recorded and watched by risk assessors who were sitting outside in a van.

Frederick asked what they were looking for and why were the police going out to the back garden.

The police officer, who was a sergeant, looked straight at Frederick and leaned in close. 'Mr Smyth, you know the truth. You and your wife should know that a level three assessment is the most serious level of child abuse. Either you, your wife, or both know why you're on a number 3.'

The police officer was right. The latest evidence, backed by research, showed that when there is abuse or harm in the family, the family, or someone close to it, know why the children are removed. It is up to them to work it out.

The sergeant spoke again, 'The days of looking at why abuse has happened are gone. We only deal with the consequences. I have been warned by the Chief Inspector that this is a difficult case and that you worked for the Dependency Unit. I must tell you that, from today on, you and Mrs Smyth are dependency figures.' The Sergeant folded his arms across his chest and rocked back and forth on his heels. 'I must say, Mr Smyth, that you should have had more respect for your employers. You should be ashamed.'

A police officer went up to the sergeant and said that the risk assessment was complete. Lidia just stared speechless. Two people came through the door, each with a computer.

'Hello, I am Simon and this is Joanne. We're Development Planners.' He smiled at Frederick and Lidia in turn.

Frederick asked, 'Why are you seeing us at a Development Planner level?'

Simon explained that due to Frederick's previous level in the Department, the Department decided to be completely objective. 'We are offering you the opportunity to discuss any issues with us.'

Joanne then spoke, 'We understand how difficult this is for both of you but, Mr Smyth, either yourself or your wife or both have committed serious harm to your children. We are looking for further evidence today.'

Without waiting to be asked, Joanne sat down in an armchair placing her briefcase and laptop on the floor by her feet. 'We have also been asked by the Department to let you know that your children will be staying with the Florence family permanently.'

At this Lidia looked up at Joanne. 'Where's the evidence? You haven't even spoken to us. Have you interviewed the children?'

Simon looked at Lidia. 'Mrs Smyth, by the time a situation gets to a number three everything has been looked at and the decisions have been made. On issues such as this, the Department is aware that one of you at least will be responsible for significant abuse.'

Lidia and Frederick stared at the two Development Planners.

'Getting angry won't help. The situation is very difficult for us, too, We've seen and read some of your work. I probably shouldn't tell you this but the Department has offered us counselling. They are worried about how we manage the questions and the interview. However the decision was made and is final.'

Despite what Simon said, Lidia could feel her temper rising. 'This is preposterous, you can't do this!'

Joanne replied icily, 'You should have thought about that before you harmed your children.'

Frederick said, 'What is it we've done?'

Again the response was the same, 'You know what you've done, not us.'

'But we have not done anything!' Lidia shouted.

'That's what they all say,' replied Joanne.

Simon explained that there was a very small possibility of Lidia and Frederick seeing their children again and for that to happen, they had to own up and declare how they abused the children. The Department would view such an admission as them accepting responsibility and they could then work with the parents.

Joanne said they needed to discuss Frederick and Lidia's responsibility regarding financial support for their children.

'The Florence family,' Joanne said, 'needs to have the resources to look after your children.' Lidia and Frederick would have to sell their house with any equity going to the State and the Florence family.

Lidia felt the blood drain from her face. She had planned to split from Frederick but how was she to survive afterward? She asked the Development Planners where they would live. The response was even worse than she had expected. Simon said that because of the circumstances, they would be deemed to have made themselves intentionally homeless.

Joanne said that they would be assessed and would get minimum money for basic survival but would not receive housing support. With a hint of sarcasm she said, 'Mr Smyth, I would have thought you would appreciate the action being taken. You are one of the greatest advocates of the dependency program and the rules should not be broken.'

Frederick and Lidia were then asked about bank accounts, jewellery and anything they owned of value. It took a while to go through the inventory.

When the Development Planners had completed their tasks they explained how Lidia and Frederick needed to live their new lives, and they would get a sum of money that they would be allowed to live off for basic survival. All the rest of the money would go to the Florence family.

Lidia had felt so very low after the children had been removed; now she felt completely helpless.

The Dependency Planners thanked Frederick and Lidia for their time, packed up their laptops and briefcases and left.

As soon as they had gone, Lidia said she would be leaving the next day. Frederick did not try to talk her out of it. He still couldn't quite believe what was happening to him.

Lidia arranged to meet Sophie who was going with Lidia to her flat in Spain, and the tickets had already been bought.

Frederick had never felt so lonely in his life; he could not see any of his family as he fell out with them several years ago after he accused his brother of being a scrounger and sponger. The main reason why he didn't want contact with his family was something he would never share or talk to anyone about, but would this would come back to haunt him?

Can Openers

The only person Frederick had a relationship with was Joseph. He liked Joseph because, like Frederick himself, he was a complex person. At work Joseph was ambitious; he wanted to go up the ladder and would do anything to gain promotion. Joseph was openly gay and had to fight against discrimination. Considering he was very insecure about many areas of his life, to come out openly was very brave. Even Frederick had respect for Joseph, even though he often was confused by his own sexuality. Joseph never questioned anything about the department's values and was very focused; this made some of his peers suspicious of him. But outside of work Joseph was liberal in his views, he had sympathy with those who were less fortunate and, on occasion, even put up homeless people in his flat. Joseph was a most contradictory young person.

Frederick thought about Joseph now, and wondered if Joseph would offer some comfort to him and some accommodation until he could get back on his feet.

Lidia went upstairs to their bedroom. She pulled a suitcase down from the top of the wardrobe and packed clothes and any valuables she had hidden away. They had both kept quiet about some valuable jewellery they had hidden when being interviewed by the Development Planners, so they would have some cash to survive. They decided to split the valuables between the two of them.

Frederick sat and pondered how life had changed for him. He always felt that anyone who kept anything hidden from the State was no more than a common criminal. He would have no hesitation in sending the police around to their houses. Yet here he was, doing the very thing he had so disapproved of in others. But what choice did he have?

Frederick decided to visit Joseph. He walked the entire way, even though it was a 45-minute walk. It helped to clear his head and calm him down. He arrived at the communal door to the apartment block where Joseph's flat was and pressed the intercom. Joseph buzzed open the door. Frederick went up a flight of stairs and knocked on Joseph's door. Joseph was surprised to see Frederick standing there but invited him in.

They both went in to the sitting room. Joseph thought Frederick had aged, he looked stressed and worn out, he seemed a different person, as though his confidence and arrogance had deserted him. Joseph was keen to know what had been going on; he heard rumours at work. He asked Frederick if everything was all right. Frederick told him everything that happened and, when he had finished, Joseph gave him a hug.

Joseph then stood back. He had lost some of the attraction he had for Frederick. Joseph told him quietly that he did not feel it was safe for Frederick to see him anymore. He said that he had enjoyed their time together and how maybe, in other circumstances, a relationship could have developed. However, he felt that this had to be the end.

Frederick sighed, his hope for comfort and accommodation was disappearing fast.

Joseph said that if he was seen by the Department in any kind of relationship with Frederick, they would dismiss him.

'I can't associate with a number three,' said Joseph. To be kind and to soften the blow, Joseph told Frederick that if he was struggling for money he would help him but otherwise he should leave. He apologised. 'I'm sure you understand.'

Frederick, with his head bowed, murmured, 'Yes', opened the door, and left.

This devastated Joseph. He loved Frederick but did not completely trust him and he knew that if he let Frederick into his life, there would always be a nagging doubt about whether Frederick hurt his children in some way. Joseph would not be able to cope with this; child abuse was such a terrible act.

As Frederick walked out on to the street, he felt invisible. He felt like a zombie in a world full of zombies. He was numb.

When Frederick arrived back home, Lidia had just gotten back from taking a number of items to Sophie's house. Frederick and Lidia didn't speak to each other, more out of shock than from anger. Lidia went upstairs into the children's bedroom; she lay down on one of the beds, picked up the pillow, and breathed in deeply her child's smell. She put the pillow under her head and cried herself to sleep.

Lidia awoke early the next morning. After she showered and dressed, she decided to say goodbye to Frederick. Everything important had been said; the parting was cold, not even a shout or a fight. Lidia left.

Frederick had not even asked Lidia where she was going, not that she would have told him. He had decided that he didn't really care, he poured himself some whisky and started to drink.

Later that day, Lidia and Sophie arrived in Spain. It was October and the temperature was still in the 20s. The beach was only a five-minute walk from where they were staying. It was a beautiful place to be. Despite the beauty of her surroundings, Lidia barely noticed the outside world. Sophie tried to cheer her up. She told Lidia that she thought Herbert was looking into the case. Lidia looked blankly at her friend.

Sophie and Lidia were in Spain together for some time. After discussing the matter, Sophie decided to go back to England to look for accommodation for Lidia. Lidia convinced Sophie she would be fine staying in Spain on her own, telling her she needed the space to get her thoughts together. However, Sophie did not realise how desperate her friend's thoughts had become.

Chapter 21

The same morning that the police and the Development Planners called to Frederick and Lidia's house, Lord Dibble asked Sir George to his office.

Lord Dibble started the meeting by saying that he had met the minister the previous day. 'He is not happy, what on earth has happened?' he thundered. 'What has Frederick Smyth has been up to? Why didn't we know about it? Can we get someone else to find the fraud on A1021a? What is going on?'

Sir George said he was as shocked as Lord Dibble, and could not understand what had happened.

'I'm most concerned,' said Lord Dibble. 'Our organisation may have been infiltrated by rival companies. We must find out what happened to Frederick. I want you to find out what he has done and report back to me.'

'Yes, of course, Lord Dibble,' said Sir George. Sir George went on to say that there had been rumours that Frederick may have been set up.

'How can that be?' demanded Lord Dibble. 'The system is foolproof and evidence-based.'

'Yes, yes, of course,' said Sir George, 'but there are some clever people out there and Mr Smyth has enemies, I believe.'

Lord Dibble said he thought there should be an investigation as Smyth had been at such a high level; they needed to know what happened.

Sir George was doubtful about the need for such an investigation but didn't dare openly express disagreement or dissent. 'Yes, of course, Lord Dibble,' he said instead. 'So who do you think should lead the investigation?'

'Dashed if I know, it's your job to identify someone, who do you suggest?'

Sir George thought about it briefly and then suggested the Head of Department, Herbert.

He explained his choice on the grounds that Herbert was known to be thorough, that when he carried out investigations he left no stone unturned. 'He should have been in C.I.D. or been a spook,' chuckled Sir George.

'Good man, get him to investigate it then,' said Lord Dibble. 'And one more thing, no one else is to know of this conversation. Get the investigation done quickly. We can't let this interfere with our other plans. We will pay the ringleader of the Can Openers at the end of the month, but we cannot go ahead with the rest of the plan until Herbert finds out something.'

Lord Dibble ended the meeting by picking up his phone and punching a number into the set, he didn't even look at Sir George or hear him when he said, 'I will get on to it straight away, Lord Dibble.'

When Sir George arrived back at his office, he summoned Herbert without delay. They were both polite, asking about each other's families and how they had been keeping, but Sir George was keen to get down to business.

He discussed the situation regarding Frederick. 'Due to the high position Smyth had in the organisation, we want you to carry out an investigation. We want you to look into what happened and make sure the people who were involved in Smyth's dismissal did not make any mistakes. You must be thorough. And we do not want anyone else involved. You report to me only; anything you find out, any rumour or tittle-tattle you hear, you bring it to me only. I want to know everything on the Smyth case.'

Herbert asked about his other responsibilities. Sir George told him to drop all his other work and concentrate on the Smyth case.

'We want to know what he did to get a number 3 risk rating; we want to know everything. These are orders from the very top.'

Herbert returned to his office and went to work straight away. He relished these tasks; he loved watching the old detective programs on the television and had watched every episode of the vintage program, *Inspector Morse*.

It took time but, by being patient and unobtrusive, Herbert eventually started to learn things about Frederick. One of the first items of information Herbert found out about involved the affair that Frederick had been having with Joseph. He could hardly believe it. Though he could not see how it was connected to Frederick's children at home. It was the sort of thing that could lead to disciplinary action, but he couldn't see how it could lead to a number 3 risk rating. Herbert needed to see Joseph and interview him as part of the investigation. He summoned Joseph to his office. Herbert was keen to make progress.

Chapter 22

Sophie was pleased with herself. She had already found a decently furnished flat for Lidia with affordable rent, and she had taken a call on Lidia's behalf from the shop where Lidia worked, offering more hours. It meant she could contact Lidia and give her some good news. Sophie felt as though she was really helping her friend.

Sophie and Lidia had talked about Lidia remaining in Spain on her own. Although Sophie was worried about her friend, Lidia needed some time to herself. It would help her gather her thoughts and sort herself out.

Lidia, however, left on her own, had descended into a very low mood and her thoughts darkened. She was on her own. Her children had been taken away, what had she left to live for? However much she tried, Lidia couldn't see any future. She spent time walking in the sunshine. In other circumstances, and at another time, this would have been a pleasurable experience.

Lidia contemplated how she could end her life and if she could be brave enough to commit the ultimate act. She thought about it from every conceivable angle. Her thinking had become so fixed; it was centred on whether she had the bravery to carry out something so serious. She thought that if she didn't kill herself it would be another negative experience.

Lidia decided to get a bus to a village a few miles away from where she was staying. The village sat on top of a small mountain with spectacular views over the valley below. There was a viewing over a cliff face, which had a sheer drop to the stream and rocks below. Some way behind the viewing point was the main village square. Around the square and off the surrounding streets were small shops and cafés. Children played by the small fountain in the centre of the village square. The day was still warm and, in the early evening light, the village was alive with activity.

Lidia went to the viewing point. There was a small fence separating visitors from a drop of several hundred feet. Lidia wondered how to get over the fence. She turned and looked around. There was a small bar only a few hundred metres away. She went to the bar and ordered a short and wine, took her two drinks to a table, and sat down, staring at the world in front of her. She watched a village that was full of life. There was some older women dressed in black, chatting; an old man came through the village with some goats, noisy with their bleating, the bells around their necks clanging almost in harmony with each other. Sitting opposite Lidia were a group of young people, she could hear from their conversation they were young Americans backpacking around Europe.

Beyond this, Lidia didn't notice much else. She thought the village could be straight out of a holiday brochure.

Lidia was getting more wrapped up in her own world; she drank copious amounts of alcohol, having ordered two more rounds of spirits and two more glasses of wine. The drink was starting to do what Lidia had wanted; it gave her the confidence to commit suicide. She looked around and thought that a person could be in paradise, but at rock bottom paradise could be a very lonely place; it could be hell on earth.

Lidia paid her bill. She left the bar and went to a bench in the square. As she sat down her mobile phone bleeped. She read a text from Sophie: 'Have got u a flat and have found out some info. Will tell u when u r back home. Sophie.'

Lidia was frustrated. 'What information? She needed to know. She texted Sophie back asking the other woman to tell her what information she had. Before she could send the text, as if ordained by fate, her mobile phone went dead.

She needed to make a choice. She could still see no future; even when there was the possibility of a tiny fraction of hope, it was snuffed out. She could see only one way out, it was her destiny.

Chapter 23

Joseph knocked on the door of Herbert's office and walked in meekly. Herbert told Joseph to sit down and then showed him a letter from Lord Dibble explaining the investigating procedure. Joseph looked perplexed.

'The department needs to maintain its reputation,' said Herbert. 'It needs to be value free and have morals.'

Joseph wondered if this summons to Herbert's office had something to do with Frederick. He didn't have to wait long to find out. Straight away Herbert asked Joseph how long he had worked in the same section as Frederick Smyth.

Joseph answered.

Herbert then asked him to explain what his relationship with Mr Smyth had been.

Joseph hesitated; he didn't know how to answer the question. He settled for telling Herbert that he had always had a positive relationship with Frederick, before correcting himself and saying Mr Smyth. Joseph added, for good measure, that Mr Smyth really believed in the values of the department.

'Do you have any reason to be upset with Mr Smyth?' asked Herbert.

'Absolutely not,' said Joseph.

Herbert offered Joseph a drink of water, which Joseph accepted.

Herbert asked, 'Since you've been at the department, you've moved up the structure very rapidly and now you're Dependency Programmer. Are you pleased with your progress? What do you put it down to?'

Joseph could feel himself flushing. He said that he was pleased with his progress. He thought it happened because he was a good administrator and was excellent at inputting into the system. He believed in the system and the values of the mission statement.

'Do you think Frederick believed in the mission statement?' asked Herbert.

'Yes,' replied Joseph.

Herbert started to fire questions off. He asked if Joseph was aware that Frederick no longer worked there. 'Do you have any views about that, Joseph?' asked Herbert.

'It was a tragedy.'

'What do you mean by a tragedy?'

Joseph then said despondently, 'Frederick's whole life is ruined.'

Herbert felt he was starting to get somewhere. 'How do you know that Frederick's whole life is ruined?'

Joseph was startled by the question, he'd been caught out. He tried to cover by saying that he meant that it must be terrible to lose your job.

Herbert asked how he knew this as Frederick may have taken a job elsewhere.

Before Joseph could even think of an answer, Herbert looked straight at Joseph, lowered his voice slightly and said in a menacing tone, 'we're aware of your relationship with Frederick. If you tell us the truth, this conversation will go no further. If you deny it, we will. And, with the evidence we have, it will be worse for you.' He paused and then said in a much calmer tone, 'to be honest, I'm not interested whether you had a relationship or not. I just want you to be truthful.' Joseph sank down into the chair, a tear rolled down one cheek. Quietly and with a slight, nervous stutter, he explained how he had loved Frederick and had been in a relationship with him.

Ever since Frederick had left his flat and Joseph had chosen his career, Joseph felt guilty, so it was something of a relief that he had now told someone about the relationship. Joseph was ambitious, he was developing into a career-man but he still had softer side to his character.

Joseph wanted to be honest with Herbert, the department knew everything anyway and honesty would be the best policy. Herbert asked if Joseph had a physical relationship with Frederick. Joseph told him that they had a relationship for two and half years but that it was finished.

'Why did it finish?' asked Herbert.

Can Openers

Joseph wiped his eyes and took another sip of water. He said that he had ended the relationship because he had not wanted to compromise his position in the Dependency Department.

'So,' queried Herbert, 'you didn't fall out because of a lovers tiff? Are you sure he didn't finish with you? Were you spurned?'

Joseph thought Herbert was mocking him. 'No!' he said sharply and angrily.

Herbert asked, 'Is there any reason you would benefit from Frederick *not* working for the department anymore?'

'Are you accusing me of something?' asked Joseph.

Herbert stated that it was his job to gain information and up to now he had been reasonable. 'I might as well be direct. Have you had any part in framing or setting up Frederick for a fall? It will be best to tell us now as we will find out the truth.'

Despite his nerves Joseph responded angrily to this, he said that he thought it was disgraceful that anyone could accuse him of anything, that there was a structure in place that had been developed on the basis of evidence-based science and that it was flawless.

Herbert nodded, he said that he had to ask his questions and thanked Joseph for his answers. 'You can go now,' he said. Joseph left.

Herbert stood and walked over to the window. He considered Joseph's responses to the questions. He thought that the Joseph and Frederick affair was terrible. Herbert had met Lidia on several occasions. She was a devoted wife; Herbert thought that this was an awful way to treat her. Herbert wondered if his sense of disgust at the affair was due to him genuinely feeling bad for Lidia or if he was being moralistic, homophobic, or a mixture of all three? Herbert didn't quite trust Joseph; he had given Herbert reasons to be suspicious.

Herbert had heard a rumour that the department was going to offer him early retirement and that Joseph was to replace him. Herbert was aware of this rumour before he had interviewed Joseph, and he wasn't happy. He didn't want to take early retirement as he had an expensive lifestyle. He had worked hard and was close to being appointed to the position of supporting Sir George, working as his right hand man, Sir George's eyes and ears. Until the investigation, Herbert had been trusted and seen as a safe pair of hands. However, Herbert knew that Joseph was a rival; Joseph was dynamic, ruthless and younger, while Herbert was now well into his fifties. If he was going to move up in his career, he needed to do so quickly. With Frederick out of the way, Herbert had seen this opportunity to move up the ladder open up before him, so when Joseph appeared on the scene, it started to worry him very much.

Herbert went back to his desk to make his notes and to look at who else he needed to interview. He picked up a pen and listed names on a sheet of paper. He put Joyce's name down; below that, he added Phil the IT expert, and Marcus the other Opportunity Planner. He was also going to interview Lord Dibble, Sir George, and Sir Harpa; he had been given the authority. There were others he needed to see but they would only need to be asked just one or two questions. He sat with pen in hand and wondered if Joseph could have tampered with the system. Could the system be manipulated?

Chapter 24

Whilst Lidia sat contemplating her future, an old man came up to her and sat down next to her.

'Don't be so sad,' he said. 'It's a lovely day.' He spoke good English.

'I lost everything,' murmured Lidia.

'There's nothing to be sad about. We are only here once,' said the old man. 'We might as well enjoy it.'

Lidia said, 'I don't want to be here. I'm finished, there's nothing to live for. Nothing, nothing.'

'There's always something,' said the old man, 'there's always hope and opportunity, however small or meaningless, even in the darkest of days.' He got up and left her to her thoughts.

She felt the warmth of the sun on her face and arms. She lifted her head up and noticed the children playing in the square. Watching them made her stiffen; she remembered the text and started to shake. Perhaps Sophie had some hope for her. Lidia suddenly broke down and cried. She became frightened by the thought of death, her sense of survival had temporarily abandoned her.

As her tears subsided, Lidia felt embarrassed. She thought about how she had started drinking to get the courage to die, and now she thought about her children; they were still her children, she wanted them and they needed her. As she sat there thinking about all that had happened, she got angry, very angry with Frederick. Her hatred towards him was at the forefront of her mind. If nothing changed, however, she could end up again in the dark place she had just left.

Frederick spent his time drinking at home. He received a letter giving him notice to leave the house. Frederick started to question his own morality. He had always been a doer, had always done his job, but had never stopped to question himself, who he was or his beliefs. He thought he had a sense of right and wrong, and believed that people had to take responsibility. 'With freedom,' he believed, 'there also had to be responsibility.' Absolute freedom for him meant chaos. Frederick was scared of anarchy or change. He both believed in and needed order.

What is, is, he thought. Society needed structure and Frederick needed that. However, he thought about how ironic it was that his own moral code was being used against him.

The more he pondered his situation and thought about what he believed in, the more Frederick became confused. His values came from a form of religious belief. He had a strong sense of good and evil. He believed in the ideology of the Dependency Department. He thought about his own personal history. He considered his ideas about the Dependency Department and how it had fit his existence and led to him to forming a view of human nature that maybe was wrong. Frederick shook his head in frustration, the whisky was making him maudlin but he carried on drinking regardless. Lidia sat on the bench in the village square. She was curious and desperate to know the information Sophie had found. She was hoping for something she could cling on to. She felt her life had ended and again questioned the point of it all. She considered how short her life had been compared to how long humans had been on the planet. She was just a speck, insignificant. But her children were her life. Maybe, if she could get through the next few hours, it might make her a better person and stronger. More hope, she thought. If she could get through this desperately depressing rut, she may be able to fight to get her children back. Lidia still thought about suicide, but those thoughts were diminished by a much stronger view that there had been an injustice. Lidia still wondered if Frederick had abused the children. Maybe the Department had made a mistake, maybe there were other families going through the same thing.

Sophie found Lidia a flat that was homely, it even had a balcony. Sophie was relatively well off, her parents had died and left an inheritance. Sophie had made friends with Lidia some years ago, they had gotten to know each other well and often Lidia would discuss her with Sophie.

Can Openers

Despite her contentment now, Sophie had had bad experiences and had gone through her own difficult times. Sophie's mother and father had died when she was in her early 20s. Despite her inheritance, or possibly in part because of it, Sophie was very vulnerable. Before her parents died, she met an older male, who she moved in with. Her family was not happy with the situation. However, she could not tell her mother about her desperate need to get away, with whoever was willing to accept her: abuse from her father she suffered from an early age. Her worst memories were when he touched her on her private parts and often made her rub her hand until he become hard. '

The man she moved in with was 25 years older and kind to her, but she realised that the trauma of her earlier childhood was making her a psychological wreck. She soon left him, as moving in with him was merely a way to get away from her father. Her parents wanted her to go back home so would not give her any support. The Dependency Department assessed her need for emergency accommodation but had refused to help her. They told her she had to go back to her parents, even though she told an adviser for the dependency unit she had been abused by her father. The Dependency Department offered her counselling but assessed her as low risk and because of little evidence offered her no support. She had no useful help from the dependency department and had to go through their demeaning assessment processes when she was depressed herself.

Because of her parents' mysterious, sudden death, in a fire at their holiday bungalow, their estate was assessed and the assets approved for distribution. This meant she now had the financial means to get accommodation, and had the support of friends, who would help her come to terms with the abuse and her loss and grief. She always said that she would never ignore any of her friends going through difficulties; she would not be where she was in life and would probably not even alive if it had not been for her friends.

Sophie thought about this as she went to meet Lidia at the airport. Lidia had arranged to come back from Spain sooner than planned.

As soon as Lidia came through customs, Sophie ran up to her, embraced her and said, 'I've got a surprise for you.'

143

Lidia half smiled, she desperately wanted to know the information Sophie had texted her about whilst she was still in Spain. As they walked to Sophie's car, Sophie told Lidia she had a flat sorted out and that the shop had offered her extra hours. Sophie then told Lidia that she would tell her something more.

Sophie felt she was in a difficult situation. On the one hand she had never been disloyal to Herbert but, on the other hand, she felt Lidia should know any information that could help her with regards to her children.

Chapter 25

Frederick needed to contact Lidia but he had no idea where she'd gone. He looked destitute. He had several days beard growth with bits of food stuck in it. He hadn't washed himself and hadn't done any laundry. His clothes looked rancid and smelled. Frederick lived in hope that he could stay in the house and just survive on the basic money he received from the Dependency Unit. He spoke to the Customer Care Officer at the Unit, asked to stay in the house for the short term, but he would have the minimum to live on.

Fortunately, and unknown to the Unit, Frederick had his share of the jewellery that he and Lidia had split between them. He could sell his share and that would be enough to keep him going for a short time. He sat at home and had a break from drinking. He thought about what he should do about his life but, like all the other times he tried to work something out, every thought led to a dead end.

His life outside of work had been centred on the children. He had taken them on days out, he had played with them. He knew other fathers who didn't bother spending time playing with their children. Spending time with his children had always given Frederick great pleasure and a sense of joy. Besides playing with his children, Frederick used to enjoy watching cricket. It appealed to him. There was a sense of fair play; if a player was a shirker or lazy they would be found out and either run out or lose the wicket.

However, since his life had been turned upside down, Frederick lost interest in cricket, along with everything else apart from the drinking. He didn't know how to get out of his despair. He was barely eating; on the rare occasions that he did eat it would be chips, but then only if he could get up out of his drunken stupor.

Frederick was becoming increasingly obsessed with finding Lidia. He thought constantly about what she had done and where she was. He needed to talk to her. The problem was that he had never taken too much notice of her when they were together. He had taken Lidia for granted. He had no idea about her life before the devastation, so he had no idea now where to start to look for her.

Chapter 26

Herbert's investigation continued. He sat in his office, working through the list of names, thinking about whom to see next. He had crossed several names off the list already.

Herbert decided it was time to speak to Opportunity Planner 22. Her name was Joyce. Herbert did not know, and could not understand, why he had been told to get Frederick to avoid going for full disciplinary action against this Joyce. Herbert had picked up on a rumour that she might be working for another organisation.

Joyce was given one day's notice of the interview. She contacted Herbert and told him that she did not want to attend. Herbert spoke to her bluntly, told her it was in her contract of employment to cooperate with any investigation fully. Joyce had no option but to agree to attend at the specified time, but she had no idea what it was all about.

Joyce went to see Marcus the evening before the interview. Marcus, on the face of it, seemed a principled person; he talked of wanting to see change for the better. He told Joyce that he had socialistic and humanistic leanings. He thought the Dependency Unit was contradictory and involved in people pushing. There was no choice or care for anyone. It reminded him of what he had read about Eastern Europe before the wall came down; there had been a culture of production for production's sake.

The relationship between Joyce and Marcus had become strained since Joyce had her disciplinary. Although Marcus was very pleased about Joyce not getting disciplined, he could not work out why she hadn't been. He was suspicious of the outcome and questioned Joyce about whether she had agreed to something under pressure.

Although the couple was still happy, Marcus was still frustrated about the issues raised by the disciplinary meeting Joyce had. Most of the time he could forget about it, but when something reminded him, he could not help but question what had happened.

Joyce told Marcus about not wanting to be investigated again.

Marcus asked her why. 'You need to go in,' he said. 'Is it about the A1201a case?'

Joyce didn't know. It might have been that this time they were going to discipline her. Marcus thought that she was only saying this to make him feel less insecure, but once again he felt guilty. He knew he needed to let the issue go or it would damage their relationship.

Marcus put his arms around Joyce, kissed on the cheek, and looked at her. 'Let's wait and see what happens.'

They kissed and then held each other's hands as they went in to Marcus's bedroom. That night they made love, forgetting the world around them.

The next morning, after Joyce had left for work, Marcus wondered if Joyce was a company plant, but he immediately felt disloyal and that he was being unfair to Joyce. He had been reading too many spy thrillers.

Marcus, however, wasn't alone in questioning Joyce's motivation. Herbert went further and had wondered if Joyce was working as a spy for Quality Control. That far from working for another company, he wondered whether or not she was checking the efficiency of the workforce for the Human Logistics, a special section that had been created when Human Resources had been restructured. Although the main part of HR had become what was called Human Care, some small specialist units had also been formed. Quality Control was well known for its practice of using people as spies among all levels of the workforce; they had immense power in the organisation.

Herbert was concerned about how best to interview her as she might be watching him and reporting back. Although his role and authorisation came from the very top of the organisation, Quality Control had a reputation for being untouchable.

Recently there had been extra competition from other multi-nationals. The Dibble Group responded by cutting costs and enforcing strict discipline among the workforce. This led to discontent; staff in other areas of the Dibble Empire had started organising against Dibble. This had made the Dibble Empire, and anyone linked to them, more paranoid and cautious. There was extra monitoring of staff, checks to make sure they did everything the "right way". However, it was difficult to ascertain what the "right way" was. Policies were contradictory and instructions were confusing; only those involved in the monitoring seem to know what the "right way" was. They determined that the "right way" was an interpretation of the evidence-based science. The problem was that the science was reliant on the fact that the questions it asked were designed in such a way as to get the answers that were required.

A culture of fear existed throughout the Dibble Empire and the Dependency Unit was no exception. Everyone was worried they would get something wrong or make some mistake. All the workers were putting complaints in about each other, criticising each other before anyone got them. It was a dog-eat-dog world. Fortunately, Quality Control made sure they were all well fed. The irony, as was well understood by Quality Control, indeed was set up by them, was that the workers who put the complaints in were also doing wrong, the system blamed everyone. There was no trust in such an alienated system with such alienated workers who had no control over what they did and had no understanding of what they are doing, but still tried nonetheless.

Herbert put his concerns to one side. He had already given some thought to the different ways he could handle the interview. He could check on her performance and use this to unnerve Joyce. He looked at the spreadsheet in front of him, from this he could see that she had not made any improvement on her targets. She hadn't even submitted a job plan to show how she intended to improve her performance.

He would ask Joyce how she intended to improve and what her timescale was for reaching excellence. If she was not working for Quality Control, he knew the questions would unnerve her. The focus on the individual and her own shortcomings, and not accounting for context, often takes away a person's confidence, it would put control in his hands. He needed the truth. If he could get her on the defensive straight away she might crumble. If he couldn't then it maybe was an indication that she is a plant from Quality Control. Maybe he could ask her some trick questions and catch her out. This may push her to let slip that she was with Quality Control. He then felt that he could just ask her whether she was with Quality Control; Lord Dibble had, after all, told him he had complete authority. It momentarily crossed Herbert's mind that Lord Dibble was setting him up to fail. Herbert quickly dismissed that idea. He picked up his pen and started to make some notes.

Joyce hardly ever saw Herbert and barely knew him. Whenever anything happened at the department someone would say, 'Frederick will take it to Herbert to make a decision,' but no one ever saw Herbert personally. Some of the staff had even joked about whether he really existed or whether he was some kind of existential being, a power to keep everyone in their place. Joyce was very worried.

On her way to his office, Joyce noticed that all the desks in the Dependency Unit were clear of all personal items. Joyce had seen a memo the day before about personal items being removed, but she was surprised at how quickly it had taken effect.

The memo had been a dictated from Central Office. There were to be no personal pictures on desks, computers, notice boards or walls. The memo said that the reason why desks and office furniture were not to be personalised was because it could take the staff's focus off the production targets. The memo reiterated the company motto: "Quality, Performance, and Excellence".

Joyce thought that the problem with going for excellence is that there has to be those who were not excellent, there couldn't be one without the other.

Joyce started to apply the same logic to other ideas. It applied to the argument about the deserving and the undeserving poor or to those who were good and those who were bad; one existed in relation to the other; one was used as a measure of the other.

She was aware there was a view held by some people that the dependency system was rotten. If you were not achieving excellence or moving towards excellence then you would be monitored. The irony was that by not achieving and being labelled a failure, it allowed someone else to succeed.

Can Openers

Therefore the champions of the system owed their status to those who were failing.

Joyce knew the department was obsessed with good quality based on the system's values of evidence-based science. However, you could only measure excellence if you had poor quality. If poor quality did not exist how could good quality be measured or determined?

The idea of taking personal items away focused the managers' minds purely on function, on targets and performance within a clinical environment.

Joyce reached Herbert's office. She knocked on the door and Herbert told her to come in. When she entered the room, Herbert asked if they had met before, she said they had. The only reason Herbert has asked the question was to try and convey to Joyce how unimportant she was.

Herbert asked Joyce to sit down. He asked her to confirm what number planner she was.

'22,' she replied.

Herbert asked, 'May I call you Joyce?'

'Yes,' she answered.

Herbert put his pen down. 'I've been asked to carry out an investigation but I cannot give you any details. I've been looking at your performance notes. I see you have been working for this department for a few years.'

Herbert told Joyce that the notes described Joyce as a steady worker and very capable.

'My concern,' he said, 'is that you have little ambition and your performance is not improving. Are you aware we are aiming for all our employees to achieve excellence?'

Joyce nodded in confirmation. What a load of rubbish, she thought; if everyone achieved excellence there would be no excellence.

'I've been looking at some of your work in detail. It has come to my notice that you have difficulty accepting the structure. You have not taken on board many of the values of the department, nor the overall mission statement. It would seem you question things and are not using the evidence-based science the department has built up over the years. If you're going to analyse the system, you must do it from a scientific base. We know what intervention and therapy works based on research. We feel that you sometimes deviate from the system. Please explain yourself.'

Joyce said, 'I thought I was keeping to policy. I will try to improve.'

'Maybe you need more training,' said Herbert. He asked how much training Mr Smyth had given her. Herbert was hoping to put her on the defensive; he was being cunning and thought she may open up about Frederick.

Joyce said that she would look at more training and thanked Herbert for pointing out her deficiencies.

Herbert could not understand her reactions. Joyce did not seem flustered about any of the questions. She appeared worried about the questions but she certainly did not fall to pieces as he'd hoped. He decided to carry on asking about Frederick.

'Joyce, do you think that Frederick gave you enough support?' he asked.

Joyce said very shrewdly that she had been working for the Department for a while so could not compare how Frederick was supporting her, as she had no experience with any other department. Herbert asked her if she thought that she may be a failing worker at present due to lack of support from Frederick.

'Maybe,' she said.

Herbert then spoke about the stress she had been under recently. 'I understand you were interviewed about the A12010a case and that there was no case to answer?' Joyce replied, 'Yes.' At this point she started to wish that she had taken someone in to the meeting with her. She was concerned that she would be disciplined, that they may have found out further information.

Joyce was confused, before the meeting he had assured her that the meeting was not about her. But now she was being asked about the previous case, she was worried that they were going to look at sacking her because of her performance.

Herbert asked what she thought about the incident involving the A1201a case, was she surprised with the outcome and by not being disciplined? Joyce tried to be as non-committal as possible. She said she had been pleased with the decision as the whole process made her feel unwell; she needed to support her child.

She thought that she had better say something more to help her case. 'Can I mention something about the case?'

Can Openers

Herbert suppressed a smile, pleased that she appeared ready to open up. She may be able to shed some light on things and may even give away that she had been involved in Frederick's demise.

Joyce told Herbert that when she heard that the IT department had found that she had made mistakes, she had felt very guilty. Being here today had helped to clarify her thoughts and she now realised she needed further training.

Herbert was getting frustrated. Her answers were repetitive. He wondered again if he was being watched and set up. She was too cool under pressure and it made him suspicious. She was giving nothing away.

He asked, without thinking about it, 'Do you think there may be industrial spies working in the Department or spies from other departments placed in your department to check on people's work?'

Joyce said that this practice was well known. She told Herbert that the staff were aware that the Quality Control department placed spies or used them to monitor their performance to make sure they were working at 100% capacity. She told him how she had heard that other large firms had industrial spies but did not know whether to believe it.

Herbert had not gained anything from Joyce. His method of questioning completely failed. He had tried to be too clever for his own good.

'Did you like Frederick? Was he a good manager?'

Joyce asked Herbert what he meant by 'good', she then said that Frederick's statistics were very high.

Herbert asked her if she had been surprised that she hadn't been sacked. He knew that he had told Frederick not to sack Joyce but did not know why the instruction had been given; he was also curious about Joyce's response.

'Maybe Frederick realised I needed further training,' Joyce said again.

Herbert said that he would have disciplined her.

This alarmed Joyce. She wished now she had brought someone to be at the meeting with her. Herbert could see Joyce was alarmed and may have spoken out of turn, so re iterated and said this was off the record – he wasn't interested in her situation.

Joyce asked him how she could know this for certain as all the questions seems to be directed at her. Herbert realised he would have to give a little bit of information away.

'I'll be upfront with you,' Herbert said, 'I want to know whether Frederick was a bully and whether you resented or held a grudge against him. All this will be off the record.' Herbert paused. 'Do you know why Frederick is not working for the department anymore?'

'No,' Joyce replied.

Herbert asked again why she thought Frederick did not discipline her. Joyce began to think that Herbert was obsessive with the way he kept repeating the same questions.

For his part Herbert felt Joyce was holding back, that he could not trip her up and get to the truth. Herbert said that he thought her IT skills were excellent and that they were good enough to manipulate the system. Herbert didn't notice Joyce flinch. She responded saying that she thought the system could not be challenged, that it was foolproof.

Herbert was disappointed with the interview. He had not advanced his investigation at all. He abruptly terminated the interview and asked Joyce to leave.

While he was speaking to Joyce, Herbert had received several messages on his transformer from Sir George who wanted to see him immediately.

Sir George's office was on the next floor up. Herbert went up and knocked on the door. As he entered the office, Sir George stood up.

'We've had little information from you regarding the investigation, and why it's taking you so long,' said Sir George abruptly. 'Lord Dibble is not happy.'

Lord Dibble was not happy as he had been forced to cancel the plan on A2101a. Unfortunately A2101a had realised that she had still been receiving benefits from the department even though she was working fulltime. It was too late to put the plan into action; it had relied on strict time limits. Although Herbert was to carry on with the investigation, Lord Dibble now had to move to plan B and C.

The Minister was particularly unhappy with the situation. He felt that what was needed was for Frederick to be given his post back quickly so they could use him to move things forward, but even they could not beat the system.

Can Openers

Although Herbert had uncovered interesting information about Frederick, he had not found out any more details about why Frederick had been dismissed or why his family had been put on a number 3 risk rating. Had Frederick been set up? Had he significantly harmed his children? Sir George still wanted to know what had happened.

Herbert left Sir George's office with instructions to carry on his investigation.

Chapter 27

Jane realised that she had been paid money from the Dependency Department even though she was working fulltime. Jane was irritated about this, she was sure she had told the Department about her change in circumstances. Jane tried to contact the Department again to tell them that she was now working fulltime, but she could not get a response. She tried phoning, writing, and emailing but no one seemed to want to take any responsibility for altering her records. In exasperation, Jane sent a special electronic flyer by registered courier so she could prove she had told the Department.

Sir George knew how often Jane had been trying to get hold of the Department. Many others would have given in or taken the money. He was annoyed – she had evidence to show that she had informed the Department of her changed circumstances. The plan needed to be cancelled.

After Sir George had spoken to Herbert, Jane received a response from the Department, which informed her she had been overpaid and had to pay the monies back to the Department immediately. Sir George still hoped that Jane would take her time in repaying the money; this would then give them an opportunity to accuse her of knowingly keeping money that she wasn't entitled to and thus had defrauded the Department. He was disappointed, therefore, when Jane paid back the money straight away. This posed something of a difficulty for Lord Dibble and Sir George, who both believed that everyone, given the chance, would deceive the system. They both thought that Jane would not be able to resist and that she would keep the money. So ingrained were these views that even now, in trusted company, Lord Dibble still used the old fashioned term Chavs in describing people like Jane.

Chapter 28

Two more weeks passed and Frederick knew he needed to appeal against the removal of his children before the time limit ran out. He had no idea why they have been taken. Everyone assumed that he knew the reason, but he didn't. He still thought that Lidia had abused the children. He knew he was innocent.

Frederick gradually started to pack his things in preparation to leave the house. Although he was drinking, he just had enough sense about him to eat a little.

Frederick used to collect antiques years ago, most of them useless. However, he had found two vases, which he had forgotten about, that had been gathering dust in the attic. Frederick had them valued in the past and knew they were worth some money. Luckily for him, Lidia had never supported any of Frederick's hobbies. She thought his antiques, and the vases in particular, were junk, so he was left with them. If he sold them and the jewellery, he could survive for a short while. Frederick recognised that there was an irony in his situation: when he had worked for the Department, any dependency clients found in possession of any undeclared items of value would be prosecuted and have any support removed.

Due to his new, difficult situation, and his complete and utter despair, Frederick had begun to question his values again. One evening he sat in the front room just staring in to space. Eventually he had got up and looked in the mirror over the fireplace. He looked at a face he barely recognised, the face of a bitter and traumatised man. His life had been centred on his family and on the Department, but in many ways the Department had come first.

Can Openers

Frederick had no real friends left except for the next-door neighbour who was now in his seventies. Frederick wondered if the neighbour had any idea what had happened; he must have noticed that Lidia hadn't been around for several weeks and that his children were no longer with him.

Frederick went into the loft and, whilst sorting out what proved to be mainly junk, he had found the two vases. He took them downstairs and then went back up to the loft to continue clearing things out. He came across some old photographs, pictures of his family. When he came across pictures of his father, Frederick felt angry. It was due to him that Frederick had had no childhood. As a child, he had lived in fear. He became insular. At school he was seen as the odd one. None of the teachers noticed him; he was just there. He was always on his own, had been bullied by the other children. He did not seem to have any redeeming attributes. Perhaps all this had had an effect on him later in life.

Just as he was putting the pictures away, he heard a bang at the door. Frederick rushed downstairs. The front door shook with the second, louder bang. Frederick rushed to the door and, as he opened it, a big boot appeared through the opening so the door could not be shut. At the door was a police sergeant with at least four other officers. 'Are you Mr Smyth?' asked the sergeant.

'Yes,' said Frederick.

'We need to speak to you, can we come in?'

Frederick thought it sounded more like an instruction than a request; he let them in.

Frederick was bemused by the situation. His first thought was maybe they knew about the vases and the jewellery. He felt panic rising.

'We have a warrant to search your house,' said the sergeant.

Frederick could not believe what is happening to him.

The officer explained that they would tell him what was going on in due course but at that moment, they needed to search the house. The four police officers went around the house, the sergeant stayed with Frederick.

Frederick thought that he had been rumbled and considered whether he should just tell them where the jewellery was. He wondered if they knew the value of the vases. He couldn't understand why so many police officers were there. Usually in situations where the Dependency Department had thought fraud had happened, two police officers would go out with a representative from the Dependency Fraud Investigation Team. However, he also knew how seriously the State took allegations of fraud. He knew they were going out in force to make an example of people and to show those who committed the offence just how serious it was.

Nonetheless, Frederick was surprised at how friendly the police sergeant was, despite the foot in the door. Usually, in these situations, they were very abrupt and acted tough; they liked to show the so-called skivers how serious fraud was. Maybe, thought Frederick, they were being a bit nicer with him, a bit more polite, because he used to be a senior member of the Department. He was surprised that they had not started their lecture on how morally wrong it was not to declare everything to the Department, how he had let his country and community down. 'The only people who suffer,' they usually said, 'are the children. There is less money to maintain them when they go to a Florence family.'

Frederick decided to stay quiet, but would confess to everything if they accused him of not declaring valuables. He knew that whatever he said would be used against him.

He had put the two vases on the mantelpiece earlier. The police hadn't noticed them – maybe they thought they were just old junk. The police looked at the vases but had not looked at the stamp on the base, had not properly looked at them. Perhaps they only knew about the jewellery. The police seemed to be pre-occupied with his kitchen. At least he had not hidden anything there.

One of the officers went up to the sergeant. 'There doesn't seem to be much cutlery.'

Frederick explained that he had packed some of it. By now, all the police officers were in the kitchen taking it apart. The Sergeant asked Frederick for the entire cutlery, specifically the knives. Frederick could not understand why the police was so interested in the kitchen.

He tried to recall if anyone knew he had the vases or the jewellery and if anyone had told on him. But, as far as he could remember, he had not.

Can Openers

The police put white suits on, literally taking everything apart. If they were trying to frighten him, they succeeded. They even ripped out all the units. The sergeant asked Frederick to go upstairs with him. As they got to the top of the stairs, the officer asked where his wife's clothes are kept. Now, thought Frederick, perhaps they were going to mention the jewellery and had been making him pay for his dishonesty.

Frederick tried to keep calm. He noticed that he was being braver and cooler than he had probably ever acted. He had nothing to lose, had reached rock bottom. Nothing else could happen to him that would be worse than what had already happened. If they find his jewellery, so be it, the money would only last 6 months anyway.

The sergeant asked if his wife had any other personal possessions. Frederick showed the police where Lidia may have kept her personal items but he said she had left him and taken a lot of her things with her.

Most of the officers were now upstairs. They were in the bathroom taking swabs with small buds of cotton and taking hair out of the plug with tweezers. Frederick thought that they were probably just making an example of him because he had been high up at the Dependency Unit and had at times clashed with the police over the handling of cases. This could be their revenge.

When they found the jewellery, Frederick actually felt relieved. Instead of accusing him of not disclosing valuables, they simply asked if the jewellery belonged to his wife, they then bagged it up and said nothing. The police carried on searching the house.

The police sergeant asked Frederick if he was leaving. Frederick said that he would have to move soon.

'Dirty business all this,' said one of the police officers.

'You must be traumatised,' the sergeant said.

Frederick replied, 'Yes, and you seem to doing a very thorough job with your search. Don't you think it slightly over the top?'

The sergeant raised his voice, 'I think we've been very sensitive considering the situation.'

Frederick then agreed as meekly as he could, hoping not to upset the police. At least, thought Frederick, they left the vases. They were worth more than the jewellery.

'Anyway,' the police sergeant said, 'you have to come to the police station. We would like to ask you some questions. It is best for you to come voluntarily as we don't want to arrest you. We would also advise you to contact your solicitor.'

This is odd, thought Frederick. This seemed a disproportionate response, just because he had withheld information from the Department. Frederick's department hadn't really been involved in the processing and business end of fraud cases, so he didn't understand how people were treated and wondered if this happened in all cases. The sad reality was that he would have agreed with the police action only several weeks ago, before his life was turned upside down.

Frederick had a solicitor but hardly ever used him. The police officer suggested the solicitor meet him at the police station. Frederick, however, could only get hold of the duty solicitor.

He could not and did not understand the seriousness of the situation. The police sergeant asked Frederick for a set of keys for the house so they could continue their search. Frederick went to look for the keys in one of the boxes he had packed.

The police sergeant said, 'Sir, we will make sure the house gets locked up securely when we have finished.'

Frederick became agitated. He started to think that the police should have better things to do with their time.

The sergeant said, 'If you come now to the police car, sir, with two of our officers, we will take you to the station.'

Frederick felt the police were being too nice, that it was totally false.

He recalled the firm but fair approach that was his hallmark at work, perhaps that was what the police were doing; but Frederick was not happy.

As Frederick left the house the rain started to pour down. It was dark, cold, and miserable outside; if there was ever a scene more appropriate for his mood it was the weather that night, dark and utterly unpleasant.

Frederick got in to the police car. A female officer sat one side of him, a male officer sat on the other side. Frederick felt that his body was in the car but his soul was somewhere else, it did not seem like reality.

Can Openers

This was beginning to feel like the second worst day of his life, after the day his children were removed.

What else could happen to me? He thought. I didn't think it could get any worse. At least I've gone voluntarily, even if the police were being sycophantic.

He arrived at the police station. It had been built back in the early 2000s and was like a concrete fort. There were hardly any windows and the building, both inside and out, was very sparse and dehumanised. Frederick had been there before when working cases with the police. On the last occasion he had been there, Frederick had gone to the administrative office and had never noticed or seen the other side. This time was different.

Frederick was taken through the entrance and was led up some stairs. All the walls were concrete and devoid of any decoration. He went into an airlock, having to wait for one door to shut behind him before the officer opened the next door and then walked along a corridor. This journey felt like an eternity. They arrived at the duty desk. The duty sergeant asked Frederick his name. To the other side of the large custody office were two teenagers who were shouting at two police officers.

The cells were lined down three corridors that all started at the custody office. There was someone screaming from one of them. The custody sergeant pointed to the cell, looked at Frederick, and said in an apologetic tone, 'Too much drink I'm afraid. Your solicitor hasn't arrived yet so you can sit in one of the waiting rooms for now.'

Just as Frederick was led off to the room, the solicitor arrived. He seemed young and scatty. The police sergeant wanted to have a word with the solicitor before the interview and Frederick agreed.

Frederick still assumed that he was being interviewed about non-disclosure of valuables to the Dependency Unit. He decided that he would plead guilty to having the jewellery. At least he still had the vases, unless they found them as well. Two police officers, a male and a female, introduced themselves to the solicitor and said they would be interviewing Frederick. The Sergeant then explained to the solicitor that the officers who would be interviewing Mr Smyth were from CID.

The solicitor went into the waiting room and spoke to Frederick, asking him if he was aware what the interview was about.

'Yes, yes,' replied Frederick impatiently; he just wanted it over and done with. 'Just get on with it.'

The solicitor told Frederick that he would stop the interview if he felt it was becoming difficult. He then spoke to the police who led them to an interview room where the two police officers sat waiting.

Chapter 29

Not much had changed over the last 20 years regarding police interviews except the role of psychology. When Frederick went into the interview room, he noticed a mirror on the wall and knew it was a two-way mirror. Sitting behind the mirror were psychologists. They could see Frederick and everyone else in the interview room, but Frederick couldn't see them. The police officer asking the questions was wearing a headphone that received instructions from the psychologists who, at times, would get the officer to ask certain questions or act in a certain way.

Frederick sat down in the small room. The police officers introduced themselves as Detective Sergeant Cone and Detective Constable Lansbury. Also in the room was the duty solicitor Mr Take, from Take and Take Solicitors.

The officers began by saying that Mr Smyth had voluntarily come to be interviewed to help with their enquiries regarding a very serious matter. Frederick still thought they were going over the top, but then, he reasoned, he had been high up at the Dependency Unit.

The officers stated, for the benefit of the recording device, who was in the room and gave the time and date of the interview. They asked Mr Smyth to confirm his address and who lived with him. Frederick confirmed his address and said he lived on his own.

DS Cone asked Frederick how long he had lived on his own.

'About two months,' Frederick said.

'Why do you live on your own?' DC Lansbury asked.

Frederick started to feel agitated. He thought to himself, *why all the questions*? It seemed so unfair, why didn't they just come out and ask him about why he hadn't declared items to the Dependency Unit? Why were they were playing games with him? However Frederick had enough knowledge about the police and their procedures to know he had to be co-operative. 'My wife, Lidia, decided to leave me.'

'Why?' asked DS Cone.

'You're aware that our children have been taken. Our whole world was centred on our children. My wife couldn't cope anymore and she left.'

'Mr Smyth, when did you last see your wife?' DS Cone asked.

Frederick shrugged and said, 'When we split up.'

'Are you sure about that Mr Smyth?' The police officer asked. 'Didn't you ever go to her new flat?' Frederick was taken aback; he didn't even know she had a flat.

The officers carried on with their questions. They started to focus on the reasons for the split and when it had happened. They asked Frederick if he and his wife had ever argued and repeated the question in several different ways. Frederick answered each question truthfully and explained that the break just happened, that there wasn't any argument. Frederick didn't acknowledge how angry he had been since the breakup.

'It's getting late and is it is unfair to carry on the interview at this hour,' Mr Take said.

The police stopped the tape.

'We will reconvene tomorrow morning,' DS Cone said. He pressed a button on the recording machine and removed some CDs from it. He then placed them on the table in front of Frederick and all the parties signed them for an accurate record. Frederick was angry, agitated, and confused. He couldn't understand what was going on.

His solicitor asked to see him before he left. Frederick went into the waiting room with Mr Take.

Before they sat down, Frederick said, 'I'll own up, I'm sick of all the stupid questions.'

The solicitor sat there open mouthed. Frederick blurted out that he hadn't told the Dependency Department everything. The solicitor puckered his lips and blew out a heavy breath, he looked relieved.

Can Openers

'I think there's been some misunderstanding,' Mr Take said. 'This matter is most serious, Mr Smyth. Your wife, or ex-wife, however you want to describe her, was found dead twenty-four hours ago.'

Chapter 30

Frederick felt as though time had suddenly stopped. He was certain the sound of his heart pounding echoed across the waiting room. Frederick turned ashen, felt his blood go cold.

'No, no!' he shrieked.

The solicitor said nothing.

'My god,' said Frederick, his hands on his cheeks. 'What were the circumstances? How did it happen? Was it an accident?'

'Mr Smyth, if you do not go voluntarily to the police station tomorrow, the police will have to arrest you,' Mr Take said.

'What for? Why would they arrest me?'

'Think about it,' said the solicitor. 'You must cooperate with the police enquiries and be here on time tomorrow.' Mr Take paused. 'Is it true that you haven't seen your wife since you split up?'

'Absolutely,' said Frederick. Then the situation finally hit home. 'Hold on. Surely, they don't think I did something?'

Mr Take said again that he needed to be at the station on time the next day. 'I think we need to leave now, I'll see you tomorrow.'

When Frederick arrived home he could hardly move. He was in complete shock, his muscles had seized up. He went over in his head how his wife might have died, but it was a complete mystery to him. He sat in the dark. He knew she had self-harmed in the past, was it possible she had taken her own life? Why were the police making him out to be a criminal? Did they think he had driven her to kill herself? He felt isolated.

Frederick desperately wanted to speak to someone. He could go speak to his neighbour or he could try to contact his brother, but they hadn't spoken in years, so he didn't know if his brother would even speak to him. He went to the sideboard in the lounge. Fortunately, the police, who were due to return to the house the next day, hadn't removed the alcohol from the house. They had, however, secured almost all the doors to rooms in the house, leaving him with access only to the toilet, living room and study. Frederick poured himself a large whisky.

He took his drink into the study and switched on his electronic link to try and contact his brother by Facsope, the updated text video link. There was no reply.

Frederick left a Facmessage to say that his situation was grim. 'I'm desperate for help, please get in touch.' Frederick clicked off the link.

He sat nursing his whisky, thinking. I've lost my wife, my children, my job, my house, and now my dignity. How can I move on after this? he wondered. Frederick felt like he was being knocked in to the ground with a large hammer. He sat in his chair thinking and drinking; unfortunately, the whisky was running low.

Frederick didn't sleep much that night, partly because he was worried about waking up, but mostly because the thoughts swirling around in his head would not give him any peace. Sleeping on the chair did not help. He kept going over and over in his head what had gone wrong, wallowing in his plight. He could not process the news that Lidia was dead; it seemed unreal, like a film.

Yes, they had had their ups and downs, but he had loved Lidia, although love often meant different things to people. He had only ever wanted to please her and make her proud of him. Maybe he could have done things differently. Maybe Lidia had done something to the children. Maybe she couldn't face the guilt and had killed herself.

He slowly convinced himself that she must have taken her own life. But then why were the police interviewing him?

It was early in the morning when Frederick got out of his the chair. He tried to scrub up but he still looked as though he had been on the streets all night. He even tried to iron his suit that he found packed away in a bag in the living room.

Frederick arrived at the station an hour later. A police officer came out and took him inside. They went through the air lock and they arrived in the inner core. There were no windows, just plain concrete floors and walls. There was a step up to the counter where the custody sergeant stood.

Frederick took a seat and waited for Mr Take, who arrived five minutes after. Mr Take asked if he could have a word with his client. They went to a side room.

'So many things had gone against me, it's like someone is out to get me,' Frederick said.

'You need to concentrate on the interview,' Mr Take said. 'Wait here a moment, the Sergeant wants to speak with you. And I'll try to find out more information from the police.'

Frederick was left on his own in the bare room. He sat on a chair that was screwed into the floor. It epitomised what his life had become. As he sat there, Frederick felt he could not carry on any more. His life had been so ordered and structured; he had a set of values and had found excitement at work. Everything had changed; he started to question his life. Frederick was frightened. It seemed like an eternity before Mr Take returned.

As soon as he walked through the door Frederick jumped up. 'What have you found out?' he demanded of the solicitor.

'The police were looking at a murder inquiry,' Mr Take said.

'What?' Frederick gulped.

'A murder inquiry.'

'What else did they say?' asked Frederick.

Mr Take told Frederick that the police would not explain anymore. 'But I'm afraid I have some bad news.'

Frederick almost laughed. 'What more could they do to me?'

Mr Take raised his hands in a 'calm down' gesture. 'The police may not let you go after the interview, but I don't think they have enough evidence to hold you. The problem is that you are top of their suspect list.'

'This is ridiculous,' said Frederick. 'They could keep me in custody? I don't believe it. They don't have anything on me.'

Frederick and Mr Take went into the same interview room they had been in the previous night. The officers went through the same procedure as they previously had and, although he couldn't see them, Frederick just knew that there were two psychologists behind the mirror again watching the interview.

'We have been told by Mr Take that you were not aware of your wife's death,' DC Lansbury said. DC Lansbury made some more sympathetic comments before becoming more businesslike and authoritative, probably taking instructions from the psychologists.

'Mr Smyth, did you become resentful and blame your wife for your children being removed?'

'No,' Frederick answered.

'We don't believe you,' DC Lansbury said. 'You need to tell us the truth.'

'Why were your children removed?' DS Cone asked.

Frederick said, 'I don't know.'

'Come on, Mr Smyth, you know the score. We understand from your department that everyone knows the reason why you are a number 3 risk rating. You're as aware of this as anyone. So, Mr Smyth, stop messing us about. Tell us why your children were removed.'

Frederick's tears rolled down his face. He hadn't even been aware that he was crying. 'I don't know why any of it happened,' he said quietly.

'So are you saying your wife had committed some form of abuse to the children?'

'No,' said Frederick.

'Can you say with one hundred percent certainty that your wife had nothing to do with harming your children?' asked DS Cone.

'Look, it is a possibility; I didn't have anything to do with harming them, so I suppose—' 'Suppose what, Mr Smyth?' the officer interrupted, 'Come on, you blamed your wife and you—'

Frederick interrupted. 'That doesn't mean I did anything!' he shouted.

DS Cone said, 'Did I say you did anything? You said that.'

Mr Take spoke at last. He told the officers he felt they were asking leading questions. 'You know Mr Smyth did not say that.'

'OK, OK,' DS Cone said. 'Let's look at it this way, you believe that your wife may have done something to your children, you must have got even a little angry?'

Frederick said he had felt more numb and shocked than angry.

DC Lansbury asked if he and his wife had a big argument, did she walk out?

Frederick explained that they had finished their relationship calmly.

DC Lansbury said, 'We have to consider the possibility that you, Mr Smyth, became angry and that you committed a horrendous crime.'

Frederick shook his head. 'No, no,' he said.

DC Lansbury continued. 'Because who else would commit murder? You were a senior executive at the Dependency Unit. You must realise how unique it is for a number 3 risk rating to come up, how very rare it is.'

'Yes, of course I do,' said Frederick.

'You know then that if a children's number three comes up, either you or your wife have harmed the children,' said DC Lansbury, 'and by definition, significant harm. If it wasn't you then it was your wife.' DC Lansbury paused. 'Mr Smyth you don't seem to have many friends. We also understand that you were abused as a child. Is this true?'

Mr Take interrupted and asked about the relevance of the questioning.

'Does it not say in your department risk assessment that if you have been abused as a child, you are a risk or higher risk to your own children,' DC Lansbury said.

DS Cone took over. 'So, Mr Smyth, I put it to you that you became an abuser. You moved from being the victim to the victimiser.'

'No, no, no!' Frederick shouted. 'That's not true.'

'So your wife abused the children. She must have done,' said DS Cone matter of factually.

DC Lansbury said, 'And that is why you got very angry with your wife isn't it? Come on Frederick, you got angry.'

DS Cone said, 'Mr Smyth, you're left with nothing, your house has been taken, you have no job, and you've become a dependency figure, one of the very people that you loathe. Come on, tell us the truth. When was the last time you saw your wife?'

'I told you,' pleaded Frederick, 'I told you it was about two months ago, when she left me.'

'Where did she go?' asked DS Cone.

'I don't know, I just don't know,' Frederick replied pitifully.

DC Lansbury asked, 'So you're telling us that a person who, according to you, has abused your children just left and you just let her go? Just like that? You didn't even ask where she was going?'

'I'm telling you the truth,' said Frederick.

'So where did she get the money to go to Spain, Mr Smyth?' asked DS Cone.

'Spain? What are you talking about?' asked Frederick dumfounded.

Did you know she had gone to Spain?'

'What? No.'

'Why do you think she went to Spain?' asked DS Cone.

'I don't know, I've no idea,' said Frederick.

'Why would someone go to Spain in these circumstances?' asked DS Cone. 'I wouldn't have thought it was for a nice little holiday, do you?'

Frederick wished the ground would swallow him up.

DC Lansbury coughed and said, 'I'll tell you, Mr Smyth, why she went to Spain. It was to get away from you. She was scared.'

'Bullshit!' exclaimed Frederick.

The officer went on. 'You were married for years and you have two children but you're trying to convince us you that do not know anything about your wife's last movements! Mr Smyth, you do not seem to know very much at all. Your children are now settled with a Florence family so, for their sake, have some honour, tell us what happened.'

Mr Take interrupted, he told the officers they were putting too much pressure on his client and were trying to force a confession.

DC Lansbury leaned back in his chair. 'I do appreciate the situation, but we are talking about a murder inquiry. Your client has not been forthcoming with his answers. Mr Smyth, we may have to interview your children.'

Frederick looked down as he twisted his hands together in his lap.

DS Cone said, 'Maybe both of you abused the children and you then blamed your wife.'

Frederick didn't look up. 'Nothing happened, I'm getting confused.'

The two officers laughed. 'Of course something happened, you ended up as a number 3 risk rating, so tell us what it was,' demanded DS Cone.

DC Lansbury said, 'How about we tell you what happened and, Mr Smyth, you tell us whether we're right.' He paused. 'You got home from work, your children had gone. You know what has happened, or your wife does. Fact. Maybe you harmed the children. But we put it to you that you have not harmed the children, so it has to be your wife.' DC Lansbury paused to see if there was any reaction from Frederick. 'You got angry, you threatened her, she left. But, before she left the house, you told her about the jewellery. She took it, cashed it in and left the country. She left because she was so scared.' He paused again, but still no reaction. 'You helped her move out so, when she came back from Spain, you knew where she lived, so you went to the flat.'

He paused again. This time Frederick bowed his head and held it in his hands. 'No, no!'

DC Lansbury continued, 'You've been on your own for two months, you've been dwelling on what's happened, getting more angry. You blame your wife for you ending up a dependency figure and losing your children.'

'No, no!'

'She comes out of her flat, she goes for a walk. You follow her down a quiet street, you sneak up on her, grab her from behind and stab her.'

Frederick was shaking and crying, and started repeating over and over, 'It's not true.'

'Maybe you didn't mean to kill her,' said DC Lansbury, 'maybe you just wanted to hurt her. Maybe you both got involved in an argument and then you stabbed her, maybe you had been drinking. Do you agree, Mr Smyth, that this is how it happened?'

'No,' said Frederick quietly now. 'I didn't know she was dead. I loved her.'

DS Cone was getting particularly agitated. 'This will not help your case. We have the evidence. Lidia was stabbed with a short sharp knife, which came from a box of cutlery at your home. The knife was the only item missing,' he said. 'Also our forensic team has categorically proved that she couldn't have stabbed herself, it had to have been carried out by someone else.'

'How do they know this?' asked Mr Take. DS Cone didn't answer. Frederick was beside himself, he began to think that he was being framed, that his whole life had collapsed and they were now going to charge him with murder.

The officers ended the interview. Nothing felt real. Frederick felt as though he were in a waking nightmare.

The officers asked to speak to Mr Take. Frederick left the interview room and waited in the waiting room. Frederick felt a sharp pain in his head, like a bolt had been pushed through the back of his head, into the temple lobes and out through his forehead. The pain was excruciating. He could hardly stand and started to lose his balance. He sat quietly with his head in his arms on the table.

Mr Take came in. He sat down and looked at Frederick whose eyes were showing an animalistic fear, an animal just about to be taken by its predator.

'The police are going to keep you here on remand and charge you with murder,' he told Frederick. 'However, they are still investigating and forensics are completing more tests.'

Frederick nodded. He was led out of the room and taken to the main desk in the charge room where the police searched him.

Everything was taken off of Frederick, even the laces were removed from his shoes. He was then taken by another police officer to a cell. The officer asked Frederick if he wanted some food. Frederick refused, he felt sick. He went over to the bench and sat. His cell door was slammed shut.

He heard one of the other cell doors open and heard a female voice shouting, 'You fucking bastard scum, you tried to touch me up, you perverts.' The woman sounded as though she was much younger than Frederick.

He listened to the shouting coming from other cells, it sounded to him like desperate people who were now caged animals. He sat and wondered what they may or may not have done to end up at this place, this human zoo.

He then started to reflect back on his life. It felt like someone had framed him, but why? He thought about his past and about some of the things he had done. He realised that some people could well have a grudge against him. This experience made him understand that things were not always what they seemed. He sat there thinking, his mood shifting back and forth between despair and self-pity.

Chapter 31

Herbert studied his plan and decided whom to interview next. It was time to speak to Phil the IT expert but, as he worked for a separate company, he would need permission from Lord Dibble first. Whilst he was making those arrangements, the police contacted Herbert. They wanted information about Frederick, explaining that that Lidia, his wife, had died. Herbert was usually relatively relaxed, but this news was unbelievable. He could hardly speak, he just sat there staring at the wall. He could not believe that someone he had known, who was always so full of life, was dead.

He felt as if she was a member of his own family, and it seemed as if he had known her forever, even though he had only met her three times. She had been so vibrant and made such an impact on him.

Herbert had an impeccable attendance record at work; he was never off sick. That day, however, he felt too grief-stricken not to go home.

He arrived home just as Sophie was leaving the house. He walked past Sophie, went into the house, and upstairs. Herbert was shaking and was physically sick in the bathroom.

Sophie went upstairs after him. 'Herbert? Herbert, are you all right?' she asked.

Herbert came out of the bathroom. 'Lidia, Frederick's wife, is dead,' he said. 'The police told me that the circumstances of her death are suspicious.'

'What does that mean?' Sophie asked.

Herbert told her that was all the information he had. Sophie looked at him, turned around and went downstairs without saying anything. She wanted to know more but she had always been very practical. She bit back her tears and wondered who would make the arrangements for the funeral. She wondered, too, whether she should tell Herbert how friendly she had been with Lidia and what she'd done for her. Above all else, she needed to know more about what happened.

Chapter 32

A week after Lidia's body had been found and the day after Frederick had been remanded in custody, the daily edition of the local paper dropped through Herbert and Sophie's letterbox. There was a short article about Lidia on the bottom of the front page. The headline read: *"WOMAN STABBED TO DEATH! A female body was found in a pool of blood following a brutal stabbing"*.

The rest of the article gave no more than a few scant details; it stated briefly the name of the dead woman, the area where the body was found, and that a man was helping police with their enquiries.

Sophie read the article. She didn't know what to do. She had had regular contact with Lidia and was fully aware that she may have been one of the last people to see her alive.

The article was asking for anyone who had any information to contact the police. Sophie now started to be led by her conscience. She would have to go and see the police, but what would she tell Herbert? She has broken his trust. She then started to think of poor Lidia.

Both Herbert and Sophie were shocked by Lidia's death. Herbert appeared to be completely overwhelmed and unable to concentrate. It seemed a little odd to Sophie considering he had only met Lidia a few times.

Sophie hardly spoke all day, although she felt she would have to sort out the funeral and discussed this with Herbert. Herbert hadn't known that Lidia and Sophie had been close friends, but he had his suspicions they were close, heightened further as Sophie was seemingly so keen to organise the funeral.

Can Openers

Sophie thought about who the next of kin would be and, even though they had split up, realised it was Frederick. She wondered if anyone had seen Frederick. Other things were starting to play on Sophie's mind; she was aware of other information and wondered whether this had any bearing on what had happened to Lidia. Should I tell the police? She wondered. Sophie wanted to go see Lidia's body at the morgue.

That evening Herbert and Sophie sat in silence, each lost in thought. Herbert was trying to prepare himself mentally, composing himself so he could go to work tomorrow. He realized that his investigation might now take on more significance. As they sat in the lounge there seemed to be a tension between them that had never existed before or, if it had, neither of them had felt it. Herbert thought that Sophie was hiding something; Sophie felt that Herbert was acting strangely and out of character.

As the evening wore on, Herbert thought about work and whom he would be interviewing the next day. He had arranged to interview Phil from IT in the morning having received the go-ahead from Lord Dibble. Herbert tried to concentrate on what he would ask Phil. He needed to find out if it was possible that Phil had misinterpreted information going into the computer and if he was expert enough to fix the outcomes. Herbert knew this was a long shot, even he didn't really believe the computer could be tampered with, and that it was foolproof. For now, though, Phil was the least of his worries.

Chapter 33

Mr Take had been relentlessly trying to get bail for Frederick. He was in final discussions with the police. It was unusual to get bail in these circumstances, but the police accepted that Frederick could be bailed. The main condition they applied was that a computer chip be inserted in his arm. It was no bigger than a small splinter. The chip would track Frederick's whereabouts and keep check on his physical condition. For instance, if the chip indicated that Frederick was sexually aroused a signal would be transmitted to the tracking station. The police would be alerted and then they would immediately check him out. Frederick also had to be available for interviews.

Frederick had been in the cell overnight. Around lunchtime, Mr Take visited him. He told Frederick that he gained bail and that he could go home. Mr Take explained the bail conditions.

The police were not entirely happy with the situation; they had reservations about letting Frederick go because they were convinced that he had murdered Lidia. Unfortunately, they still didn't have all the evidence together.

On his way out, Frederick had to sign for his few possessions before he could go home.

He entered his house and went in to the front room. The house was a wreck from the police search; they had ransacked every room. Frederick looked at the mantelpiece, the vases were still there, thankfully intact. They were worth a few thousand pounds and were the only antiques he'd bought that he might make some money on. He knew a dealer who offered him £15,000 for the pair a few years ago. Frederick decided to sell the vases with the hope that he would get enough cash to ensure that when he had to move out of the house, he could get a flat instead of having to live on the street.

Seeing the vases intact had lifted Frederick's spirits for a while, but he soon went back to utter despair, as though he lost all hope. Even if he got a decent sum for the vases, the money wouldn't last very long. What was the point, he wondered, of carrying on anyway? He lost his wife, his children, his status, and his dignity. Frederick was desperate for a shot of whisky but there wasn't a drop of alcohol left in the house.

He was exhausted. He went upstairs to his bedroom and lay on the bed. He drifted off to sleep and didn't wake up until almost midday. Frederick got up. He didn't bother washing; he had definitely lost that habit. He slipped on his clothes and went out to the mini-market on the corner of the street. With the last of the cash he had, he bought several bottles of whisky. He went back home and started drinking.

Frederick sprawled out on his armchair, a whisky bottle in one hand and a mug in the other. He looked around him; he had nothing left except the vases. 'What a dreadful life I've got,' he thought.

'I've got nothing to live for,' he said out loud to the empty room. He poured some more whisky in to the mug. He looked at the furniture that no longer belonged to him, it was now owned by the Dependency Department, which would sell what they could. They would give a percentage of the cash to the Florence family and the rest would go to Dibble Care.

Frederick stood up unsteadily. He took the vases off the mantelpiece and put them away in the sideboard before he drank more. As the day progressed, so did his drinking, and his mood became darker.

The Dependency Department was coming to value everything the following day. He had also received a letter, which he hadn't read, but knew it was a notice to quit. He neglected himself for weeks. He had several days' beard growth again, his clothes smelled as he had given up doing any laundry, and he looked years older. He was now the person whom he ignored at the train station on the way to work.

Somehow Frederick found the motivation to get out of his chair though he could just about walk. He found his coat draped over the chair, put it on, and walked out the front door onto the street.

He started walking with no thought to where he was going, and he just kept walking. Eventually he found himself by the local canal. He was surprised that he made it that far in his state. Frederick sat on the wall that separated the towpath from a patch of wasteland. There was no one else around. On the opposite side was a large brick wall that was all that was left of an old paper mill, a relic of the old industrial history of the area. Frederick held his head in his hands and cried. He had no one to talk to; he was alone in the world. He never felt so lonely. Frederick looked up searchingly at the sky. The evening light was turning to darkness and the sky was becoming overcast, dark clouds were moving in.

As he sat there, he became aware of a person walking along the bank, he could just make out that it was a woman, but she wasn't yet close enough for him to see her face.

The evening walker noticed a shadow in front of her; someone had moved off the wall and towards the canal edge. She knew that the bank at this part of the canal was steep, if someone fell in, he wouldn't be able to get out. As she got nearer she could see the man more clearly, he looked down and out. She was certain he was about to jump into the canal. She watched him briefly, aware of the potential dangers a lone woman faced in such an isolated area. She decided to take a chance and went over to the man. Even though she stood a few feet from him, she could smell the alcohol on him.

Frederick hadn't looked at her directly but he was aware she was there. 'Just leave me alone,' he said. 'I don't want to be in this life anymore, it's shit.'

'What's happened?' she asked. 'Come and sit on the wall. Come on, come away.'

Frederick stood there, tears streaming down his face. His arms were wrapped around him and he was rocking backward and forwards.

The stranger said again, 'Come and sit on the wall.'

After what seemed like an age, Frederick moved back from the slope's edge. He sat on the wall and broke down, crying and shaking. Even though the stranger wanted to help, she could not help but notice that this man needed a bath. She asked him what was wrong.

Can Openers

Frederick started to tell her some of the things that had happened. This was something he had only done once before, he was usually very reserved and private. He told her that his children had been taken by the Dependency Department, he was losing his home, and his wife was dead.

The stranger listened sympathetically; she didn't berate him or judge him in any way. If anything, the stranger took pity on Frederick. She asked him when he last had a good meal. She also wanted to ask this man when he had last had a bath last, but she was too polite.

'Come with me,' she said. 'I'll get you something to eat.'

Frederick looked at her. He didn't know what to do, why should anyone take pity on him or want to help him? Who was this stranger? What did she want?

'Look,' she said. 'I don't want to pry or interfere; it's just that you look and sound like you've been through a terrible time. Let me get you some food.'

Frederick nodded slowly.

'I'll cook you something, you can have a wash, if you want, and then go on your way.' Frederick nodded again.

The stranger surprised herself. She wouldn't normally ask a complete stranger back to her house, but this man looked desperate and his story was so sad. He was probably harmless, though, and he did seem to be telling the truth, there was something genuine about his grief. They walked along the towpath; she led the way, he followed like an old dog trying to keep up with its owner.

Frederick had not asked her name and he couldn't remember if he had told her his. He had started to sober up, however.

Chapter 34

When they arrived at her house, he sat on a chair next at the dining room table, leant on, and lay his head on the table. The woman cooked him a meal, a pasta dish, and it didn't stay on the plate very long. After he had eaten, she gave him a mug of tea. She asked him if he had somewhere to stay. Frederick did not hold back from telling her almost everything, it felt to him as though the floodgates had opened.

He said that he was soon going to be homeless because his house was going to be taken, although, he said, his intention was to get enough cash together to rent a flat. He started to cry again.

'I wanted to kill myself,' he sobbed, 'but I couldn't even do that properly.'

Frederick veered between complete hopelessness to having a plan for his immediate future, though it did amount to contemplating suicide. His suicidal thoughts were so overwhelming that he thought he could actually kill himself, at the same time he felt as though he had no energy to even carry out the ultimate act.

The woman felt sorry for him. He obviously needed help.

'I can make up the spare room if you want,' she said. 'You can have the room for a small weekly rent. That would help me out as well.'

Frederick looked at her, lost for words. This was the only positive thing that had happened to him in months. He was too depressed to even be suspicious of her.

'Ok,' he murmured. This was one chance he could not refuse. 'Can I come on Monday?'

'Yes, of course you can, if you're sure you'll be all right in the meantime.'

Can Openers

Frederick wanted to ask her name but was too scared, in case she had already told him. How embarrassing would that be, he thought. She might get upset, and he needed the room she had offered him. He told her his name was Frederick and she nodded, but she did not respond and instead continued with the previous conversation.

'It's a deal then,' she said. 'There is one thing I would ask, though.'

There was bound to be a catch, he thought. The old Frederick came to the surface, his complete distrust of others. He waited for what she had to say.

'I don't know quite how to put this,' she said, 'but would it be possible for you to have a bath and let me wash your clothes?' She smiled at him, evidently embarrassed.

Frederick looked at her and smiled for the first time in what felt like months. He was so relieved; if that was the only catch then he didn't mind. He agreed straight away, saying that he was not the slightest bit upset at what she had asked.

The stranger was not so much a stranger now but more like the women with no name. She told him he could move in Monday evening. Frederick agreed and shook her hand.

'Just have a bath before you come round, else the deal is off,' she said, half joking.

He left, saying over his shoulder that he would see her on Monday. He still didn't know her name. He looked at the house number; he needed to make sure that he didn't forget the address.

It started to rain but he hardly noticed. For the moment, he had a slight lift to his shoulders and, for a few steps, there was a noticeable change. It was not quite a spring in his step, but his walk was not as flat and despairing as it had been when he'd left his home. Maybe things could improve. However, as the rain got heavier, his shoulders drooped. He started thinking again of all the terrible things that had happened to him and became increasingly self-pitying. I could, he thought, lose my freedom as well. At least I've got somewhere to go on Monday. He wondered then if he would be free on Monday, and whether the woman who was taking him in would have bothered if she knew he was facing a murder charge.

Frederick arrived home and went to bed. For the first time in a long while he slept soundly. He was woken up by someone phoning him. Frederick picked up his phone. It was Mr Take. Although Frederick was sleepy, there was a noticeable excitement in Mr Take's voice. He told Frederick there had been significant developments in the case.

'Can you come to office at 11.45 am?' Mr Take asked.

Frederick's heart sank; they are going to charge him for the murder. What was he to do? He had the vases, if he could get some decent money for them, he could leave the country. Frederick had forgotten about the chip in his arm and he felt desperate.

'Yes, all right, I'll see you later,' he said and put the phone down.

Frederick quickly got dressed, went downstairs, and retrieved the vases from the sideboard where he had put them the previous night. He wrapped the vases in newspaper, put them in a shopping bag he found in the kitchen, and went to the dealer who had made him an offer in the past.

Frederick walked in to the dealer's shop and went to the counter. The dealer knew him, but had not seen him for a long time. He tried making conversation with Frederick asking how he was keeping and that he thought he had moved out of the area.

Frederick did not want to get into a conversation. He put the shopping bag on the countertop. He pulled out one of the vases and unwrapped it to show it to the dealer. The dealer remembered the vase; in fact he had often thought of it, it was rare example of its type. The dealer knew that Frederick had been an enthusiastic amateur collector and that this was a prize piece.

Frederick said to him, 'When I came here before you offered me £15,000 for it. Well, you valued it at that price.'

The dealer certainly remembered but said, 'I think so,' as if he could only just recall. The dealer was shrewd, he wanted the vase; he knew it would probably fetch more at auction than the price he had valued it at. But he was surprised that Frederick had come back and didn't seem to have had it valued elsewhere.

In different times and in different circumstances, Frederick would have had the vases valued elsewhere to get a range of quotes. He had felt when he first got it valued a few years ago that the vases were worth more than he was offered. But he had little time and needed the money.

Can Openers

The dealer took the vase from Frederick. He looked at it closely, turning it this way and that, checking it closely for any cracks or chips, checking it for even the smallest flaw. He upended the vase and looked at the back stamp. He handed the vase back to Frederick and then leaned down and pulled out a book that he kept on a shelf under the counter. He thumbed through its pages until he found the one he wanted. He studied the page closely for a few minutes. He closed the book and put it back on the shelf. He went over to an open laptop at the far end of the counter and clicked some buttons before pausing to look at the screen. It was all for show. The dealer had no need to look in the book or even check the computer. He knew how much the vase was worth. But the dealer had been in the game for a long time.

He closed down the laptop, went back to Frederick. He told Frederick that the previous offer had been made a few years ago, that the value of antiques fluctuates over time, that some go up in value, others go down, others remains the same.

The dealer was trying his luck. He could tell by looking at his customers how to approach a deal and the intuition he had gained from his years in the trade gave him the impression that Frederick needed money immediately. The dealer offered Frederick £9,000 cash, for the pair he said.

Frederick flinched. '£13,000,' he said.

The dealer said, 'I'll give you £10,000 for them. It's a good price.'

Frederick needed more, so he hesitated. The dealer couldn't be certain but he knew that Frederick's hesitation could be an indication that Frederick was going to turn down his offer and go elsewhere. It was a risk, in fact Frederick was on the verge of accepting the offer and was just thinking if he could manage to try and do a runner from the authorities on this amount and how far he was likely to get.

The dealer, however, didn't know this. He thought that he didn't want to lose out for a second time on the opportunity to acquire these two vases. 'Ok,' said the dealer, 'I'll give you £12,000 for the pair. It's my last and final offer.' The dealer knew it wasn't anywhere close to his final offer and that he would have gone higher still but, to his surprise, Frederick accepted.

The dealer asked Frederick to wait while he went to the bank to get cash. Frederick waited impatiently in a café nearby. Once again, and for a short period of time, Frederick was actually pleased. He had shifted the price up from £9,000. He then thought about what the solicitor might have to say. Were the police going to pick him up at any time? Was the solicitor going to tell him he had to go back to the police station so he could be charged with murder? His mind started to race. The money from the vases might help him to go on the run but where would he go? The reality of his situation started to sink in.

I've got a chip in my arm, he thought, they could find me anywhere. He was looking at the rest of his natural life in prison. Dark thoughts once more entered his head.

The dealer returned. Frederick watched as the man opened up his shop and went in. Frederick left the café and walked over. The dealer locked the door behind him. He placed a small black holdall on the counter, opened it, and then started placing bundles of cash on to the counter. He and Frederick counted out £12,000. Frederick handed over the shopping bag with the two vases in it. The dealer took out the vases, unwrapped them and double-checked them. When he was satisfied, he carefully placed the vases on the counter. He then put the £12,000 into the black holdall. He zipped it up and handed it to Frederick.

'Keep the holdall,' the dealer said, 'you can have it for free.'

Frederick thanked him and left the shop. He walked the short distance to the train station, entered the main hall and went up to the bank of left luggage lockers. He placed the holdall in one of the lockers, shut the door, and removed the key. He placed the key carefully in his jacket pocket.

Chapter 35

Frederick left the station and walked back down the high street to the solicitor's office. He hadn't wanted to take the money with him to the solicitors because of the possibility that Mr Take might take him down to the police station since the solicitor was responsible for him.

Frederick thought that the police or the Dependency Department had been following him for a few days now. He noticed cars parked outside the house that he didn't recognise as belonging to any neighbours. He wondered if he was becoming paranoid. He admitted to himself that he didn't really know what to think anymore. If he were being watched, had they watched him take the vases? Would it count as evidence stacking up against him? Maybe they were going to charge him with fraud and murder. He was becoming panicky and upset again.

It was about midday by the time he made it to the solicitor's building. Each step he took up the stairs to the office was taking him closer to his fate.

A secretary at a desk as he walked in smiled pleasantly at Frederick and asked him to sit down on the leather sofa. She pressed a button on the intercom on her desk. A few seconds later Mr Take came out of his office and invited Frederick in.

The office was small. It contained a desk with an executive type chair behind it, and another chair in front clearly intended for clients. The office had nothing in it that could be described as grand; it was just basic and functional.

Mr Take opened the conversation with a few comments about the weather. Frederick didn't respond; he just wanted to know what the solicitor had to tell him.

Mr Take got down to business. The police had contacted him, he said.

Frederick sank down into the chair, his stomach tightened and he started to tense up.

'The police have told me,' said Mr Take, 'that they want to drop the bail. They have also dropped the charges against you.' He spoke slowly so he could be sure that Frederick took in the news. 'They have also taken you off any legal framework but they may want to interview you again.'

Frederick stared at Mr Take for a moment, trying to absorb this new information. It sounded like good news, but he couldn't be sure. 'Where does this leave me?' he asked.

'You're now a free citizen,' Mr Take said. 'The police have told me that you are still a suspect, but you are not the only suspect and you are further down on their list than you were previously. This is a massive step forward. If the police want to interview again, they will contact me and I will get in touch. You will need to go to the police station later so a nurse can remove the chip in your arm.'

Frederick nodded. Mr Take leaned back in his chair and told Frederick that the new development was a great relief. Mr Take thought the police might have new evidence. Frederick wasn't completely off the police radar but the situation was a tremendous improvement from before.

'What is your new home address?' Mr Take asked.

'Would my vismoblie be a sufficient contact point?'

'Yes, so long as you contact me straight back when I try to get in touch.'

Frederick agreed.

'I will send you my bill,' said Mr Take.

Frederick left the solicitor's office with an enormous sense of relief. This time while going down the stairs, he had a little spring in his step. His mood had been swinging from one extreme to another, from desperation to almost feeling ecstatic. His life had become a rollercoaster. However, for the first time for months, he had some positive things happen that finally gave him a glimmer of hope.

Chapter 36

Herbert arranged to see Phil. Herbert hadn't been able to sleep the night before and he got up, dressed, and went to work early. On the journey in to work, he couldn't focus on the task ahead; he was incredibly stressed from the news of Lidia's death. He thought about Frederick and wondered if he knew about Lidia's death.

However, like the professional he was, when he arrived at his office and settled in at his desk, he started to focus on the task in hand. He had to try to find out why Frederick had been given a number 3 risk rating. He wanted to see if he could relate the number 3 rating to Lidia's death. Had Frederick harmed his children or had it been Lidia? Herbert wanted answers.

Herbert also needed to respond to the police, but he had so little information. Perhaps, after interviewing him, Phil would be able to do an audit trail. Herbert knew it might be difficult; the system was so secure that once an action goes to a number 3 rating, the computer took over and the systems worked separately. The programs had all the outcomes stored away. This was so that decisions could be value-free and not prone to human error, human emotion, or human sentimentalism. However, it meant that to find anything out was near impossible. Even the top executive leader had extreme difficulties finding out anything other than the outcome.

Phil knocked on the door and Herbert invited him in. Herbert was in no mood for playing games; he got straight down to business.

'Hello, Phil. I've asked you here because I am investigating concerns about events surrounding what happened to Frederick Smyth. You know he has left the department, do you have any idea why?'

Phil said, 'No.'

'I know you had some involvement with Frederick and you worked closely with him at times, particularly in relation to the A1201a case.'

'Yes,' said Phil, 'that's correct, we did.' Phil had a short temper and at times could be loose cannon. He was not sure what he was being interviewed in connection with. He was not entirely happy being in Herbert's company. Although he had no particular axe to grind with Herbert, he never understood why he and Frederick had been told to back off the A1201a case and take no action against Joyce the Opportunity Planner. It was something that Phil had simmered with for a while now.

Phil blurted out, 'According to Frederick, you told him not to find Opportunity Planner 22 guilty, so why am here? I believed him; I was also getting pressure from my management.'

Luckily for Phil, Herbert was not in the mood to play mind games. 'I'll be honest with you, Phil, I was told by very senior people to make sure 22 was not guilty, they had other plans.'

'For what?' asked Phil.

'That, I don't know,' Herbert answered. Phil looked at him in disbelief. 'They don't tell me everything. As far as they're concerned, I'm just a cog in the wheel.' Herbert then explained that he was told something about three different plans, but didn't know the details and didn't understand what was going on.

Phil told Herbert he didn't believe him and asked again if he knew what was going on.

Herbert said, 'Look, I need to put something to you. Given your knowledge of IT and the way the system works, could anyone have hacked the system to set Frederick up?'

'Unlikely,' said Phil.

'Could you do that?' asked Herbert.

Phil looked at Herbert not sure what he was implying. 'Why has Frederick left the department?'

Herbert paused. 'Because he had a number 3 risk rating on his family.'

'No way,' said Phil, shaking his head, 'that's unbelievable. Frederick wouldn't harm anyone in his family or do anything to bring any disrepute to the department.' He shook his head again. 'He was Mr Department, a corporate man. He believed in the mission statement. But then, the system is always right. I suppose anyone can abuse their kids, but this is shocking.'

'Do you think it is possible for him to have been set up?' Herbert asked.

'No, no, it's not possible, it's...no, it just doesn't seem possible.'

Herbert made notes on the pad in front of him.

'There are rumours going round,' Phil said, 'that the story in the paper about the woman, the one who was stabbed to death, was Frederick's wife. There are rumours that Frederick has been charged with her murder. Is it true?'

The colour drained from Herbert's face, his mouth dropped open. He looked as though he was going to collapse.

'Are you ok?' asked Phil.

'I'm not feeling so well,' he replied. 'I'm fine, must be a virus or something.' He took a sip of water from the glass in front of him and loosened his tie.

'Look, I need your help. I've been asked to look into something, I've been given high-level permission for a root and branch investigation; my jurisdiction is very wide. If you can help, it could mean a promotion for you and help with your career. I will guarantee it.'

'I'll see what I can do, but the only explanation I can see is that Frederick must be guilty. The difficulty is that we may have to accept that the only person who knows what happened is the guilty party. Number 3 ratings do not lie.'

Chapter 37

Frederick gathered his clothes together over the weekend. He had some cash and was not yet reliant on the Dependency Unit for money. Despite the recent upturn in events, he was feeling low. He thought about Lidia often. Everything was unreal. He had not really had a chance to grieve; she had left him and was now dead. He could still barely believe it. He thought about the arrangements for the funeral. A huge void had opened up in his life and his heart ached. At the same time he was astounded that someone had offered to help him, had given him a room. He would have to pay rent on it, but even so.

Frederick wondered about the police investigation, nervous that the police might call him back. He felt aggrieved about the way they had treated him. His job at the Dependency Unit seemed so long ago. He no longer had the evangelical zeal with which he used to carry out his work. All of the ideas he had held, his moral compass, were in crisis. Before, every day had been a crusade against the underclass. He blamed State dependents for their situation; he used to argue that the situation they were in was entirely their own fault, because of their inadequacies and reliance on benefits. He used to think about these issues every day. But since the number 3 risk rating and the great upheaval, he had been so wrapped up in his own situation that all the other issues were forgotten. He concentrated only on survival. He felt guilty about his children and what happened to them. He wondered where they were and how they were getting on. He hoped they were happy. He wondered if Lidia had hurt them but then felt guilty for thinking ill of the dead. He never questioned whether the system was wrong, in fact that thought never crossed his mind, but it didn't matter, he wasn't interested in any crusade anymore.

Frederick checked to see if the room was still available. Lady No-Name, as Frederick thought of her, texted him back to say it was.

Frederick started on the whisky. Fortunately, he had sorted his items out and much of his packing was done. He spent much of Sunday in bed, not getting up until early evening. He made an effort to make sure his clothes were clean and spent hours in the bath, trying his best to scrub up. How bad his hygiene had become had been a shocking realisation, but it was salvageable. He was able to get himself ready for the next day in just a few hours.

Monday came around soon enough. Frederick booked a taxi to take him to Lady No-Name's house. Before then, he had another bath and finally the smell coming from his body washed off.

When he arrived at her house, Lady No-Name came to the door. One of her children came running up behind her and told Frederick, 'My name is Daz.'

'Hello, Daz,' said Frederick quietly.

Lady No-name smiled at Frederick, stood to one side, and waved him into the house. 'I'll take you to your room,' she said. She helped him carry his luggage up to the small spare room, dropped off his bags, and asked if he wanted something to eat.

'Yes, please,' answered Frederick quietly again. He didn't really know these people and didn't know what to say to them so followed Lady No-Name downstairs to the kitchen in silence. As he walked through the door, another woman was in the kitchen putting a coat on to leave.

'I'll be going then, Jane,' she said.

What a relief, thought Frederick, I now know her name.

The other lady stopped and looked at Frederick. 'How rude of me,' she said, 'my name is Iris, nice to meet you.'

'Hello,' Frederick said. Iris picked up her bag and left, waving and saying goodbye. After Iris was gone, Jane asked Frederick to sit down at the table. They discussed how much he should pay for the room and Jane agreed that he could pay whatever he was able to afford, so long as he paid her something each week.

'Don't look so worried,' said Jane. 'Make yourself at home.'

Frederick explained again that he had lost his house and about what had happened to his children. He thought it best to be honest.

Jane told him that she had been involved with the Dependency Unit and that she thought they treated people disgustingly. 'Luckily,' she said, 'I'm not involved any more so I have sympathy for you.' Frederick decided not to mention that he used to work for the department, Jane must have had a bad experience. And that was all in the past.

'You can stay as long as you like, it will help me financially,' Jane said.

Jane asked Frederick if he had ever hurt his children. Frederick's eyes filled with tears. He told Jane that he had loved his children so much and how his heart ached for them now. Frederick started sobbing. Jane handed him a tissue. She felt he was completely genuine. Jane leaned around the kitchen door and shouted to her children who had just run out of the house.

'I've got to go out,' she said to Frederick, 'I'll see you later, and you get settled in.' She grabbed a coat and rushed out of the house to catch up with her children.

Frederick could not believe how trusting she was; she had left the house with him alone in it. Frederick went upstairs to his bedroom and started to unpack. He put his clothes in a drawer. He then put his suitcase, which had the cash hidden within the lining, at the bottom of the wardrobe and placed a few clothes and some other items over it.

He lay on the bed. He heard Jane come in some time later and he heard her children come upstairs to bed.

There was a knock on his door. It was Jane. She spoke to him through the door, asking if he wanted to come downstairs and join her for a coffee. He went downstairs and sat with her in her sitting room. They agreed to a few basic house rules, that Frederick would keep his room clean and tidy, that he would leave the bathroom and the rest of the house as he found it, that sort of thing.

Once that was out of the way, they started chatting. Frederick asked about Jane's children, how old they were, whether they liked their school. Jane asked Frederick what he did for work. Frederick wasn't expecting it and nearly let slip, he dodged it by pretending not to hear the question.

'Because of what happened, I'm unemployed,' he said.

'If you need work, there might be jobs coming up where I work. It may only be casual work but it's better than nothing. Winter's coming and soup production is going up. I'll let you know, if you're interested,' she said brightly.

'Thanks,' said Frederick, 'thanks very much.'

Jane went to get them some more coffee and a snack. When she had sat back down Frederick asked her where she worked. Jane told him she worked for Dibble Canning. Frederick knew the Director of Dibble Canning, having met him, but he would never come across him again as a casual canner. The organisation was so big he would not even notice Frederick. Frederick thought about calling himself by his second name "Kevin". He realised that he could start that now.

'I like to be called by my middle name of Kevin, it's what most people know me as,' he lied.

'Kevin it is, then,' Jane said. They chatted some more and then Jane said she needed to go to bed as she had work the next day.

Frederick followed Jane upstairs and went to his room. When he got into bed and put his head on the pillow, he felt human again. He hadn't had a drop of alcohol, and he felt pleased to be in a family home. He lay in the bed and thought he could only have respect for someone like Jane. She had opened her home to him, fed him, and had listened to him patiently while he talked about his anxieties and concerns.

.

Chapter 38

Time went by and Frederick and Jane got to know each other better. Frederick made an effort to be reasonable. His mood had lifted slightly. He was still low, but it seemed to only affect him during at night. He would wake early each morning after having dreadful nightmares. They seemed to be linked to the abuse he suffered as a child. There was a recurring dream he had from which he would wake up hyperventilating.

He dreamt about his father humiliating him, putting him down and then beating him with a stick, or anything he could lay his hands on. In the recurring dream, the room he was in expanded and Frederick shrank to a tiny size. He would go to a mirror and seeing, instead of his reflection, a monster staring back at him.

The longer he stayed at Jane's, the more Frederick started to look back at his life, at who he had been and what he had become. The monster in his dreams played on his mind and he started to look at the way he had acted at the Dependency Unit. He had lost faith in humanity and felt that everyone was out to get something for nothing. He realised that he had lost touch with his own humanity.

One day Jane asked him if he would be around as she had some friends coming over and she would like him to join them. Frederick had not touched any alcohol since he had been at Jane's. This had been difficult for the first two or three days, he had craved whisky; he was worried about alcohol being available at the get together.

Can Openers

Frederick spent his days walking the streets or sitting in the library so he wasn't in the house all the time. He was also keeping on top of his cleanliness and the domestic chores he had agreed to with Jane. He was also trying to find out about Lidia's funeral, but this could be months away as the coroner had to examine the body.

Frederick decided to ring his solicitor Mr Take. Frederick wanted to check if he had heard anything from the police or anything regarding his wife's funeral.

'No, I have not heard anything, and I have no new information for you,' Mr Take said. 'Perhaps you should just focus on moving on with your life.'

Although he was worried about the alcohol, he didn't want to hurt Jane's feelings; she had been so kind to him. It had been a long time since Frederick had bothered about anyone else's feelings.

When the day of the get together came round, Frederick made a big effort. He decided he would go out and buy some wine and a chocolate cake. He then changed his mind and decided he would make the cake himself. When he first got married he used to bake and cook until his job took over his life.

Just before the meal, Frederick had gone to his bedroom and lay on the bed in tears thinking about Lidia and his children. He really wanted to know what had happened and why his wife had died. He wanted his children back, too. Now that he felt slightly better he wanted, and needed, answers. He wanted his children back, whatever it took.

This was the first time in months he had felt strong enough to try and analyse what had happened to him. He questioned if it was possible that it was neither Lidia nor him who had abused the children; he knew that he was innocent, after all. Maybe a mistake had been made. Or maybe someone was setting him up; he had moved up the ladder of the Dependency Unit and had probably made enemies in the process.

Jane's two children had gone over to a friend's house for a sleep over. Jane told Frederick that the children really liked him.

'You must have been a good dad,' she said.

Frederick's eyes filled with tears.

'Kevin, you really don't need to worry or be embarrassed about what has happened to you. Most of the people coming tonight know exactly how bad the Dependency Unit treat people. Many people on this block at some point have had dealings with them, either directly or through family or friends.' She went to the kettle and switched it on. 'Most people who go to the Dependency Unit aren't dependent but desperate. The department sees them, deals with them, and takes their confidence away. They blame the poorest in society for their own poverty or mental distress.'

Frederick nodded, not saying anything.

'When it comes to those who own companies like Dibble,' said Jane, 'they rely on the unemployed and stigmatise them. They use the Dependency Unit to separate the so-called deserving and undeserving poor.' Jane paused while she poured the hot water from the kettle into the two mugs she had prepared. She poured some milk into both mugs, stirred the contents and handed a mug to Frederick.

'Do you know why they do this, Kevin?' she asked. He shook his head. 'They do it to make those in work feel insecure and more likely to accept that they have to work harder for lower wages or risk ending up a dependency figure and worthless in society's eyes.'

Frederick kept on nodding but remained silent. He was interested enough to just want to listen.

Jane said, 'Wait until you meet Iris, she goes on about ideology all the time, but what she has to say is interesting. She's bound to talk about the propaganda put out by the wealthy: those who want us to believe their ideas so they can divide us and stop us from organising amongst ourselves.'

Frederick asked if there was any truth in the system. 'But don't they use research to back their evidence up?'

Jane explained that the Dependency Unit was there to create divisions among people. She told Frederick how they wanted ordinary people to look down on each other. They wanted those with permanent jobs to fear or look down on those with temporary jobs, and they wanted everyone looking down on the unemployed. She explained how they were all encouraged to compete with other races and cultures.

'One of my friends,' said Jane, 'is at the bottom of the pecking order. What those at the top don't realise is that what they want us to believe doesn't always work out; not everyone thinks or wants to see people in the way they try to encourage us to.'

Jane told Frederick that the following Monday she and her friends were going to protest outside a Dibble care home, as they didn't recognise the union. 'Why don't you come?' she asked.

Before Frederick could answer there was a knock on the door.

Iris came in. 'Hi, folks,' she said, 'How are you, Kevin, how are you getting on at Jane's Ritz? Is she taking care of you?'

Frederick said that Jane had been brilliant and he had settled in. 'I couldn't have asked for more.'

'That's great,' said Iris.

The door opened again and another woman walked in. Jane said, 'This is Gina.' And she introduced her to Kevin.

Gina always got to the straight to the point.

'I believe you're the lodger. Have a drink?' she asked.

'Yes, thanks,' said Frederick.

'I've heard things have been difficult for you and you've been on the wrong side of the Dependency Unit?' Gina said.

'Yes,' said Frederick.

Iris came over and butted in. 'Let's have a break tonight and let our hair down. I've got some good news: I think love is in the air for Gina! Go on, tell us about him.'

Gina blushed. 'He used be an electrician but he lost his job and now works as a canner and yes, before you ask, he is a union member and he is a Can Opener. He's really nice,' she said. 'How is your girlfriend keeping?'

'Oh she's fine,' Iris said. 'Jane, how's the Can Opener movement going?'

Jane said the movement was spreading, that they were calling for strike action at all the Dibble enterprises over the minimum wage. 'The national union,' she said, 'is balloting not only plants in this country but right across the Dibble empire, including the USA. They're even unionising care homes in the USA. The company's arguing that if they pay us then Gleto, the multinational drugs company, will get in a foothold in the market and jobs will have to be lost.'

Iris and Gina nodded. Frederick kept quiet, fascinated by the discussion.

'Anyway, Iris, how are the preparations going for Monday?' asked Jane.

'There's been a day's action being called by our members,' Iris said. 'The homes that are organised are joining with the residents inside and the Can Openers outside for the regional day of action. The action is not just about the union, it's also about how the residents are treated, and their rights.'

Iris turned to Frederick and said, 'Kevin, why don't you join us on Monday. This is about the residents as much as the workers. It's about dignity in later life. We're starting our campaign to challenge the injection.'

Gina said, 'If you come along Kevin, it'll help you get back at the Dependency Unit for the way they've had a go at you.'

'Yeah,' said Iris. 'Come on, come with us. This is your chance to get back at the bastards.'

Frederick was confused. Jane sensed he might be uncomfortable and changed the subject. They all talked for a few hours. At one point the conversation centred on Gina, who was asked by Jane to tell Frederick her story. Frederick listened intently, horrified as she described how she was tortured in Africa.

Gina explained how when she had come to Britain she was not treated as a full citizen. She talked about how she was attacked in the streets and how the courts treated her. Frederick started to feel embarrassed. He had treated people with disdain when he had worked for the Dependency Unit. He hadn't realised how many genuine people there were.

Gina then asked Frederick what his experience had been with the Dependency Unit. Frederick couldn't tell them he had worked for the Unit. He didn't know how they would react, and was concerned they would turn on him. However, he found all of the women to be warm, genuine and interesting. He thought he could at least tell them he been a Dependency Manager, it would be the truth. But when he saw such thoughtfulness in all the women's expressions, when he considered the way he felt warmth and companionship with them that he had never felt before, he decided he couldn't tell them. He lost his nerve. How could he jeopardise everything he had gained?

So he ignored that part of his previous life, told them instead about what had happened more recently; that he lost his job. Everything that had happened to him since then

Can Openers

shocked them enough to distract them from asking him any further questions about his former working life.

Chapter 39

After interviewing Phil, Herbert decided to take the rest of the day off. He felt too distressed to carry on that day. When he arrived home, Sophie was upstairs. She had been crying. Herbert asked her how she was. Sophie told him tearfully that she had made friends with Lidia.

'A few years ago, if you remember, we had a dinner party with Lidia and Frederick. We've been friends ever since and I've being meeting her quite regularly.' Sophie wiped her tears away. 'When she lost her children, Lidia came to me. I helped her. I found a flat that she could move into. She was so distressed about losing her children. She had often talked about killing herself and felt suicidal.'

Sophie looked at Herbert, she expected him to be angry with her for being deceitful and for not having told him about this sooner. They rarely kept things from each other.

Herbert listened to what Sophie had to say. He didn't get angry; he was calm. Sophie wanted him to at least question her. She couldn't understand his reaction, he didn't ask her anything. She asked him if he was mad with her.

'No,' said Herbert. 'All you did was show how kind and generous you are.'

'Aren't you angry that I went behind your back?' she asked.

'No, not at all. You did your best for your friend. Your kindness is why I love you.' Herbert went over to Sophie and put his arms round her. They embraced.

Sophie pulled away and said, 'There's more I need to tell you.'

Can Openers

'What else is there?' he said.

Sophie took a deep breath. 'I've let you down Herbert,' she said. 'Because when you're stressed you talk about work sometimes. I've always been loyal to you, you know that. The thing is, you told me information that I then passed on to Lidia.'

Herbert blanched, he thought he was hearing things. 'Which information did you pass on?'

Sophie burst in tears, she sobbed into the already damp tissue she had in her hand. 'I promised Lidia that if I knew any information about Frederick, I would pass it on to her. Anything you told me, I passed on.' She paused, her tears lessened. 'To be honest, Herbert, I was not expecting you to say anything as you hardly ever talk about work, but I promised Lidia. I feel like I manipulated you to get information for her. I am so sorry.' She started sobbing again.

He pressed Sophie for more details. 'What information did you give to Lidia?'

'Well, you mentioned to me about an affair Frederick had had with someone called Joseph, another worker at the department.' Sophie cried even harder.

Herbert couldn't believe his ears but he knew he needed to stay calm if he was going to keep Sophie talking like this, getting angry with her would be pointless and counterproductive. He put his arm around her again to comfort her.

'I went to see her in a café one lunchtime,' sniffed Sophie. 'Lidia had just moved into her flat and was trying so hard to move on, despite such terrible circumstances. She had told me she had started to feel better, but she still seemed subdued. I was really worried that she may do something silly, possibly even try to kill herself. I knew she had been put on anti-depressants and although they helped lift her mood a bit, I know she still had suicidal thoughts.' Sophie blew her nose into a fresh tissue. 'I'd been reading about medication and the information I found out really concerned me. When people take anti-depressants their mood lifts, but it's a dangerous time because they then have the energy to kill themselves. I'm worried she went off and committed suicide. I should have brought her back home.' Sophie was now sobbing again, 'I told her what you told me and now I'm so worried that it sent her into despair; after everything else that had happened. I am so, so sorry Herbert.'

All Herbert could do was pat Sophie's hand, inside he was seething.

'She got so very angry, she lost it in the café. She said she wished she could see him, that she wanted answers. She was talking about Frederick of course. She didn't know where to find Joseph but she was worried that if she did ever come across him, she would cause him harm.'

Herbert tried to be supportive. 'We may never know why she died but you only did what she asked.'

'I know,' said Sophie, 'but I'm worried that she may have killed herself. The papers are implying that Lidia was murdered. I'm also worried that I'm probably the last person to have seen her alive. Although if she found Joseph, maybe he was the last person to see her alive. I just don't know.'

Herbert told her not worry and he hugged her again. He seemed so understanding.

Sophie said, 'There's something else I need to tell you. I hope I've done the right thing,' she said, 'but I went to the police today and told them everything.'

As soon as Sophie told him that, Herbert exploded. 'You did what? Why? What on earth do you think you were doing?' he shouted at her. He went mad. Sophie had never seen Herbert get so angry, so quickly.

Chapter 40

There was a bang on the door. Joseph went to the intercom but the picture was very blurry. He went to the door, as he opened it, the door was bashed open and Joseph was knocked to the floor.

'Get down! Get down! Stay on the floor!' shouted a uniformed police officer. Joseph didn't dare move as more police officers flooded into his flat. A police officer ordered him to get up. When Joseph stood, he was pushed up against the wall, his legs were kicked apart, and he was patted down.

One of the officers flashed a warrant card and then a search warrant at Joseph. 'You are under arrest for the murder of Lidia Smyth. You will be taken to a police station for questioning. A solicitor will be arranged for you, and will inform you of your rights.'

Joseph did not even have time to speak; he was handcuffed and led to a police van outside.

'Where are your house keys?' one of the officers asked.

'On the console table in the hall,' said Joseph, and indicated with his head.

'Our officers searching your flat will pick up the keys before they leave, you can sign for them at the station later.'

Joseph was then pushed inside a police van.

When they arrived at the station, Joseph was taken to a tall counter. A sergeant on the other side of it told Joseph he needed a lawyer. Joseph had never been in trouble before and had never needed a lawyer. He explained this to the police sergeant. The police sergeant told Joseph that a duty solicitor would be called for him. The handcuffs were removed and Joseph was asked to empty the contents of his pockets. He was then instructed to take the laces out of his shoes. He was then asked to stand up straight with his legs apart and his arms outstretched. Joseph did as he was asked and wondered what they were going to do to him; Joseph was relieved that he was only patted down. He was led to another room where he was introduced to a police doctor who examined Joseph. The police were making sure everything was being done by the book.

Joseph was then taken to a cell. He felt totally cut out from the outside world. There was nothing to do to pass the time, indeed he had no idea how much time had passed since his watch had been removed. There was nothing to do except sit and think.

Joseph thought that everything had been going so well for him up to then. Since Frederick had left the department, Joseph had taken on more responsibility and done more to try and make himself indispensable. As a result, he came to the notice of senior managers like Herbert, but also those even more senior at the Dependency Unit. Sir George got to know this career-minded, corporate young man who was bright, worked hard and would do anything he was told for the department. In a short time he was put forward for a series of successive promotions, clearly being groomed for appointment to the Board, just like Frederick. Joseph wasn't surprised that he had got so far in the organisation.

What Joseph gave no thought to was that others in the organisation might have similar ambitions. He had no idea at all that anyone might see him as a threat let alone as a rival. Joseph had no idea how unsettled and unnerved Herbert was by his rapid rise up the corporate ladder.

Unaware of any of this, Joseph could only dream about making it to the Executive Office floor level. He had no idea of just how close he had come.

Keys turned in the lock and the cell door was pushed open. Joseph was summoned out of the cell and told that he had to go and see the duty solicitor had arrived.

Joseph was introduced to the duty solicitor who explained to Joseph what his rights were. He informed Joseph that he was going to be interviewed and then led Joseph to an interview room.

Once he was inside, two police officers sat behind a table introduced themselves as DS Cone and DS Lansbury. The two officers looked smug and self-satisfied. Any outsider could be forgiven for assuming that this attitude was typical of the police, there would have been at least a grain of truth in this assumption. However, the truth was more complex and only the police fully appreciated the impact of the intense rivalry between the police force and the Dependency Unit.

Chapter 41

Joseph looked around him. The walls of the interview room were bare aside from a mirror on one wall. He couldn't be sure, but Joseph thought it might be a two-way mirror, he had seen them on the crime dramas on the TV. Joseph didn't know that on the other side of the mirror were two psychologists.

Joseph no longer looked like a well-groomed, young executive. His clothes were crumpled and he had rough stubble on his chin, dark circles under his eyes, and his uncombed hair was sticking up at odd angles.

DS Lansbury explained the interview procedure to Joseph.

'Where were you at 8 in the evening on the 20th?' DS Cone asked.

Joseph hesitated, very uncomfortable. 'I was in my flat,' he said.

DS Cone looked at him. 'We have information saying that you were not in your flat and you were, in fact, on Cotton Street. You were there weren't you?'

Joseph looked to his left at the solicitor and then looked down at DS Cone. 'I'm not prepared to answer the question.'

DS Cone met Joseph's gaze. 'We have a witness who saw you talking to Lidia Smyth and saw you go into an alleyway with her.'

'I'm not prepared to discuss that.'

The officer said again, 'We have witnesses who saw you talking to Mrs Smyth. So, why did you meet her?'

'OK,' Joseph said. DS Cone asked Joseph to repeat what he just said, Joseph said again, 'OK.'

'Were you having an affair?' asked DS Cone.

'I'm not prepared to say,' said Joseph.

At this point the two detectives stopped the interview for the evening. DS Cone told Joseph that he was to be detained and would stay in the cells until the following morning. The solicitor left the police station.

Chapter 42

Herbert was at work when Sophie answered a knock at the door. It was the two police officers that Sophie had recently spoken to about Lidia. One of the officers told Sophie they needed to ask her some questions to help with their enquiries. They asked if they could come in. Sophie quickly agreed to their request. She thought she may have been the last person to see Lidia alive and wanted everything out in the open.

Sophie led the two officers into the sitting room and invited them to sit down. One of the officers took a portable recording device out of a small bag. The other officer led the interview. He told Sophie their names. Sophie smiled at him and asked 'How can I help?'

'We'd like you to tell us again what you told us yesterday and if there's anything else you can add, please try.' Before she could answer, the officer asked what had happened to her eye; it looked puffy and swollen and was black around the edge.

'I tripped over one of the children's shoes and bashed my eye,' she said. 'May I phone my husband before we start?' she asked.

'No problem,' said the officer.

Sophie picked up her phone and dialled Herbert's number. Herbert answered almost straight away, 'I'm in a meeting,' he said.

Sophie told him that the police were there and wanted to question her. The line was very crackly. '...*crackle*....can't say....*crackle*....thing....*crackle crackle*....to go....*crackle*...' the line went dead. Sophie hadn't quite been able to catch what he had said or maybe she chose not to hear, she thought he must have said that he couldn't say anything because was in a meeting. At least I've told him, she thought.

Both officers were shrewd enough to recognise that if she went to the police station her husband would not have any influence, so they asked her to come to the police station.

As soon as Herbert was out of the meeting, he tried to ring Sophie but she had her phone turned off. Although he was pleased she contacted him earlier, he was now desperate to speak to her. He was worried that the police or the department would find out that he had told his wife confidential information. That information should have been given only to Sir George, and if it got out that he had told someone else, even his wife, Herbert knew he would be dismissed. He worried that he could lose his job, and just as he was really starting to go places.

Herbert tried Sophie's number again. Her phone was still turned off.

Chapter 43

At the police station, Sophie sat in the interview room with the two officers.

The lead officer told Sophie that she may have been the last person to see Lidia alive but she was not a suspect.

'Can you tell us again what happened that day?' asked the officer.

'Yes, as I explained yesterday, I had told Lidia that if I found out any information I would let her know.' Sophie started rambling. 'My husband has never spoken about work before. But something happened, or he found something out, and he seemed genuinely shocked.' Sophie became tearful. 'I think that's why he mentioned it to me. I think he thought that it would go no further.' Sophie paused and fished a tissue out of her pocket, wiped her eyes, and blew her nose. 'I wish I hadn't told her. She was so upset. I'm worried that what happened to her had something to do with what I told her.'

The police officer asked Sophie to explain exactly what had happened and what she had told Lidia.

'I told her that Frederick was having an affair with someone from work, a man called Joseph.'

'And how did Mrs Smyth react to this? What did she say or do?' asked the police officer.

'Well, she said she needed to see Joseph.'

'Is that all she said?' asked the officer. 'Did she say anything about seeing her husband?'

'Oh no,' recalled Sophie. 'She was very angry, very upset. I don't think she believed me at first, but when it sunk in that I was telling her the truth she was very upset. She did say Frederick's a bastard, from what I remember. I'm sure she called him other things as well, but I'm not sure who she directed her anger at.'

'Can you tell me what you mean by that?' asked the officer gently.

'You need to understand,' said Sophie, 'that Lidia was completely obsessed with her children; they were her life. Knowing her, she would be angry if she thought that this affair resulted in her losing the children. She said to me that she wondered whether Frederick was to blame for it. She wondered whether the department knew about the affair, and had taken the children because there was dishonesty in her family and sexual deviance. They were not your standard moral family or heterosexual couple.'

'And she said that to you, did she?' asked the officer.

'Oh, yes. Her husband worked in the department, don't forget, so she was well aware of the evidence-based science that showed that if the children were at risk of significant harm, the children are removed. But she really did not have a clue as to why they were removed. So she thought that Frederick must have harmed them.'

'Ok, that's very helpful,' said the officer. 'Is there anything else you can tell us about what she said to you or of her state of mind?'

Sophie explained that both Lidia and Frederick on the face of it brought their children up with a strong moral education and strong values, even though Lidia had despised Frederick.

The police officer asked Sophie if Lidia had told her anything about Frederick's childhood.

Sophie shook. 'Not that I can recall, no. She didn't tell me anything about that, I would've remembered.'

Sophie asked the police whether they would be asking Herbert to come to the station. The lead officer leaned forward. 'Can we ask you how Herbert knew about the affair?'

'Herbert knew about the affair because he had been investigating something at work that had involved Frederick getting a number 3 risk rating,' Sophie said.

'Did your husband tell you why the Department thought Frederick should have been given a number 3 risk rating? Is he investigating it because they may have made a mistake?' asked the officer.

'Oh no, nothing like that,' said Sophie sounding indignant. 'The Department doesn't make mistakes, it's the people who work for them that do.'

'We may have to interview your husband,' said the officer.

'Do you have to?' asked Sophie, concerned.

'Yes we do, we need to speak to anyone who may be able to help us. Why are you worried about us speaking to your husband?' asked the officer.

'I'm worried that he's discussed confidential information with me and might be in trouble with the Department.'

'I can't do anything about that,' said the officer in a tone that sounded like smugness.

The lead officer whispered to his colleague, 'That Dependency Department isn't as clever as they like to think. We might not need to interview this Herbert, we might have enough evidence.

The officer turned back to Sophie and asked her what she thought had happened to Lidia. Sophie started to cry again. 'I think she took her own life,' said Sophie, through her tears.

'What makes you say that?' asked the officer.

Sophie told the police how Lidia had self-harmed and had threatened to take her own life on several occasions.

'If you knew that why then did you tell her about Joseph?' asked the officer.

'I had to tell her, she was my friend, she had a right to know.'

The officer then asked if her relationship with Lidia was more than just a friendship.

'No!' said Sophie, sharply.

The officer persisted. 'You were rejected by her would you say? You wanted more and she did not?'

'Absolutely not,' said Sophie firmly.

'Thank you for your co-operation,' said the officer, 'you can go now. We may have to interview you again, we will be in touch.'

Sophie had told the police everything, about the support she gave Lidia in getting her to Spain, in finding a flat for her, in everything. And now they'd turned everything on her. Sophie was outraged they asked if she had wanted an affair and Lidia had refused. She prided herself on her honesty and integrity so it upset her when these values were questioned.

Can Openers

The police had offered her a lift home, but she had declined. Sophie left the station and went out in to the cool damp air; she decided to walk home, as she did she thought about Lidia and whether she been responsible for her death. Sophie thought about the questions the police had asked her. She had only gone to them in the first place because she thought it was the right thing to do and she had wanted to help; now she felt as though she wanted nothing more to do with the police.

When Sophie arrived home, Herbert was waiting for her. He asked where she had been. When she told him she had been at the police station and had told them everything, Herbert became very angry. Sophie hadn't seen him like this before. He shouted at Sophie asking her why she hadn't even discussed it with him. 'Where is the trust in this relationship?' He screamed at her.

She shouted at him for the first time, 'Someone has died and all you're worried about is whether you broke confidentiality.'

'You stupid fool!' shouted Herbert back at her. 'Our lifestyle, our holidays, everything we have, where do you think the money comes from? We could lose everything.'

'What do you mean?' Sophie asked. 'Lidia is dead.'

Chapter 44

Frederick enjoyed meeting Jane's friends. He had even gone to the care home protest. He had remained on the edge but he read the placards and heard some of speeches.

He had also gone for an informal chat at the canning factory about part-time work as a canner. He had given his name as Kevin. They said that when the production level rose, they would contact him for a formal interview.

On the way back, his solicitor called him to let him know that the police wanted to re-interview him. Frederick knew he was still a suspect but it still upset him; for the first time in months his life had turned a corner, but now everything could go wrong again. Frederick was desperate to find his children and get them back. The upturn in his life helped give him the strength to fight back, not to be the victim. He would find them. Using technology, he could get on VideoFace and start a search. It would be a breach of the conditions, however, if he got caught attempting to find or contact his children. That would result in a lengthy prison sentence. So much for human rights, thought Frederick. He had always been such a stickler for the rules, but he was becoming increasingly fed up with going through the proper channels. He had tried to contact the Dependency Unit but no one ever got back to him.

Jane and the others argued that the system was set up to victimise the poor. Frederick had begun to have some sympathy with this view and he now often found himself questioning his former beliefs.

Frederick wondered why he had been so rigid, why he had created a whole world centred on the values of the department. All those morals had turned on him. He was still confused; he didn't really know what to believe anymore. He couldn't see the world in the same way as Jane and her friends did but, probably for the first time in his life, he started to question things that he had previously taken for granted.

He had made decisions in the past that he would not make now; he wondered whether or not this made him a bad person, whatever that meant. Everything about his life had changed, the only thing he knew with any certainty was that he no longer knew where he belonged any more, and he no longer knew where he fitted in.

Frederick decided to meet his solicitor. They would have to meet at the police station but he had no choice. Otherwise they would have him arrested, just as he was getting his life back on track.

When Frederick arrived at the police station, his solicitor was waiting for him. The two Detectives wanted to go straight to the interview room. By now Frederick was used to the procedure. The recording device was switched on. Behind the mirror were the two psychologists.

Detective Cone asked Frederick where he was on the day of Lidia's murder.

'I have been asked that question before,' said Frederick. 'And my answer is the same.'

'We have more evidence,' Detective Cone said. 'Could you tell us about an affair you had while you were still married to Lidia?'

'I'm not prepared to answer any more questions on the matter,' Frederick said.

'Mr Smyth, you had an affair with a man called Joseph while you were still married to your wife Lidia,' Detective Cone said to Frederick's astonishment. 'You're a disgusting man.'

Detective Lansbury switched off the recording device and asked Detective Cone to step outside for a moment.

'What do you think you are doing?' Detective Lansbury asked once outside the interview room, 'We won't get anything out of him if you carry on like that. Go and get a coffee, I'll get someone else to finish the interview. We need him to give us the facts. We don't want him to clam up on us.'

Detective Cone didn't say anything but stomped off down the corridor. Detective Lansbury went into the mess room and looked around. He spotted Detective Renton. Renton was openly gay. Renton wasn't the only gay police officer based at the station, but he was one of the most experienced men they had. Renton agreed to assist with the interview.

Back in the interview room, Detective Lansbury introduced Renton, and explained that the other officer had been called out on another case.

'Mr Smyth,' asked DC Lansbury, 'when was the last time you saw Joseph?' Frederick didn't answer. 'Look Mr Smyth we're not here to make any judgments about you, we just want to get to the truth.' Detective Lansbury stopped the tape and asked to have a word with Mr Take. Frederick reluctantly agreed. Although Frederick was angry with police, he was much calmer than he was before.

Detective Lansbury said, 'Mr Take, it is important that your client speaks to us. We're looking at whether he was an accomplice to a murder we believe may have been committed by this man, Joseph. It may be that your client is innocent, in which case we can eliminate him from our enquiries. The fact is, Mr Take, if he doesn't answer our questions we will assume he is guilty and we will charge him with murder.'

Mr Take asked, 'What's your evidence? I need more information and I need to speak to my office.' The interview was suspended while Mr Take went into the waiting room and called his office to speak his senior partner. The senior partner's advice was to try and get a deal with the police. If Frederick was guilty then see if they would be more lenient if he pled guilty.

Mr Take called Detective Lansbury to one side and asked what they would offer his client if he pleaded guilty. Detective Lansbury explained that the courts were likely to be more lenient if Frederick pleaded guilty, it could mean that they may argue diminished responsibility.

'We would support that if Mr Smyth plays ball with us,' said Detective Lansbury.

Mr Take went back to the interview room and spoke with Frederick on his own. He explained to Frederick that it would be in his interests to answer their questions. 'If you're guilty,' he said, 'the police would do a deal. I've spoken to my partner and he thinks there is room for a deal. Apparently the police are down on their targets so it's in their interest to accept a guilty plea in return for supporting a lenient sentence.' Mr Take paused. 'Are you guilty?'

'No,' said Frederick quietly but not convincingly. Frederick said that this was his personal life and was annoyed the police was pressuring him to answer questions, even though he understood why.

Mr Take told Frederick that the police wouldn't be interested in him if they didn't believe they could get a conviction. But the police were, however, in a double bind. If they found Joseph and Frederick guilty, their point tally went up. Because they would be murder convictions, they would jump right up the police league table.

'The truth of it, Frederick, is that this could be your saving grace.'

Frederick explained how unhappy he was that one of the officers had treated him like a leper and had acted so abrasively towards him.

Mr Take said, 'That officer will not be involved in interviewing you anymore. You could be charged for murder. Be careful and please take my advice.'

They were interrupted by one of the police officers poking his head around the door and asked if they were ready to continue. Frederick said he was ready. He and the solicitor returned to the interview room where the officers were waiting. The recording device was restarted. The two psychologists were sat behind the mirror.

Detective Lansbury said, 'Mr Smyth, could you tell us about the relationship you had with Joseph?'

Frederick said he had been in a relationship.

'Are you still in a relationship with him?'

'No.'

'When did the relationship finish?'

'The relationship had finished just after my children were removed,' he said, sadly.

'Do you think your relationship with Joseph had anything to do with your children being removed?' asked the Detective.

Frederick said he didn't know why his children had been taken from him.

The Detective raised an eyebrow. 'Everyone knows why something like that happens,' he said. 'Perhaps you're in denial?'

Frederick didn't answer.

Detective Renton spoke for the first time. He had a calm voice and coolly asked Frederick to give him the precise details of what had happened when he and Joseph had broken up. Frederick told him that he had gone to Joseph's flat, that he had been very distressed because his marriage had ended, that Joseph had said he thought that being in a relationship with Frederick could jeopardise his career and they should never see each other again.

Detective Renton asked if there was anything else he wanted to say.

'No,' said Frederick.

Detective Renton stopped the tape. The two detectives were friendly enough. They thanked Frederick for helping them with their enquiry and told him he was now free to leave.

Mr Take asked what would happen next.

'We may need your client to come back,' said Detective Lansbury. 'It depends on further information we receive. Even if we find that your client is not a suspect anymore we may need to interview for evidence in court.'

The psychologists behind the mirror were now looking at body language responses and arguing between each other about who they thought was guilty; they were split between the two suspects.

On the way out of the station, Mr Take told Frederick that he had interviewed well and expressed his hope that this would all be concluded very soon. 'At least you're not the only suspect,' he said.

Frederick was more worried than ever. He had thought that he was off the police radar but now it seemed he was high up on their list of suspects after all.

He walked home. He tried to put thoughts about the murder enquiry to the back of his mind and instead thought about the job in the canning factory. He could do with starting work soon; the money from the vases wouldn't last forever. He also thought about contacting the Dependency Unit again to find out about his appeal. Deep down he knew he was unlikely to get a reply, but he had to keep on trying.

Frederick still thought the Dependency Unit had some sense of justice. Jane and her friends argued with him that there was no justice, that the Department abused their power in order to make the poor blame themselves for their own poverty. Frederick felt conflicted; he could see both arguments but was unsure which he should believe.

Chapter 45

Neither Joseph nor Frederick realised they had been at the police station at the same time. The police now went to his cell to fetch Joseph for his interview.

At work, Joseph had been promoted to the role of Postmodern Executive Manager. Since taking on that role, he had started talking in senseless platitudes. He would speak to his staff about things like how important it was to quality assess and how they could improve efficiency. Joseph had the impression he was an intellectual, a mover and shaker and started to believe he was better than the others. He didn't realise that most of the staff thought he was a plonker.

Joseph went into the interview room with his solicitor. Joseph didn't put on any act; he now looked a broken man. Stress had aged his otherwise youthful face.

One of the detectives started the interview. He said he was going to put a statement to Joseph and wanted him to say whether or not it was true.

'We believe you killed Lidia Smyth by stabbing her. She had gone to see you to speak to you about the affair you had with Frederick. You had a knife from Frederick and Lidia's house, suggesting that this murder was planned between you and Frederick. You callously stabbed her, committing premeditated murder.'

Joseph's solicitor raised his hand to stop the interview. Joseph said he wanted to speak to his solicitor. The police refused, they wanted to outline the evidence they had against Joseph. He told them that he wouldn't say anything until he had spoken to his lawyer alone.

'We have enough evidence to charge you with first degree murder,' said Detective Lansbury. Detective Renton left the room, returning in less than a minute carrying a parcel. He placed the package on the table. Wearing gloves, the detective opened the package and pulled out and unwrapped an item. He placed the item on the table, careful to only touch the very ends of the item.

'Do you recognise this?' he asked. He didn't wait for Joseph's response, 'It's the knife that killed Lidia.'

Joseph started to cry. The psychologists behind the mirror analysed every reaction Joseph made.

Detective Lansbury hadn't said anything so far. He looked at Joseph. 'This is the murder weapon and it has your fingerprints all over it. Forensics also found your handprints on Lidia's clothing, as well as your hairs.' He paused. 'We also have witnesses who saw you and CCTV footage of you with Lidia moments before the murder took place.' Detective Lansbury paused again.

Joseph said nothing.

Detective Lansbury sat up straight in his chair, coughed, and assumed his most professional manner. 'We will be charging you with pre-meditated murder. You can make a statement if you wish. You have asked to speak to your solicitor alone and maybe it is time that you did so.'

The detectives left the room and the psychologists cut off the mirror. Joseph broke down. He was shaking and could hardly speak.

'I did it,' Joseph gasped, 'but I didn't mean to, it was an accident.' Joseph slumped in his seat and held his head in hands. 'I'll plead guilty. I'll tell the police everything. But please help me, it was an accident.' Joseph looked up at his solicitor.

'Look,' said the solicitor, 'you tell the police and I will see what I can do, but how was it an accident? You need to compose yourself and explain everything, don't leave any detail out.'

The detectives came back in and said they wanted to continue the interview. Joseph nodded. Detective Lansbury explained how the evidence was stacked up against Joseph. The solicitor interrupted and said his client was pleading guilty and wanted to make a statement.

The detectives looked at each other and nodded.

Joseph started shakily. He told them he wanted to tell the police the facts. Joseph was shaking. He looked round at the

Can Openers

small room and felt the walls and the ceiling getting closer.
His life was finished.

'It was an accident,' Joseph said.

'What do you mean?' asked DC Renton. 'How can it have
been accident? Take us through it Joseph.'

Chapter 46

Joseph explained that he had left his flat at about 7.30. He was going to go to the local store for milk.

As he started to walk he felt like he was being followed. He had gone about two blocks when a shadowy figure came out of nowhere. A woman approached him from behind and asked if his name was Joseph.

He had turned round to see who was talking to him. He thought the woman must have taken some kind of substance; her eyes were popping out of her head.

'I thought it was a druggie scrounging money,' said Joseph, 'She came up very close, looked me in the eyes, and said she wanted to ask me some questions. She was acting really strangely. I got nervous, thinking she was going to mug me or something. I walked away from her. I turned back round and started to walk faster. She kept up with me; she was determined to stop me. But how did she know my name? I didn't understand what was going on and started to panic.'

'Go on Joseph, you're doing OK. Tell us what happened next,' said DC Renton.

'She moved in close to me and pulled out a knife. She was holding the blade directly pointing at my crotch. I was terrified. She told me that if I did as she said no harm would come to me, otherwise I would have no balls. She was mad. The blade looked sharp, all she would have to do was to push slightly and it would have gotten me,' Joseph said quietly.

Joseph paused, took a sip of water.

'We ended up in front of an alleyway. I asked her what she wanted. She said if I didn't shut up I was a dead man. She told me to move down the alleyway. She made me go first. I felt the blade right in my back, digging into my skin.' Joseph looked pleadingly at the detectives.

Detective Renton nodded at him and asked him to carry on.

'I told her she could take anything she wanted, that I only had a small amount of cash on me no cards or anything. She made me walk down the alleyway. When I got to the wall at the end she forced me to put my nose against it. She told me not to move, told me one false move and she would slit my throat. I started to think she was a mass murderer or something; she seemed professional, maybe a psychopath. I couldn't work out why and how she knew my name. I was so scared. I wet myself, y'know?' Joseph started to cry again.

There was silence in the interview room.

'"Do you know who I am?" she asked. She whispered menacingly in my ear, "You try to move and I will slit your throat." I didn't know what to do. "I'm Lidia Smyth," she said. At this point I did not know who Lidia Smyth was, I was so scared. "Who?" I said. She then said to me, "Lidia Smyth, you know, the wife of Frederick Smyth, the wife of the man you fucked." Man, I could've died there and then. I said to her, "look, can we talk? Please move the knife?" I begged her. She moved the knife slightly away from my neck so at least it wasn't touching my skin. But it was only a millimetre difference. She said to me that we'd talk and then she'd cut my throat.'

Joseph rubbed his neck as if he was remembering the feel of the knife against his skin.

'Go on, you're doing fine,' said Detective Renton.

'As we were standing there, there was a loud bang at the end of the street and a boy walked past. We were both distracted, she jumped at the noise and she'd moved the knife away from me, I then took the opportunity. I grabbed her wrist and pulled it as hard as I could, but she wouldn't let go of the knife. I had hold of her wrist and managed to pull and twist her arm, yet she still wouldn't let go. I shouted at her to drop the knife. I just wanted her to drop the knife and I was going to run away. But she struggled. We scuffled and I had hold of her wrist worried that she would stab me. We both lost our balance and she fell.' Joseph started sobbing. 'I fell on top of her. The knife went into her. It went right into her stomach.' Joseph used his sleeve to wipe his eyes.

'She went limp. She gurgled, there was blood everywhere. I panicked. I should've called an ambulance but I was so scared I ran. I was just defending myself; she was going to kill me. I've never been so scared.'

'Is there anything else?' asked Detective Renton.

Joseph put his hands on his cheeks and shook his head from side to side as though in disbelief, the tears still pouring from his eyes. 'I've had nightmares ever since. I didn't know she'd died. I thought someone might have found her and called an ambulance. I lost the plot.' Joseph got very distressed saying he did not mean it; he started shouting that he had acted in self-defence, that it was an accident.

'I cannot believe I've killed someone,' he said. 'I didn't mean to kill her, please believe me, it was a mistake.' Joseph sat there sobbing into his hands, his shoulders heaving up and down with the force of his grief.

The detectives sat in silence, then the solicitor spoke. 'This isn't murder it's self-defence. The murder charge should be dropped.' He didn't say it but he expected the police to charge Joseph with manslaughter.

Detective Lansbury said that he and Detective Renton needed to speak to a senior officer. He asked the solicitor and Joseph to remain in the room and then switched off the recorder. The detectives needed to speak to the psychologists and then to the State Prosecution Service.

The rest of the police station had become aware that the murder enquiry was entering its last stages. These cases, particularly toward the end, created an atmosphere like no other at the station; there was a palpable tension in the air. The other officers watched every movement in and out of the interview room. They watched as the two detectives came out and walked along the corridor. It was clear to everyone from their body language, that the two detectives had got a confession.

The detectives were on an adrenaline high. They would be in the papers; they would be heroes on the force for a short while. The stats would be up. But they had to speak to the psychologists first.

The detectives went into another room, the two psychologists stood up as the detectives entered.

The psychologists reported that they thought Joseph was telling the truth. They had analysed the interviews they said and there was 95% likelihood that Joseph was telling the truth. Detective Lansbury was irritated with the psychologists; they were getting paid to state the obvious. What really irked the detective, though, was they had an air about them that suggested they thought they were more important than the detectives.

The officers left the psychologists and went in to a small room. They had some influence on what to charge Joseph with. Although elated with the confession, they weren't entirely happy with the situation. They wanted to charge Frederick. They knew that a murder charge probably wouldn't stick, but they had really been hoping they would get two convictions for the price of one. It would've given them the best statistics in the department. They argued with each other about the way forward. They thought Joseph was telling the truth, but debated whether to drop the charge from murder to the lesser one of manslaughter, the one more likely to stick. But it would mean their performance reviews would suffer and it would mean less kudos for the department.

If they ignored the psychologists and tried and make the murder charge stick, Joseph would have to fight it in court. Even if the courts convicted him of manslaughter, they would have done well. If however, they went for a manslaughter charge at this stage, Joseph could get off with self-defence in court, and then they will not have reached their case targets. The detectives made up their minds. The inspector would go for murder; he was obsessed with targets.

While the detectives debated, Joseph was talking to his solicitor. He wanted to plead self-defence in court. His solicitor agreed. He believed Joseph was telling the truth, there was no reason he wouldn't be.

After some time, the detectives returned to the interview room. They asked Joseph to come with them. They took Joseph to the duty desk. The office was unusually quiet. Everyone watched as the custody sergeant formally read Joseph his rights and then told him he was charged with first-degree murder.

Joseph felt as though the breath had been sucked out of him. 'No! It was self-defence. You can't do this.'

The custody sergeant ordered two officers to take him down to the cell.

'I'm not a murderer' Joseph shouted repeatedly on the way to the cell, 'I'm not a murderer.'

The following day Frederick read in the newspaper that a man in his early 20s had been charged with the murder of Lidia Smyth. Frederick wept as he read the newspaper article. After he had calmed down, he felt relieved. He could now concentrate on proving his innocence over the number 3 risk rating. He had formulated a kind of plan.

Chapter 47

Ten months had gone by and the trial still had not taken place. The body was in the morgue and the police would not release it until after the trial. Frederick had to give a statement, but the police told him that he was not a suspect; it was a huge relief to Frederick that he was not involved in the trial beyond the statement.

Over the past ten months, Frederick had changed. He had adapted to his new life, which seemed better than it had for many years. He felt happier than he had in a long time. The only cloud on his horizon was that he could not know where his children were, or even see them.

He no longer felt the anger or turmoil inside that he had held for so long. He now enjoyed his life. He had more insight about himself than he ever had before. He understood that the shock of losing everything, even possibly his liberty, had humbled him. He had humility now that had never existed when he worked for the Department.

Frederick started work as a canner, a job he would have looked down on in the past. He even got involved in the Can Opener movement. He had long discussions with Jane and her friends, which, over time, had widened his view of the world. He had also been involved in taking action over the minimum wage and been on protests. For the first time he understood some of the views Iris had. He could see that there was exploitation and agreed that the world was made up of classes, that those at the top of society were there due to that exploitation. Frederick opened himself up to new ideas. He could not now believe what he had done at the Dependency Unit. He now felt embarrassed about having been a Development Planner. If someone offered him that job back, he would not want it.

He also became very close to Jane, but he couldn't bring himself to ever tell her what he used to do and how he had gone after people whom he only knew as numbers. He had been a coward; he had made people's lives miserable and had hidden behind as the numbers to make it easier to victimise them for their poverty.

He had, however, told Jane about the abuse he had suffered as a child, how frightened he had been and how he could never speak to his mother about it for fear it would wreck the family. He told Jane that he felt that he would probably not have been believed anyway and would've got the blame for causing trouble. He wondered if this had been the reason why he had lost faith in humanity, but he had learned since being with Jane that everyone has history, personal or otherwise, and it shouldn't be allowed to determine their future.

When he had worked for the Dependency Unit, Frederick had trusted no one. He had thought everyone was cheating the State and he had gone on a moral crusade. The Department had encouraged him to act that way. He had truly believed that the customers were consciously making lifestyle choices. He had blamed the smokers for smoking, the drinkers for drinking, and he had blamed the obese for their obesity. He had categorised people so they could be put into separate groups and scapegoated whenever it was convenient.

Since getting to know Jane's friends, Frederick had learned that Iris had been involved in campaigning activity for many years starting with the Occupy movement. Iris had explained it to him the slogan of 1% and 99%. A few had the power and they used that power to exploit the rest. Frederick started to think about the world and opened his mind up to new possibilities. He could see that humans had only achieved anything when they had acted together.

The Can Openers were one of the most democratic organisations he had ever been involved with. When the Can Openers had challenged their own union leaders and Dibble, it had been like watching flowers grow from seeds.

Frederick had learnt that democracy grew when people took power in their own hands instead of handing it to others and then sitting back while those people made all the decisions. The ones in power relied on those beneath them not having the confidence to challenge things. In every way, the powerful try and make the powerless believe they are inferior. As Iris would say, 'it's ideology, you know.'

Frederick listened to these discussions and started to feel happier. He could not believe that he ever was at the Dependency Unit or been part of their activities. He felt much calmer and had even got a solicitor from Mr Take's firm to help him fight the Dependency Unit for his children, but so far without success.

Frederick didn't know that the Can Opener movement was starting to have an effect at the Dependency Unit. He didn't know that some workers there had started to question the values of the Unit. He did know, however, from his own recent experience, that when you start to question an organisation that is highly autocratic, it could have an impact out of proportion to the question itself. Frederick was now Kevin the Can Opener.

Chapter 48

Something else had happened to Frederick recently that would have a big effect on his life. Ten days prior, he was coming out of the supermarket when he had bumped into Herbert's wife, Sophie. He had said hello and spoke to her. She hadn't recognised him at first; he looked younger, different. Sophie then realised who it was and hadn't wanted to speak to him. But, being Sophie, she did not want to be seen as impolite. They felt awkward at first.

'I'm pleased we bumped into each other,' said Frederick. Sophie nodded and then smiled. There was a brief, uncomfortable silence. He decided to say what he wanted to say to her, before the opportunity was missed. 'Look' he said gently, 'we both know what happened to my wife and I would like to tell you more. Can we meet?'

Sophie wanted to tell him to get lost but, at the same time, he didn't seem to be anything like the Frederick she knew previously. Sophie was having a difficult time with Herbert, nothing had been the same after she had gone to the police; their relationship had become very strained. Sophie considered telling Frederick that he had treated Lidia badly, she wanted to call him a bastard but she couldn't. He intrigued her.

When she finally agreed to meet Frederick, he bombarded her with text messages about when they were going to meet. She finally agreed to meet him in a café bar.

Frederick had got there fifteen minutes early. The café had a relaxed atmosphere with soft lighting. There was one other couple sitting at the bar.

Can Openers

Frederick started to worry that Sophie may not come, but she arrived fifteen minutes late. She came in and said hello to Frederick. She went to the bar and bought herself a drink. She made sure the drinks were brought separately. After all, they weren't friends.

Frederick asked Sophie how she was keeping, trying to keep the tone light.

'I'm surviving.' she replied.

Frederick started the conversation by apologising. He apologised for the way he acted and the way he had approached his life. He told her about the Dependency Unit and the Victorian attitude he had had towards his family, and Lidia in particular. He spoke for a while. Sophie thought that she would hate him. However, the more he spoke, the more she warmed to him. Sophie wanted to ask Frederick questions about Lidia. But first she told him that she helped Lidia.

Frederick interrupted Sophie. He told her that whatever Lidia had said about him was the truth. 'I lost my humanity, I became detached,' he said. 'But I've had time to think. I had lost touch with reality, the department had become my reality.'

'Did you know about her self-harming? Did you know how very unhappy she had been?' Sophie asked.

'I am to blame. I had become a robot,' he said.

Frederick than began talking about his children. 'Sophie, I would never hurt my children. I love them so much. I miss them.' Sophie knew that Frederick had been a good dad; it was the one good thing Lidia had ever said about him.

Sophie asked about Joseph. The discussion was frank and honest. They were waiting for the trial. Towards the end of the conversation, Frederick told Sophie how desperate he was to find out why they had been put on a number 3 risk rating and lost the children. He told her how hard he had tried to find out what happened but had gotten nowhere.

'Do you think Herbert could help me?' Sophie looked blankly at him so he backtracked. 'I understand if you don't want to ask him. I know I've acted like a monster in the past, but I've changed. Maybe I deserve everything I get but please will you help?' Sophie still didn't answer; Frederick tried again. 'I did love Lidia but it became distorted, the love became oppressive.'

Sophie couldn't tell Frederick that Hebert was conducting an ongoing investigation on him. She hadn't been interested since the death of Lidia but now, having met Frederick and knowing Lidia as she had, she believed that neither of them would harm their children. She started to become curious and suspicious about why they had ended up with a number 3 risk rating.

'I'll see what I can do,' said Sophie, finally. 'Give me some time. I can't make any promises, but I'll try and help you. I'll contact you if I find anything out.'

The meeting with Sophie was so important to Frederick. However, a few days later, another significant event happened that Frederick hadn't anticipated.

Jane and Iris were helping to organise a public meeting about the Dibble Homes. The meeting was to expose how badly both the residents and staff were being treated. The Can Openers were involved, along with various staff and Dibble Home residents.

Frederick listened to Jane and Iris discussing the meeting, what he heard had changed his views completely. He realised that Dignity in Old Age was a con, that the injection was nothing more than a way of culling the elderly. Frederick also learned from Jane and Iris that the homes were run solely for profit, there was no staff care and the pay didn't amount to a living wage. Everyone was exploited.

What Frederick learned about the Dibble Homes reinforced his anger at the system. Part of his anger was because he had been conned for years by the Department, it ruined his life. What tempered his anger was his belief that the movement he was now involved in was honest, a force for positive change.

The Dignity In Old Age option was nothing more than state murder. He agreed with what Iris said about the Dependency Unit using words like "choice". Frederick understood that choice wasn't something that could be handed down from above. He now believed that real choice only ever existed when it was fought for.

In this system, Frederick thought, choice represented little more than being presented with a set of options that the powerful deemed to be suitable. Frederick had started to understand the Dependency Unit, like all other State departments, had a role to play in making choice seem real.

Can Openers

Frederick now understood that the Dependency Unit had been developed as part of the response to a crisis in the economic system. It blamed the poor for their situation, thus making it easier to justify the rationing of welfare. According to Iris, Frederick was starting to think and act like a socialist.

Frederick had only ever been to one public meeting before and it had had no impact on him. At the time he had been in utter despair, just after having been sacked, and the meeting had offered him no hope at all.

However, this meeting was going to be different and Frederick wanted to support Jane, especially as she was one of the main speakers. They were all excited about the meeting. It was very unusual to have the General Secretary of the National Union and one of the main organisers of the Can Openers on the same platform. There were also speakers from local groups and Dibble Home residents. The meeting was to take place in an old hall in the centre of town.

Frederick hadn't realised how important Jane's role was in organising the Can Openers, or that the movement had started in Jane's workplace and that it had been Jane who, with her arguments and passion, had given confidence to her colleagues.

Jane left early for the meeting; she wanted to get there early to have enough time to prepare herself. Frederick arrived later with Iris.

He went up steps to the hall and went past people giving out leaflets and selling papers. The meeting must have had several hundred people in attendance, it hadn't yet started but already nearly all the seats were filled. Frederick found a seat in the second row from the back, wondering what to expect.

From where he sat he could see the entire old hall. He noticed a familiar-looking couple walk in together. He could not believe it, it was Marcus and Joyce. Fortunately he was sat near the back and they didn't appear to have seen him. He watched as they walked towards the front. Frederick felt weird. He had never thought that the Can Openers would hold any interest to people in his old department. He thought he knew the effect that working in the department had on people, that Dependency Unit staff were blinkered.

Frederick slumped down in his chair and held a leaflet up to his face as if he was reading it very closely. He knew there was a chance that they probably would not have recognised him now anyway, he wore glasses, his hair was longer, and he dressed differently. Even so, Frederick was nervous and uncomfortable. He had treated Joyce and Marcus abysmally in the past. How could he begin to explain to them his life after leaving the Dependency Unit? Who would believe him?

Frederick had different views about life and the system now, but he wasn't going to express them publicly, he wasn't that confident yet. If he had been he would've talked about the illusion of choice.

Frederick considered telling Jane what he used to do for a living. As he sat there watching her on the platform getting ready to speak, he thought that maybe he needed to tell her sooner rather than later. He needed to tell her how wrong he had been and that being with her and her friends has changed him for the better.

He listened to the speeches but was preoccupied with how he would tell Jane about his previous life. When Jane got up to speak he listened to her more intently than he had the others.

She spoke about power and how it needs to be democratised. 'Everyone should have power,' she said. 'The Can Openers have shown the way for mass democracy.' There was a round of loud applause. 'What I want to see is a world where the priority is peoples' needs and not profit.' When she had stopped speaking Jane got a standing ovation. Frederick glanced at Marcus and Joyce sitting near the front. He spent the rest of the meeting making sure they didn't see him.

As the meeting ended he spotted Jane talking to Joyce and Marcus. He slipped out of the hall wondering why Jane was talking to them; he was a little paranoid about it. He still had some of the tendencies of the past but tried hard to overcome his previous complete distrust of people. He had to keep what he described as his dark side under control.

Frederick went back to Jane's house. He stayed up so he could tell her what a brilliant speech she had made. He wanted to tell her how about himself, that he had been part of the Dependency unit. He had told Jane at least two thirds of his history, now he wanted to tell her the rest. He knew it would be a risk; he would have to take whatever her response might be.

Can Openers

He had lived with Jane long enough for her not to judge him just on his past but to look at the position he was in at the present and how he was dealing with his life. He heard one of Jane's friends say on a previous occasion, 'You can't change your past but you can change the present, the past has an effect but it does not necessarily determine your future.'

Chapter 49

Marcus and Joyce had moved in together over the last year. Their relationship had deepened and together they had become involved in organising workers at the Dependency Unit. They had also supported wider issues, like the campaign against the lethal injection in old age, and they supported the Dibble workers' minimum wage campaign.

Joyce had come to be seen by other Opportunity Planners as a Can Opener. Joyce and Marcus had wanted to see the leader of the Can Openers and hear her speak because they had been told what a brilliant orator she was. They were shocked when they saw her and realised that it was the same person they had assessed as Case Number A1201a. They did not grasp it was the same Jane; she used both her maiden name and her married name inter-changeably.

As Jane got up to speak, she noticed Joyce and Marcus sitting in one of the rows of chairs close to the front. She wondered whether Joyce was there as a spy. She was determined to go up to them at the end of the meeting and confront them.

As soon as the meeting was over, Jane pointed them out to Iris and said she thought they might be spies. Iris, however, knew them. She told Jane that Marcus had been working for years with the group who opposed the lethal injection. He had often passed information on to them, even though it put him in great danger of not only losing his job but of receiving a custodial sentence. Joyce, explained Iris, had more recently gotten involved in the movement and had tried to stop the Dependency Unit from taking money off customers who were

Can Openers

in severe hardship. She been caught recently, but fortunately had not been dismissed.

'I'll go over and speak to them,' Jane said. As Jane walked towards them, they got nervous and jumpy, like two cats being approached by a German shepherd.

Straight away, Jane reminded them they had met before when they were assessing her. She thanked them for coming to the meeting and explained how pleased she was that they had become Can Openers. She shook their hands and left.

Jane got home late and Frederick was waiting up. He said that he thought her speech had been brilliant. Jane had found it quite an unusual experience; she had did not realise how extensive the Can Openers movement had become or who had become involved. She told Frederick that she had spotted two people in the crowd who had assessed her when she had been a customer with the Dependency Unit. The woman still worked at the Unit and was now a Can Opener.

'I never told you,' said Jane, looking down, 'my husband died of cancer. This person, Joyce, came to my house and assessed me. She put me through hell, but fortunately I was seen as a dependency figure and it enabled me to have enough cash to live on.' Jane paused and looked up. 'I had always thought that this Joyce was a jobsworth, but she came to the meeting with a guy called Marcus, who had been the other assessor. That had been one of the worst times of my life. I even saved this.' She went to a cupboard drawer and pulled out some papers.

'I kept everything. Did you know that the Dependency Unit don't treat you as a person, they treat you as a number? I can remember mine by heart, it was A1021a,' she said laughing.

Frederick's mouth dropped open with shock. Of all the people who had supported him, that had given hope in the world when all he could see was despair, and saved him from possible suicide, it was the same person who had kept him awake at night, the same person he had spent trying to get her self-reliant so his figures would gain him a promotion. He rubbed his forehead and told Jane that he had a headache and was going to bed.

Frederick was shaken. He could hardly believe it, this woman who he was so fond of, was probably in love with even though he would never admit it to himself, had turned out to be Case Number A1201a. He had finally met her.

A dark and terrible cloud settled over Frederick. What he had done back then had been a terrible thing; he hadn't seen people as human beings but as customers with numbers and treated them accordingly. All he had seen was products to be manipulated. He thought of himself as a monster and wondered how others would see him.

Although he was scared of telling Jane the truth about his past for fear of what her reaction would be, he knew he couldn't keep it secret forever. He may come across Joyce and Marcus again. It would be far better to tell Jane than let her find out by accident.

Chapter 50

Herbert was sitting at his desk. He had just been to get a sandwich for lunch when the phone rang. It was Phil.

'I need to see you urgently,' said Phil. 'I've got information that will help you and might solve your investigation. Can I come and see you?'

Herbert was more than interested. 'Can you come now?' he asked.

'I'll be at your office in one hour.'

An hour later Phil arrived with a small suitcase full of files. Phil showed Herbert the files and told him that everything he needed to know was in them. Herbert could see that Phil was nervous.

'I've put my head on the block for this,' said Phil. 'We've not had this meeting, I've not given you them.' He pointed at the files. At that Phil got up and left, shutting the office door behind him before Herbert could even respond.

Herbert wanted to read the files straight away but he wouldn't be able to concentrate in the office. He decided to take the files home and read them there.

Sophie was there when he arrived home. Their relationship had gone from cool to icy. In the past she would've given him a hug when he arrived home, not anymore since what happened to Lidia. They were courteous to one another, but acted as flatmates rather than lovers. Even so, Sophie noticed that Herbert looked preoccupied.

'You look excited about something,' she said.

Because of this rare interest, he opened up to her. 'The answers I've been looking for are in here, I must read these papers.' As soon as he said it he regretted it, but then quickly decided it wouldn't matter. Sophie was scared of him these days, she knew better now and wouldn't give confidential information to anyone. Anyway, he thought, who does she know who would want it?

Herbert went to his small study upstairs with the bundle of files. Sophie realised that Herbert must have information in the files about why Frederick and Lidia had ended up on a number 3 risk rating. Sophie also knew where Herbert kept the spare key for the safe where he often kept confidential information. Sophie rarely had any reason to go to the safe but, since her relationship had deteriorated with Herbert, she no longer cared. It would be useful to find out if there was any information in that safe that she needed.

Herbert settled down with his files. Once he'd had a sense of justice but it eroded over time. Ambition had gotten the better of him, ambition had worn down Herbert's sense of justice, but it was greed that had killed it off entirely.

Chapter 51

Frederick had started the day after the meeting with Jane feeling apprehensive, steadily going to downright nervous.

Jane had been at work all day and they met in the kitchen. She wanted to tell him about something that had happened at work that day which she thought was strange.

'The manager on my section and someone else I didn't recognise asked me in for a meeting. They said it wasn't a union meeting or a Can Opener meeting and that I would be OK attending on my own.' Jane was so excited and couldn't wait to tell him. 'They asked me, of all people, if I would be interested in a management position.' She laughed.

There was a knock on the front door, one of Jane's children ran to answer it and Iris walked in. She came into the kitchen, a big smile on her face; she told Jane how well her speech had gone down and how happy she was that they had organised the meeting.

Jane was pleased. She told Iris that she had been offered a management position, that they had explained it would be a new post; her job title would be Management Care. 'They'll double my salary.'

Iris and Frederick looked at each other and then looked at Jane, but didn't speak.

'Shall I tell you what they said?' asked Jane.

'I'm all ears,' said Iris, quietly.

'They started off by saying how important for Dibble the Can Openers movement had become, that they had learnt from it. They said one of the major themes that had come from the Can Openers, as far as they were concerned, was that they had not been a fair employer. Can you believe it?' asked Jane. 'They went on to tell me that they hadn't looked after their main asset, their staff. They want to officially recognise the Can Openers. What they want me to do is work with staff regarding their welfare and support. They want me to develop policies and equality opportunity schemes, and look at the jobs so they can be evaluated to make sure that everyone gets a fair pay.' Jane told Iris and Frederick that she thought that they might have won.

'Why didn't you tell them to get lost?' Frederick asked.

'I told them I'd consider it and get back to them,' said Jane.

'You should have told them to get lost,' Iris said, angrily. 'While them bastards run the company, fair and equal procedures is about taking power away from the Can Openers. We will have a say on the policies only if you stay as our leader.'

'They also said that they'll give secondments to the Can Openers so they can work fulltime for the union,' said Jane. 'Look, Iris, we have to be practical here, they're not only recognising us, they're letting us have an equal say in policy.'

Iris stood up, her hands on her hips, 'They're trying to cut the head off the Can Openers, don't you realise?' she almost shouted at Jane. 'There's no such thing as fair pay for a day's work.'

Jane looked puzzled.

'Look,' said Iris, 'we create the wealth for Dibble and they steal it. That is not fair. They still own us at work.'

'We have to be pragmatic,' said Jane, 'I'm going to take the offer back to the Can Openers and see what they say.' Jane looked directly at Iris. 'It's our strength, we've forced them to change.'

Iris shook her head. 'These policies and procedures just involve doing things to individuals; nothing will change. We've got them to back off but now they just want to tame us and get us to operate on their terms. They want the workforce as separate individuals rather than as the collective. Don't you realise that everyone who goes over to management changes and either becomes like the rest of them or has a breakdown? They have to take part in efficiency savings and cuts, creating competition amongst the workers so they are scrapping with one another for the crumbs. There's a cost to the managers in terms of their own emotional and psychological health.' Iris paused and then said, 'or they just become bastards.'

Can Openers

Frederick nodded. He, himself, had changed in more ways than one, he had become Kevin.

Chapter 52

Herbert had spent the rest of the day reading the files. What he read shocked him. He thought about Frederick's life. How, after being given a number 3 risk rating, he had probably lost everything. Herbert wondered how he managed to survive. He still found it hard to believe and accept that Frederick had an affair with Joseph, though.

Herbert was pleased he had put pressure on, and threatened, Phil. As a result, he found out things about Phil that would compromise his job if the Department got wind of it. With this hanging over him, Phil thought he had no choice but to go outside the normal procedure so he could get the information Herbert wanted.

Herbert read files well into the night, barely sleeping. He'd made copies of the files and stored them safely. He had written a set of notes of their contents and those would form the basis of a report for Lord Dibble. Herbert also kept a copy of the summary notes, just in case he needed them.

Sophie guessed that there was something important in the files. Herbert looked tired and worried. She couldn't understand why, since he found out what happened to Frederick. He'd been working on the case for more than a year so he should be relieved.

'Have you finished your investigation?' she asked.

'Yes. But I can't divulge any information. Besides, the documents didn't have much to offer anyway,' he said. He was much calmer than she had expected him to be.

When Herbert went to work, Sophie checked the safe. There were no documents and no files. He must have taken them to work. Sophie didn't believe Herbert, she was certain the files were important. He must have found out why Frederick and Lidia had been put been on a number 3 risk rating.

Sophie didn't give in. The following day when Herbert went to work, she checked inside the safe again. This time, a file was inside. Sophie took out the file and started to read. She became increasingly shocked. She decided to photocopy the whole thing. After she copied the file, she read it again, this time more slowly, taking in the contents and finally grasping what had happened.

Sophie texted Frederick to let him know that she had information and could she meet him as soon as possible. Frederick texted back to say he could meet the next day but, as he was working in the morning, they had to meet at the café in the afternoon. Sophie agreed.

When Herbert came home later that evening, Sophie had decided to cook Hungarian goulash for tea. This was something of a departure, she hadn't cooked for him for a long time, they led had almost separate lives. This, however, was his favourite dish. While Sophie was in the kitchen, he went to her handbag and took out her mobile phone. He had never done this before but the trust between them had become so strained.

He took the phone into the bathroom and locked the door. Herbert was nervous – this wasn't the kind of thing he would normally do. He was actually sweating. Sophie called out that dinner was nearly ready.

'I'm just having a quick bath,' he shouted back. He went through the recent messages, both received and sent. She shouted something again. Herbert got out of the bathroom and put the phone back before she started to suspect something.

He slipped out of the bathroom, crept up to his office, and opened the safe. Herbert was puzzled, something was wrong but he couldn't work out what it was. He suddenly realised that he had left the document face down. Could Sophie have found the spare key to the safe?

He went into the bedroom and quickly changed his clothes. He went downstairs into the dining room. They sat at the table. Herbert looked at her. Sophie was calmly eating her dinner.

'I know you're in contact with Frederick,' Herbert said suddenly and quietly.

Sophie dropped her knife and fork in surprise; they clanged on the plate, the noise only serving to emphasise the cold silence that had grown. Sophie didn't like lying to Herbert; she had come to fear the consequences.

'Yes, it's true,' she confessed.

'Why are you meeting him tomorrow?' he asked menacingly.

'I don't have to tell you,' she said.

Herbert slammed his hand on the table making Sophie jump. 'I demand to know why you are meeting him!' he shouted.

Sophie got frightened. She couldn't look at Herbert. With her head down, she hesitated before replying. 'Frederick has changed; he regrets what happened to him. He seems like a completely different person. He just wants to know why his children were taken from him; he wants to know if Lidia caused them harm or if they think he did. He just wants information about his own life.' Sophie regretted she had let this slip out.

'What have you found out then, Sophie?' he asked, a sharp edge to his calmness.

'Nothing,' she lied fearfully.

'I know you've been in my safe,' he said.

'Yes,' said Sophie, 'but I only did it for a favour, to help someone out.'

Herbert curled his lip. 'Like you tried to help out Lidia?' Sophie started to cry. Herbert held his hands up. 'I'm sorry,' he said.

He went over to Sophie and put his arm around her shoulder. This time Herbert spoke soothingly. 'I'm not angry, I'm sorry for shouting. I feel sorry for Frederick.' Herbert seemed sincere, but years of doing investigations had made him able to put an act on when needed to get information out of people. Sophie had come to learn this about Herbert, so she couldn't be sure if he was being genuine.

Sophie stopped crying, wiped her eyes, and told Herbert apologetically that she had read the report and had arranged to meet Frederick to tell him what it said.

Can Openers

'Well, he has a right to know,' Herbert said. 'I'll come with you. We can tell him together. Come on, there has been enough misery this year, we'll do this together.'

Sophie looked up at Herbert and felt that they had a connection, for the first time in months.

Herbert helped Sophie clear and wash the dishes; they talked until late in to the night. Later they made love.

The following day, Herbert couldn't concentrate at work. He left the office mid afternoon and walked around the shops. He needed to calm himself before the meeting with Frederick and Sophie.

Herbert got to the café fifteen minutes early and sat in the far corner out of the way, he could see people coming in the café but they wouldn't easily be able to see him. Sophie arrived, sat down at a table, and waited. Frederick arrived a short while later, Sophie waved to him, and he went over to her and sat down. Frederick was excited, worried, and apprehensive all at the same time. He needed to know what information Sophie had.

Sophie then explained about Herbert. 'I told him you're a changed person and I think he believes me. He wants to tell you himself the information he found. I think you can trust him.'

Frederick had little choice but to agree if he wanted to know what information they had.

Sophie dropped her phone on the floor. As they both bent down to pick it up, Sophie passed Frederick some papers, a copy of the report.

Herbert hadn't seen Sophie pass anything to Frederick. He went over and joined them after a short time. He felt awkward but knew he was doing the right thing. He asked Frederick how he was.

'I'm OK.' Frederick was bemused, the situation felt surreal.

Herbert decided to get to the point. 'I've found out why you and your family ended up with a number 3 risk rating. I have to say I was shocked.'

Frederick stared at Herbert; he thought that if Herbert didn't tell him immediately, he was going to burst.

'I can tell you why you've not been able to get any feedback for over a year from the department. Would you like me to go through the file first?' Herbert asked.

'Yes, yes please,' said Frederick trying not to sound impatient. Frederick had to shake off a feeling that he was starting to act the way he had when he worked at the Dependency Unit, subservient to his superiors. He didn't want to be seen or treated as second class anymore. 'I have a right to know, what happened wrecked my life. It cost me my children and my job. It's a scandal. Why? If there's any justice then I've got a right to know what happened.'

'OK,' said Herbert. 'But you need to stop shouting, it's drawing attention to us. What you're asking me to do is not Department policy, you know that. I'm going outside the rules.'

Frederick looked at Herbert, willing him to continue.

Herbert straightened up in his seat. 'I'll read you the report regarding the output analysis from the empirical evidence. I will read you the feedback from the system itself,' said Herbert, somewhat self-importantly. 'It says that the customer in this case cannot appeal. There is to be no further contact between the Dependency Unit and the person C421 or any of his family unit. C421 is you, Frederick.'

Herbert took a sip of his coffee. 'The report says that this is because the case has been proven one hundred percent. The reason is because C421 accepted that a Level 3 response was needed, therefore C421 was put on a number 3 risk rating and his children were removed. No further contact is needed, case proven.'

Frederick frowned. He couldn't understand it, it was baffling.

Herbert could tell from Frederick's expression that he was struggling to understand the situation. 'I can explain what has been done; I've read the whole file. In easy terms, the fact is that when you were a development manager, you pressed the number 3 on yourself and your family.'

'I still don't understand,' said Frederick.

'OK, listen,' said Herbert. 'A teacher at your children's school overheard one of your children say to another child that her daddy was going to kill her. To be honest, from what I understand, you were just playing with your kids, one weekend.

'About the same time, in the Department, there was a mad rush on meeting targets. The case, for some reason, came to you; you signed it off as a number 3 risk rating but didn't realise the case related to you and your family. From what we can ascertain, it is clear that if anyone had looked at the case thoroughly, it would *not* have gone to a number 3 risk rating. Unfortunately, the system does not recognise human error. The program saw that you had agreed for your own children to be taken from you. The program is set up in such a way that when a person accepts that he or a family member has significantly harmed the children, a number 3 is activated.'

Frederick was stunned. He couldn't speak or move. He could not believe he had made a mistake like that, and he was responsible for the children being removed. He remembered the rush on meeting targets. The pressure they had been under had been unbearably intense. They had had to work late, even through their lunch breaks, to get through the cases, upload the data, and meet the targets within the deadline. It had reached a point where Frederick was just signing off cases without really looking at them, he had agreed to anything that came across his desk. He had been obsessed with meeting the targets and getting his figures up. How many others had he put through the same fate and the same grief just by agreeing a rating without looking first?

Sophie and Herbert looked at each other and then looked at Frederick, waiting for him to say something.

Frederick didn't say anything. He reflected on his fate over the last year. He had nearly been locked up for murder, his wife was dead, and his children were gone. His life had been ruined; and it had been his fault, he thought with horror.

Herbert broke the silence. 'I've been asked to go for the promotion,' he said. 'I think I'll get it. I'll see what I can do to help. Maybe we can meet at your house and discuss options.'

Frederick nodded. Herbert said they may have to wait until after the court case to meet, but they would be in touch. With that, they left the café.

Frederick was numb. He found it hard to accept that he had been that monster. He felt tortured by the one question he couldn't answer, 'Why didn't I check? Why? Why? Why?'

As he walked from the café, Frederick started to calm down to think about what Herbert had told him. 'I have to be pragmatic. I may not be able to get Lidia back, but perhaps with Herbert's help I can get the children back. If I can get the kids back, it might go some way to making amends.' He might also feel more relaxed about the world, he might see hope where before he just saw despair. Maybe, just maybe, he had a future.

Chapter 53

Herbert and Sophie left the café before Frederick. Sophie linked her arm with Herbert's. She thanked him. Herbert looked at her and smiled, but he was far from happy. Herbert felt depressed, like he had sold his soul to the devil.

The day before Herbert and Sophie met Frederick, Herbert attended a meeting. It was no ordinary meeting.

That day Herbert had left home early. Sophie thought he had gone to work, she didn't know he had taken leave. Instead he had gone to what was probably the most important meeting of his life. He arrived in London two hours later.

Herbert waited outside Baker Street Tube station. He had received an e-mail instructing him to wait there, that someone called Sed would meet him. After a short wait, a young-looking man arrived and introduced himself as Sed. He didn't shake Herbert's hand. He waited for Herbert to confirm his name before saying curtly, 'Come with me.'

They walked in silence, Herbert following Sed along various streets. They came to the local university, into a quiet building. Herbert was worried, the last time he had attended the meeting it had taken place in a completely different building. This was all a bit cloak and dagger.

'I need to frisk you,' Sed said apologetically. Herbert felt like he was going through airport security. Sed asked for Herbert's mobile phone and watch, promising they would be returned when he was finished. Herbert knew better than to argue with someone like Sed. Herbert couldn't quite place Sed's accent but could tell he was of Eastern European descent, and built like a Russian weightlifter. Herbert did as he was told.

'We have to make sure you're not followed. I'm sure you can appreciate why,' he said

Herbert nodded.

Sed then indicated towards a door. Herbert walked over, opened it, and he and Sed entered a small room. It looked like an abandoned student residence. Herbert was instructed to leave all his personal belongings in this room, including his clothes and shoes. They had other clothes for him, oddly enough in the correct size. Herbert put them on. When he was ready, they left the room. Sed gave him a keycard so Herbert could get his belongings when he returned later.

They made their way by tube to Canary Wharf. It was now midday; the meeting was to take place at 12.30 pm. They reached a skyscraper building that seemed to be made entirely from dark mirrored glass. They went into the building and up to a bank of lifts. They took one to the fourteenth floor.

The lift opened to an entryway leading to offices rented by a multinational company. It was decorated in a modern, minimalist style. Herbert was taken to a reception area.

'I've got to go. You will have to wait until they call you,' Sed said.

Herbert took a seat. A TV screen came on opposite to where Herbert was sitting. A face appeared and said that they were ready for him. A door opened to the side of the reception area. Herbert stood up and went into the room.

Herbert had met the people in the room before, but he had always met them on a one-to-one basis, never all together.

Three men sat behind a vast desk. The man in the middle smiled a shark-like smile. 'Hello, Herbert, help yourself to biscuits and coffee, or some to sandwiches at the back of the room.'

The room was huge. Herbert went over to a sideboard and poured himself some coffee.

The man in the middle spoke with an American accent, built like an American footballer. His arms were as big as tree trunks and he had a bulldog face with a thick neck. He looked as if he could pick Herbert up, tuck him under one arm, and carry him around. He reminded Herbert of a bear.

'How're ya doing?' the bear asked.

'Fine, thank you,' Herbert replied politely.

'We're all very happy, very happy indeed, with the information you have obtained for us,' said the bear.

'Yes, I want to talk about that,' Herbert said.

'No problem,' the bear said. Herbert was always nervous around this man; he was ex CIA and very well connected.

'We're so pleased with you,' the executive-looking man in an armani suit said. 'Do you have any more news on Dibble's plans for A1201a? How is your investigation going? We were glad to find out that your rival, Joseph, is now in prison. This means certain promotion for you.'

Herbert told the three men that he had some more information regarding the outcome of the Smyth investigation. Then he paused, unsure of how to say what he wanted to say. Finally, he blurted, 'I want out. I don't want to be involved anymore; I've given enough. '

The bear leaned his head back against his chair's headrest and looked down at Herbert. 'Now, now, now, Herbert,' he said patronisingly. 'That kind of talk won't get us anywhere. Give us the information we want and then we will then consider your request.'

Angry, Herbert stood up. 'I want out now. I don't want it to be considered. I'll walk,' he said.

'Sit down,' commanded the bear. Despite his anger, Herbert sat down straight away. 'We want the information now.' There was a clear threat in the ex-CIA man's voice.

Herbert sighed and then proceeded to tell them what he knew.

'Smyth had pressed the number 3 on himself,' he said. And he told the three men what else was in the file.

Mr Executive said again how pleased they were with him. The third man hadn't spoken yet, but from the way the bear and the executive kept looking at him, he seemed to be the leader.

'We're very impressed with the way you dealt with Joseph,' the bear said.

'All I did was what you asked of me. You asked me to make sure that Sophie got the information about Joseph so she would pass this on to Lidia,' Herbert replied.

'We're most pleased with the outcome. We have always wanted our spy to be at the top of the Dibble tree and, with Joseph out of the way, there's nothing stopping you. We just wanted to discredit Joseph, but setting him up for murder was pure genius,' said the executive.

'I didn't know that Joseph would kill Lidia,' explained Herbert, anxiously. 'All I was expecting was a bit of a scandal and for him to be discredited.'

'Well,' said the executive, 'you leaked the information and the outcome exceeded our expectations. Now, we have some information for you.'

The executive looked at the leader, who nodded as if to indicate he should proceed.

'We've had agents following your wife, following both you and your wife, actually. She has been seeing Smyth behind your back. In.'

Herbert felt the blood drain from his face. He swallowed. He had not realised just how ruthless these people were.

'I'm leaving,' said Herbert. 'I want nothing more to do with any of this.'

As Herbert got up to leave, the bear also stood up, moving to the office door to block Herbert's way. The bear pointed at the chair Herbert had vacated.

'Sit,' he said, as though talking to a puppy.

'Your wife is going to meet Frederick and we think she has the information about what has happened,' said the executive. 'You can be careless, Herbert, with your secret files. Fortunately, we've intercepted her text messages and she's meeting him to give him information. What we want you to do is go with Sophie, meet Mr Smyth, and befriend him. We want you to tell him how sorry you are about his predicament. When you come back, we will let you know why we want you to take this course of action.'

Herbert just wanted out, but knew that wasn't an option right now. When he had first met the agent from Gleco, the world's largest multinational drug company, and Dibble's biggest rivals, it had all seemed relatively harmless. All he had to do was pass a bit of inside information over and in return he was handsomely rewarded with things like all expenses paid golfing holidays. Herbert justified it on the grounds that he wasn't passing them too much; it wasn't as though the information he was giving was overly sensitive. He was only doing what others had done over the years, taking money from drug companies and going on paid holidays. Doctors buy their drugs and got perks from the drug companies. What harm could it really do?

Can Openers

Herbert was in denial that what he was doing was fundamentally different that, in effect, he had become involved in industrial espionage. He became even more deeply involved as he had climbed the corporate ladder. Greed had gotten the better of him. Gleco was a massive company; they wanted a share of the Dibble market and were prepared to pay to get it. Herbert wondered what he had got himself into. He felt threatened. Here he was, dealing with some extremely ruthless people who didn't take no for an answer.

'We want you to go with Sophie tomorrow to meet Frederick,' the executive said.

Herbert, feeling as though he was taking his life in his hands, said, 'No.'

The man who had not yet spoken then indicated to the other two men by raising one hand. He then looked at Herbert. 'You've got no choice, buddy. You owe us a lot of money, all those expensive golfing holidays do not come cheap, and there's interest on that money we've loaned you,' he said.

'Our shareholders expect loyalty and some of them are not very nice people. They will not be happy if you are not loyal. Once you're in, you're in, and that is that, big guy,' the bear said.

Herbert knew he was in too deep. The money they paid him and the holidays they had given him hadn't been a reward at all, they had all been a trap.

'We understand you're going to get promoted at the Dependency Unit. We've transferred £200,000 to your account. Treat yourself; buy your wife something nice. All we want is for you do as we ask, nothing hard, just little deeds,' the executive said.

'How will I explain to my wife where the money came from?' asked Herbert.

'Not to worry,' said the bear cheerfully. 'We've got a stake in the lottery franchise and, guess what? Your ticket was one of the winning tickets! Well done, Herbert.'

'I don't want the money,' said Herbert.

'Too late, big guy, you have it already,' the bear said. 'No one will suspect you're getting the money from us. You're a rich man, Herbie, enjoy it. So long as you're nice to us, we'll be nice to you.'

'I want out,' Herbert said, this time his voice was small.

The bear went up to him 'We're getting a little tired of this,' he said quietly. 'If you don't carry on with us, your life will be ruined. We will make sure you lose everything. We will tear you apart. I know that it's a cliché to ask this, but capiche?' He roughly pushed the back of Herbert's chair with his large, bear-like hand.

'Let's take things a step at a time. Let's see how you get on with the next task then, after you have met Mr Smyth, we can discuss further,' the quite man said, in a much more emollient tone.

Herbert felt he had no choice but to do what they asked. Herbert didn't think he was a bad person; he had just gotten too greedy. But now he was up to his neck in industrial espionage.

He decided not to touch the money that he knew was now in his account. He also decided that once he had completed this task, he would try to get out again. What they asked him to do wasn't that difficult, he already sympathised with Frederick. He was annoyed that Sophie was getting information but that was the least of his worries. He decided he had better check Sophie's phone to make sure that what the three men told him wasn't just bullshit.

Before leaving, Herbert had agreed to carry out their wishes and had asked the three men again whether he would have a choice about leaving after doing this task. They told him they would consider it but that Herbert should check his account as the money may go up afterwards.

Then they reminded Herbert that he was up for retirement in five years.

'What do you owe the Dependency Unit?' they asked. 'We ask you to do a few little errands for us; we get information and you become a wealthy man.' I

Herbert left with the card to the room by Baker Street in his pocket. He went back to the room and changed back to his own clothes. He made his way home. On the train he sat and pondered. All he had done over the years was pass statistics and give them information about routine, everyday work activities. Now they seem to be rewarding him with vast sums of cash and threats. It worried him. As one of the main investigators of staff in the department, he had been on a training course some time ago, run by the dependency unit, about industrial espionage. It stayed with him, and it was playing on his mind how rival firms recruit people as sleepers. They get paid for doing virtually nothing until needed, then get asked to do at times dangerous tasks. He couldn't help but wonder, *what am I being set up for?*

Chapter 54

After Herbert left, the three men had a discussion. One of the men was ex-CIA, another was on the board of Gleco UK and the last man, the quiet one, was on the board of Gleco USA.

The US Board member was no ordinary board member. He made his money from the black economy but was now putting his money into legitimate businesses after running the mob in his area.

The three men discussed how the meeting had gone. They concluded that Herbert would continue to be a loyal agent for many years to come, that he would not have the guts to leave. The Gleco USA executive, smirking, was utterly contemptuous about Herbert. 'Herbert has not got a clue about the millions of dollars we made after he passed us information regarding the opportunity planner who ended up with half a dick after a blow job.' They all chuckled.

The three men were involved in a very lucrative private equity firm. Herbert had investigated the case involving the cousin of Gina who was forced to give sexual favours to an opportunity planner. The outcome was for a new computer program to be put in place.

When Herbert found out about the case, he told the above men. He let them know at an early stage that the department was going to look at a new computer system, enabling their private equity company to work with IT firms and offer investment before any rivals. Thanks to the tip-off, they now sat upon a percentage stake in the latest IT Company that had a contract for the dependency department. Having the information gave them a massive advantage in the

Can Openers

market. Herbert was involved in dirty and murky waters, barely aware of what was yet to come.

The executive told the other two that he had been contacted by Dibble for joint strategy discussions. The three men agreed that the markets were tight with little room for manoeuvre.

'It's a dog eat dog world out there, guys,' said the bear.

They concluded, though, that they could work with Dibble on one issue at least, the issue affected them all.

'So we're agreed. We will work with Dibble to smash the Can Openers. They're even starting to get an influence at Gleco,' the quieter man said. They all nodded in agreement.

They then talked about Herbert's role.

'We've asked him to befriend Mr Smyth, who's living with the main organiser of the Can Openers. Even Dibble isn't aware of that,' said the bear with a broad grin.

'One of our agents picked up the information by accident whilst watching the head of the Can Openers. Mr Smyth has been watched for weeks,' the executive added, 'the Can Openers helped us at one time; they didn't know it, but by taking on Dibble they left a gap in the market when their production levels went down. We moved in and gained.' The executive laughed.

'Yeah,' said the bear. 'But now they're organising within our organisation. We cannot be complacent.'

The quieter man agreed. 'We need to join with Dibble to smash them,' he said. 'Gentlemen, we will have a meeting with Dibble. We will also have an agent befriending the ringleader of the Can Openers by making friends again with Smyth. Let's see if he can engineer a meeting with Jane. Then we can formulate a plan.'

Chapter 55

After the meeting in the café with Herbert and Sophie, Frederick was very low and angry with himself. As soon as he got back to Jane's, he went straight up to his room; it was the lowest he had been since meeting Jane.

'How could I have been so stupid?' he asked aloud. 'I've lost everything in my life and all because I pressed for a number 3 on the computer.' He remembered the moment it happened. All he needed was a number 3 risk rating to get his stats over the 51%, he rushed to get it and had been so close. He had become obsessed; he pushed people. And his actions had unintended consequences

The department, he realised now, was a sham. All they had been doing was blaming the poorest for the greed of those at the top of society. The Unit had been able to treat people as they had because ordinary people had not been organised. Frederick learned that ordinary people, people like him, had only gained rights and choices when they organised and fought for it.

At least Herbert was going to try and help him to get his children back; that thought lifted Frederick's mood a little.

Frederick was a better person for the experiences he'd had and the changes he had gone through. He understood wider issues and how they related to the individual, how individuals make differences but not out of circumstances of their own choosing. This made him feel better about himself and the world around him.

Since meeting Jane he was more content as well, more relaxed and less grumpy.

Frederick heard that Joseph's trial would start in two weeks, after a delay of nearly two years. Frederick felt partly

Can Openers

responsible for Joseph's incarceration and for Lidia's death. Frederick would give a truthful statement in court.

While he was on his bed contemplating all this, he heard Jane come home. Her two children were outside playing. Frederick babysat for Jane from time to time. All of Jane's friends commented on how great he was with the children. They all loved Frederick, whom they knew as Kevin.

Frederick realised there was one more thing he needed to do; he had to tell Jane about his past life at the Dependency Unit. He decided to write a note about how his life had changed. He would tell her how it was him who had been pushing for Jane to become self-reliant and how he had believed that Joyce had been protecting her. He was going to tell her how his children had been taken from him because he had pressed number 3. He would tell her how he had treated people as commodities, treated the customers as just numbers.

He would tell Jane how wrong he had been and that, after being with her, he had realised that another, better world was possible. He would tell her that he used to be a monster but he had gotten his humanity and dignity back.

He walked down the stairs. Jane was sitting down alone, her children with Gina. She looked up at him. 'I need to tell you about the decision I've made about whether to take the manager's job,' she said.

Frederick held up a hand to stop her. 'I need to tell you something about me first. You see,' Frederick sighed, 'I am not who I was.

He started to explain his dark days as a dependency manager, leaving no stone unturned. When he spoke about A1021a he explained in graphic detail. He said that he did not know who Jane was, that to the department she was a number, and how he had no concern for her as a person just a dependency figure. When he was talking about the opportunity planner, Joyce, Jane realised everything he was saying was true.

After the last meeting, she had spoken to Iris about Joyce and Marcus. Iris had told her that Joyce had approached members of her group who were opposed to the dependency department, asking for advice about technology to try and keep case A1021a under 50%. Marcus and Joyce opposed the system, but neither had come across each other until, coincidently, the department put them together. They never completely trusted each other until they joined the can openers and realised they had both been opposing the system for a long time. Iris had reassured her that they could both be trusted.

Jane knew when Frederick was talking about Joyce it was accurate. It was a shock to find out that the dependency manager in charge at the time was Frederick himself.

Frederick explained everything. Jane said nothing and just stared, sitting rigidly upright and showing little emotion. Her fingers tapped on the kitchen table As she checked to see if Frederick had finished. He had. Her face went from pink to red; she could not look at him anymore and walked out the back door. She needed space and finally went to see Iris. Frederick stayed in the kitchen, head in his hands

Iris opened the door and Jane stumbled in. She told Iris what had happened; she was so angry, spitting out her words and barely pausing for breath. Several hours later, and as darkness turned to light, Jane realised she respected Frederick for telling her the truth and had to accept that he had changed, otherwise she was no better than the dependency department.

After a heart wrenching night, she found herself outside her own kitchen back door. She took a deep breath and composed herself as she entered. The house was silent. She put her bag on the kitchen table, knocking on the floor an empty packet of paracetamol. She went upstairs and knocked on Frederick's bedroom door, but there was no answer. When pushed slightly ajar, it revealed only an empty room. Fearfully, she rushed downstairs calling, 'Kevin!'

She launched herself in the front room to find him lying on the sofa in yesterday's clothes, with an empty whisky bottle at his side. 'Kevin, wake up!'

He groaned and looked up. 'Do you hate me?'

She smiled, kissed him on the lips, and knelt next to him. 'Frederick is in the past,' she said. 'You are Kevin, my friend and can opener.'

As she went out of the room, he put his head back on to the cushion and smiled.

Author Profile

Malcolm lives in North West England with his partner and cat. He enjoys playing the saxophone, hill walking and running. If you're hiking in Snowdonia or the lakes you may find yourself passing him on a mountain path. He is a social worker for an emergency duty team and has been working in the public sector for over 30 years. He is a socialist, political activist, shop steward and supporter of social work action network. Mal's novel reflects his fear of what could happen if we do not stand up for the welfare state and where the present policies on austerity could lead.

Publisher Information

Rowanvale Books provides publishing services to independent authors, writers and poets all over the globe. We deliver a personal, honest and efficient service that allows authors to see their work published, while remaining in control of the process and retaining their creativity. By making publishing services available to authors in a cost-effective and ethical way, we at Rowanvale Books hope to ensure that the local, national and international community benefits from a steady stream of good quality literature.

For more information about us, our authors or our publications, please get in touch.

www.rowanvalebooks.com
info@rowanvalebooks.com